MW01229399

A **MYTH** or *the* undeniable **TRUTH**?!

******

Were the Black Negroid the Adored but Forgotten Ancient God's?

Author

Tahaisa Benita G

A word from the author!

DNA and blood heritage will be proven to be a valuable tool to hush all to silent and to accept the undeniable truth of the beginning of mankind, which will force historians to revisit and rewrite our history on earth, giving glory to the ones that deserves through their heritage and legacy to be called 'THE ONES THAT DISCOVERED PLANET EARTH'! But in their agony to accomplish their mission to save their own planet they committed an abominable act by playing God, which had redounded to their own descendants being enslaved on planet earth!

Our heavenly Father has blessed all of us with the power to love, forgive and to overcome and move on to a better place that will give us all peace in our hearts with our own truth!

So open your heart and your mind for changes to come and do not be consumed by fear, because fear will only prohibit you to see the beauty of it all and jeopardize the materialization of such beauty in the acceptance of others, whom you might think does not look like you or have the same values as you have! Let us all be 'Sweet People', as the 'Children of Curaçao' for our own spiritual growth and express each and every day a warm and loving gesture, as little as it may seem to be, to make a positive contribution in the daily life of others, yes grab that God given opportunity of being whole and free yourself from any insecurity and hatred in your heart.

The author,

Tahaisa Benita G.

One of the 'Children of Curaçao'

In deep appreciation and acknowledgment,

To my youngest brother, who had the audacity to question the veracity of the information provided to us by our educators, which had fired up the flame of hope in me, to maybe still be able to fulfill my lifelong spiritual purpose in life.

To all members of my family and friends, who stood by me and listen for years to my unrelenting rambling that there must be another not yet known reason, for the enslavement of our ancestors and the attitude of the Dutch Government.

To my deceased Mother and Father, who taught me that life is more than your eyes can see, to always follow my instinct, the importance of knowledge and to just not trust only one source and to keep on digging till your mind and soul are completely satisfied.

To all my children and grandchildren, who gave me the strength and inspired me, not to leave them with the unanswered question of whom we are as a nation and as a race, our real history and our legacy and the role of our ancestors on planet earth.

To my husband, who has cautioned me to have patience, to be resilient and with an open heart to be able to forgive who ever has done you harm as a way of life, enabling me to convey in this book the final message that there is always hope for a better tomorrow.

About the Author.

This is the first book of the author. The author took two years to complete this book. All the names used in this book are not the real names of the persons in question. This book is a recollection of events of the author's life and what she believed since she was a child to be her spiritual purpose on earth.

The author was convinced that she would have to sacrifice a normal happy life to be able to fulfill her spiritual purpose in life. That she would have to travel and live in Africa were it all began, to live a life of hardship to find truthful answers to her lifetime quest. The truth about the real reason why her ancestors were enslaved, the truth of who they are as descendants of the enslaved ones, the truth of all the hatred and why her race is still being oppressed and also why there are still Africans living a primitive life?

But the same man that she fell in love with, that had convinced her to not to get trapped in the hatred that was done to their ancestors and digging up painful accounts of the cruel acts that was bestowed upon them and to let it go and let life happen, turned out to hold the key to her fulfilling her lifetime quest and to over time help her achieve the mind set and the clarity of her and also his spiritual purpose on earth.

The Publisher,

The Haflid Group.

How it all came to be!

It was at one of our many family gatherings, that we found ourselves discussing the existence on earth of various different races and where my youngest brother stated that it all did not add up that all these different races could have come from the same source, either if it was as stated by scientist from the first race on earth, the Negroid black race or as is documented in the Bible from the first humans Adam and Eve, whom presumably would have been from the white Caucasian race, this according to the Roman Catholic Church. My youngest brother had also some very interesting remarks and questions in regards to in particular the huge unexplained differences between the white Caucasian race and us the black Negroid race, which definitely intrigued me.

What is the reason that there are different human races, with very specific differences on earth? It was also astonishing for me to contemplate the fact, as brought up by my brother, that all the other races in contrary to the Negroid black race, has straight or somewhat very light curled hair, a more lean body and a more flat butt. This was indeed a mystery, where did these sudden changes in appearance of these apparently later emerged races came from and how did these changes occurred if they really did came from the same source as is now recently established by scientist through DNA, which is from the first homo sapiens or the black Negroid race. But why does the church then depicts the first biblical humans on earth Adam and Eve as being white or Caucasian? Are they not supposed to be black as now is established by scientist that the first humans were black Negroid people out of Africa? And as my brother stated, how did the nose, the lips, the hair texture, the forward chin, the body and the butt changed then, when they established themselves in the North and became the other races?

It was there and then that I immediately felt that there is something not quite right, in this whole coming from the same source information that was presented to us and decided that this is worth a further investigation, in particular now that there is DNA evidence to work with, to verify the information that was or is still presented to our children in the education system. And could this mystery of the differences with the black Negroid race, also answer the question that I have been struggling with, all my life? The question why my ancestors were enslaved because they were from a particular race and why they as the first race did apparently not progressed and are still essentially living like bush men?

Will I be able to solve my lifelong quest if I solve this mystery of the differences of the other races with mine race the black Negroid race? So after a few weeks after our family event, I decided to start my investigation to find a suitable and more logical explanation for the strange differences in appearance of the black Negroid race, the presumably first race on earth, with all the other races, that as scientist have established came afterwards. Although the evidence that I found was shockingly clear as water to me as of the very beginning, I could actually not believe or accept it myself.

This undeniable truth definitely also answered the long nagging question of a plausible real sense making explanation for the deep seated fear and hatred of specifically the white Caucasian race, towards the black Negroid race. Which hatred was fully expressed in the enslavement of my ancestors in the so called "Trans-Atlantic African Trade Slave" and genocide. And afterwards the prevailing institutionalized segregation efforts to keep despising and isolating the Negroid black race, by same countries that had previously enslaved my ancestors.

The hesitation that I first felt to share this information was not based on any doubt of all the evidence and correlation of the evidence found, but more importantly, am I going to disrupt the sacred believe system of the faithful ones, the ones that believes as I do and always will, in one almighty God and his begotten son and our savior that we call Jesus Christ, with the publishing of this book? Would the revealing of the existence of some technical very much more advanced beings that apparently came from the sky or from another solar system, created humans in their image, were adored and called 'The God's' by these same ancient humans, but are now without themselves, the descendants of the enslaved Negroid race being aware of it, living casually on earth and being controlled within the system, despised as an inferior and corrupted race by the other races, did give me some major concerns of the impact of this revelation of the truth to the world.

But more importantly why were these, more technical advanced beings, being called 'God's' in ancient time, was that specific denomination not reserved for the one and only God? But then I remembered what my mother had explained to me as a child, because I was so confused that the word God was translated in various other languages differently. So my main question as a child was, how would the real God, our Holy Father, our Lord and the

Master of our lives, know if you are praying or calling out to him, if he does not have just only one name in all languages exclusively for him? And my mother said to me 'It is not important what name you give him or what word you use to call upon him, my child. He will always instantly know that you are calling upon him for protection, comfort or his blessings. You know why my dear, because we all are connected through an invisible line that goes right through our soul directly to him our Father in Heaven.'

If it were not for the remarks brought up by my brother of the unexplained differences in all the races, the nagging questions that has persecuted me my whole life, of the real reasons for this deep seated hatred of the white Caucasians towards us, that our ancestors had to be enslaved just for being a black Negroid and the unbelievable cruelty and experiments done to and upon them for over centuries and the still existing and simmering hatred of some white Caucasians, why it seems that the Negroid race has stopped progressing as a race and the still continuing discrimination and humiliation of my people I would not had challenged myself to start this journey through time and space in search of this undeniable truth.

Discovering this truth, was a spiritual mission that I have set out for myself since I was about eleven to twelve years old, when we got to the history lessons of the enslavement of my ancestors that changed me from a happy and bustling young girl to a deep in her own thoughts, laden with fear and not trusting young girl and made me wonder why an entire race could condemn another race to eternal servitude and do the most despicable acts to them, just because they were mine race, the Negroid black race. Why in heaven's sake would they feel compelled to just enslave and dehumanize another race, just for being another race, my race? Would I be ever able to trust them, would I be able to forgive them for what they had done onto my ancestors, and do we need to still fear them? Would I be able to hold in my anger and disgust when confronted with them?

But fortunately I fell in love with Den, now my husband that wanted to protect me the best way he could. As from the first day that he saw me and I smiled at him, when I just started High School and he was finishing High School, he fell in love with me, but sensed an underlying sadness and fear of something and perceived that it was his duty to protect and love me. I was not even aware that others knew that I had moments of deep thoughts of fear and sadness and that he a very popular senior would notice this and be interested in a shy young girl like me, who came the first year of school with her hair in two braids, like an Indian girl.

I was then 13 and he was 17 and he became one of my best friends and he tried to convince me that reliving the hatred done to our ancestors and digging up the past will only hurt me and obscure my chances to have a happy and meaningful life. He was convinced that I needed to let it go, for me to flourish and become the woman that I was sent on earth to be. But I was determined to get to the bottom of this and did not had the need to 'flourish into a woman' or whatever that meant, because I was just not interested in man or getting married or having children. I wanted to be free so that I could fully commit myself to my spiritual mission, finding the answer of the real reason for the enslavement of my ancestors. Because if it really was about making money or the aim to make more souls convert to Christianity, why the hatred then? A hatred that just did not seem to subside and also seem to feed negatively and affect both races the white Caucasian and the black Negroid race. I was convinced that if I could find an answer to that specific question, whatever it maybe, this would help to heal the wounds and restore the relationship between both races.

But looking back I truly believe that Den was right, I was too young, too angry and very much distrusted and feared every white male I knew at that young age and he taught me how to separate the past and to give each person, without looking at the color of their skin a fair chance to gain my trust, my compassion and my love. So it was destined for me to let it go for a while and let life happen, to reach the maturity to be able to fully comprehend, forgive and be enlighten with the wisdom to convey this knowledge and the message in this book to the rest of the world of this undeniable truth. The truth about the beginning of mankind and the real reason why my ancestors were nearly annihilated of the surface of planet earth, enslaved and dehumanized by the white Caucasian race, because as an old saying goes, 'The truth as ugly as it may be, will always set you free!

Chapter 1.

My unrelenting eagerness to know the reason why!

If my mother was born some centuries ago she would probably have been burned alive as a witch, since she was gifted with the ability to communicate with the dead at will. My mother was a very humble, spiritual, and unselfish women who besides dedicating her life to her children and her husband maintained an open house policy were anyone was welcome to drop by and share our meals at any time of the day, although we were considered a poor family. I remember a time that my sister and I had to cut at night cardboards to place in our shoes to cover the wholes at the bottom, so that we can wear them the next day to school. My mother quit her job as a teacher when she got married, which was very common and expected from women in those days, but she always maintained the urge to educate and share knowledge. My father an autodidact, with a fierce appetite for knowledge, unfortunately had a great flaw and that was alcoholism and it was best as my mother would say to avoid him in that state of compromise.

Just a few weeks after I was born I was taken urgently to the hospital by my parents due to dark coloring and unnatural bloating of my tummy and the fact that I was suddenly falling in and out of consciousness. After quite a few hours of intense examination and observation the doctors informed my parents that I was being poisoned from within, due to an unexplained blockage of my intestines and they estimated that I would not last more than one to two months. My mother was inconsolable and was begging my father to take me back home. But the doctors would not sign the release papers, since they argued that I would then die sooner and they could not take that responsibility. 'What difference would a few days or weeks earlier make', argued my father, 'her mother wants her home and I am taking her home'. Despite the threat of the doctors, that they would call law enforcement, he went to the intensive care unit unhooked me and took me home. At home my mother had already prepared a treatment she had envisioned with the help of some passed away family members.

This treatment and the fact that my father, stood up to the doctors and took me home, as is evident saved my life. I was told this story since I was a little girl over and over again, by my father. And had wondered what my contribution if any to my family, my community or the world in compensation for being saved from an impendent death, at such a young age would be.

Growing up I was always getting sick often, but for a very short period of time sometime only a few minutes and surprisingly more when I was visiting the doctor's office. My mother one day decided to explain to me that maybe I was experiencing symptoms of sicknesses of other people, which was a mystic gift and that I should try in my mind to hold these off, because I was not really sick I was just transmitting the symptoms of other sick people to my body! She had explained to me that the mind has great powers to sense and also control the body and that I could control this too! I thought then that maybe it was my calling to become a doctor because it would be easy for me to diagnose the patients, but that idea was immediately drawn out of my head, when I was about 10 years old and saw our neighbor's child with her face full of blood, when their old dog took a bite at her face!

And then when I was about 11 or 12 years old, I thought it would be definitely my mission to be a social worker and that I would probably land in Africa to assist the communities who were deprived of equal opportunities! Because one day my primary school teacher noticed that I was distributing bread to other class mates and stated 'So are you our own little social worker now?' I did not understand what she meant by that and explained to her that Shanika, Corina and Mildred are not in the best of mood and always wants to fight or bully the other girls, because they are so hungry! And that my mother does not mind to prepare two complete loaf of bread called 'French breads' cut in four equal pieces as long as I ate my part too and also two bottles of homemade cold thee with lemon that we all can share!

It first started that I noticed that Shanika was silently staring at us when we ate at about 10.00 o'clock in the morning, stating to the teacher that she already ate sufficient at home early in the morning, but she always was irritated and mean to us and putting her head on her desk a lot! So one day I asked her if she would like to share my bread with me, because one whole bread was definitely too much and that my mom would be mad if I throw it away! The next day two other girls who always fought and bullied everyone in our class also asked me for a piece of bread and I decided to break the bread in four pieces! Since that day I was not bullied any more for my name, which sounded a lot like a delicious Chinese dish! Although I was taught by my mother to reply to them positively with a smile, like 'delicious dish, do you want some' or 'no potato with chicken this time' the intensity lowered but it still was annoying, because I was definitely not a Chinese dish! After some days my mother noticed that I was very hungry when I came out of school and ask me what was going on! Since that day she took care that I had not one but two full breads cut in half to take to school, so that I would have four pieces to share with my three other classmates. Shanika and I became good friends, but the other two girls Corina and Mildred although they bullied less, they still were pretty mean when they wanted to be.

My whole family also after what happened with my grandmother thought that I had the internal strength, the determination to take actions and the patience to cope with the profession of a social worker. I have been spending since I was about 11 years old some days of my summer vacation at my grandmothers Rose's house, were she lived with my uncle Stan. Her house was situated in the country, while my own family lived in a government housing project in the suburbs. She and my mom always used to get up each and every day at exactly 5 o'clock and this without an alarm clock. And since I was in the country we went to bed very early, because we were very tired at night after finishing the different chores with animals and also playing constantly outside, I guess it was not very difficult to also wake up early. And it was actually very adventures to stand outside so early when it was still dark outside and brush your teeth, while you are holding a tin of tuna that you are now using as a cup with water.

After being there for a week or so, one night my grandma started to get nervous and erratic and suddenly begin packing as though she was going on a very long trip. After a while she asked me to accompany her to go to one of my aunt's houses that were not very far. When we arrived there she asked my aunt for her earrings since she needed them for this trip. My grandma and my aunt started arguing. My aunt was telling her that she was not going anywhere and that she had actually gave her the earrings since some years ago as a gift. Then my aunt and her husband took my grandmother and me back to her house and they started to unpack her suitcase. My grandma got very upset and started screaming and crying that she needed to prepare herself because 'they should be arriving soon, to take her on a journey' and that she really needed the earrings because her husband, my deceased grandpa gave her these earrings and she wanted to wear them to honor him, when she embarks on her journey with her husband and other family members. My aunt again start arguing with her telling her that she is not going on a journey, that it is all in her head and that she should change to go to bed. My uncle Stan came home and one other aunt that was also living nearby also came and they all try to convince mine grandmother that she does not need to pack but that she needs to change and go to bed. After what seems various hours of my aunts and uncle arguing with my grandmother, she finally got tired and went to bed crying.

After my aunts left, I asked my uncle what was happening and he explained that my grandmother was having as the doctor explained signs of dementia and that I should not worry, maybe tomorrow and maybe just another more night she will again have one of these episodes and if that occurred I should just go and get my aunts if he is not yet at home. Early in the morning the next day I went to my aunt and asked her if we could exchange earrings, because it is important to mine grandma to wear the earrings that grandpa gave her and I showed her my beautiful gold earrings a family heirloom that my father has given me to wear to go to church or other special occasions. Which I never wore because I did not like wearing gold earrings, I thought that they were to pretentious and preferred wearing earrings with colorful beats.

When it became dark and my grandmother was looking for her suitcase I gesture to her 'Look Nanna it's already packed and here are your earrings, I have already also laid your beautiful Sunday clothes on the bed so that you could wear them and all your snacks are also in your purse. See Nanna everything is ready for you to take your journey, with grandpa!' She looked at me and smiled very peacefully and said, 'The chocolates are for your grandpa, you know my mother and father will be also coming to accompany me.' 'Where are you actually going with them Nanna?' I asked her. 'To another more beautiful world Isa, your grandpa and my parents have already informed me that they will come to take me there.' After she changed her clothes and put on her good shoes and her earrings to be ready for her journey to the life here after I did her hair and prepared tea and we sat down and I asked her to tell me stories of her life with my grandpa.

My uncle got home and was very pleased that I have found a way to keep her calm and happy. After a while I got tired and started yawning hard, giving her a sign that I was tired and my grandma said 'Today is not the day, maybe tomorrow!' and she stood up and went to change her clothes so that we both can go to bed. All my aunts and uncles were amazed that at such a young age I knew how to handle the situation with my grandma. Their major issue was that she would get as the doctor has warned them more violently as time will progress as a consequence of dementia and they were also afraid of losing her in case their deceased father really was coming to take her, which meant that they were going to lose her. But that I was right to show them that they should respect her wishes, because she had lived her life and know and accepts that soon she will leave this life and her only request is to prepare herself for the life here after, wearing her best clothes, taking along her favorite snacks and wearing the earrings that her beloved husband had given to her!

So I really thought I had it in me to be a social worker, because a social worker is according to me, someone who knows and respect the social functioning of individuals and or communities. But unfortunately the profession advisor at my high school when I was about 15 years old, after an evaluation of the qualities that I possessed qualified me as unfit to become a social worker, because although I was very action driven I was also too straight forwarded and was lacking according to her assessment the needed empathy or as she stated the ability to feel and express pity that was of vital importance to execute the work as a social worker. But I totally disagree with her that empathy is the same as feeling or expressing pity. Because it was my opinion that expressing pity for someone is actually an act of disrespect! And although I was pretty blunt and straight forward and never on purpose expressed pity out of respect, I still believe that I had empathy and was kind and caring to others. She did however recommend that I should seek a profession in law enforcement, because of mine apparently inquisitive and analytic mind. I did not even know that I had an inquisitive and analytic mind, but I could never join law enforcement since I was terrified of guns.

I met with a friend after this assessment at school and I was expressing to her how disappointed I was that the advisor does not seem to think that I am suitable to be a social worker, but recommend that I should go in law enforcement. 'Can you imagine that Ludri, me Isa with a gun?' I commented to my friend. 'What are you going to do now, do you have other options? An option that does not require you going to Africa, to live like a nun?' She said laughing. 'No it was an advice, so I believe that I will still become a social worker and go to Africa to work as a volunteer not as a nun.' I said to her also laughing. Ludri was a friend that did not have many friends at school because she was considered to live a life of sin, the same as her mother and her older sister whom were considered call girls. But I liked her, she was very confident of herself and did not care of what people thought about her. She was funny and also blunt as I tend to be, although she was dressing a little too sexy at school and always had her hair and her face perfectly done, which was completely the opposite of my style. I never whore any make-up and always had my hair braided in its natural state to go to school in those times.

Everyone at school was warning me to stay away from her because she could drag me into their dangerous lifestyle, but I thought maybe I could learn a thing or two from her and she could also I hope learn a thing or two from me. I was since very little a very good dancer and loved to dance moving my hips in a very as observed by others provocative and sensual way and this did cause some concerns in my family. But Ludri taught me how to dance the way I loved but still send a clear message with my eyes and body that you may watch but definitely need to keep your distance. It was a way to demand respect, while fully expressing mine feminine side and I was very grateful to her that she was able to teach me that.

Falling in love with now my husband Den however a half year or so later, definitely changed my perspective of wanting to leave my country in the pursued of the needed education and ultimately voluntary work in Africa as a social worker and or scientist and to also do some research in Africa on the reasons why my ancestors were enslaved and why there are still many Africans living primitively as bush men. Den had also convinced me to seek another career path, so I would not need to migrate to the Netherlands to finish my education, because migrating to the Netherlands for study will set me up with a huge student debt. And since I was a person that was always fully committed to whatever my goals will be and had now decided to be his girl, future wife and mother of his children, there would be no space for me to pursue or execute what I first thought was my spiritual mission, going to Africa the source, to seek some really needed answers on some very disturbing questions.

But nevertheless going through life I always had an urge to someday do something that would be to the benefit of my community, to in some way give back, for all the blessings that I was fortunate to receive in life, beginning with the second chance of pulling through my ordeal of a life and death situation at a very young age and meeting the love of my life, whom has taught me to not to take the burden of the world upon my shoulders, but to embrace God's blessing, enjoying to the fullest of being his girl, his wife, the mother of his children and his business partner. And although I volunteered at various charity works and tried to make a difference in the life of a few, I definitely felt that these actions were not enough to silent that still aching urge from within, to comply with a for me then just yet unknown spiritual mission that I would need to accomplish at some point and time in my life, now that going to Africa was definitely out of the picture.

Since I was always interested in lifting up spirits by telling stories most of them as told to me by family members and adapted with my own flair, I thought that someday I will definitely find the time and the inspiration to write a book that will uplift the spirit and heal the wounds of my own people, the descendants of all the black previously enslaved ones. Because at a very young age I knew that there was definitely some discrimination going on in my own community and also family members against each other. The family members with a lighter skin tone and less curly hair as me, got a better treatment even from their own parents and the boys were also more interested in lighter colored girls. So I was looking desperately for something that I can use to break that cycle of self-discrimination and self-destruction.

This was also one of the reasons I fell in love with Den he respected and was kind and charming but not flirtatious to all the girls, the black ones, the white ones and everything in between, also the girls that did not have a good reputation like my friend Ludri. He did not condemn any girl and their behavior and also did not gossip behind their back, as was very common with other boys. It seemed also that Den did not regard the social status of anyone, he treated the teachers and the principal the same way he treated the other students at school. From him I learned that there are definitely people in this world that are color, social or reputation status blind. My mother also did not discriminate, but she was very aware of her place as a descendant of the enslaved black Negroid race. But Den was very confident of himself and not at all aware it seems that he was actually black in a world that disregarded black people as equal. Den was definitely not waiting to be accepted and regarded as equal by anyone, neither the black, the white or the rich and powerful ones!

Growing up as a young child, you could definitely say that I was obsessed to in some way or other, comprehend the underlying reason for the institutionalized deep seated hatred of the white man for the black Negroid African race, which were fully expressed in the killing of over 10 million Negroid African people and also the enslaving and dehumanizing of another 10 million both in the so called African Trans-Atlantic Slave Trade as from the 1500 and also the other holocaust or genocide the one of the African Congolese people, were again over 10 million African Negroid people were slaughter or enslaved by the white Belgian King Leopold II as from 1885 and various other mass killings of groups of African Negroid people in various other countries.

But still all of these systematic, state sponsored persecution and mass destruction or slaughter of these Negroid black people for no apparent reasons or a war between these two group of races, were never recorded in human history as a holocaust or a genocide, why was that? Holocaust and or genocides does mean the killing or destruction of a good quantity of people or humans of a certain race or ethnic group for no apparent reason.

Were my ancestors not considered people or humans on planet earth? Were they actually a breed of something else? A breed that was not equal to humans, a breed that could take humanity down, a subhuman breed as some of the white Caucasians has pointed out? Were these the reasons why my ancestors were and in some cases we are still treated this way? And why was there never an expressed apology of the head of states of the countries that initiated and maintained these actions of an institutionalized enslavement? And why has not one head of state of the countries in Africa pleaded for the safe return of their enslaved and essentially kidnapped citizens or their descendants?

Why were my ancestors after slavery not returned by their captures to their original home somewhere in Africa, by the countries that permitted these enslavements, so that they would not have to stay where they were essentially not welcome? Why was there no registry of who they were? Their real name and where they came from? Why were my ancestors not allowed to keep their own name? Why were everyone separated, children from their mothers or parents? Why were my ancestors not allowed to indulge freely in their own language, culture, believes and customs? Why all the secrecy and commitment of wiping out of their identity? What was it that we the descendant were not allowed to know?

And why was their never a compensation paid to my ancestors for their enslavement to enable them to at least have a fresh start in a country that is supposed to be unknown to them? And why was there a compensation paid by the government of certain countries to the slave owners to free their slaves? Did we as the descendants of these former slaves in essence then became property of the Government of these countries? Because it sure must have felt and still feels liked that was indeed the case! And why did these governments put segregation laws in place after the abolition of the Negroid slavery in certain countries? Why does it seem that we as a race must be constantly humiliated and maintained under these countries tight control at all times? Why does it seem that what happens to black Negroid people just does not seems to matter? What is there that the other races are afraid of that the Negroid race can do or has done or is capable of doing?

Or is it really that as they the white race claim that we are perceived as still being apelike beings or hominoids and that we would be a danger for the further intellectual development of humankind if we were ever regarded as their equal? That we will if we mate and bore children with the white races take humanity down, due to our perceived ugliness and inferior level of intelligence? But why would they then make the woman slave, hide her hair and her body, if she was unattractive to them? And why would they then rape the black and therefore through their eyes ugly and inferior woman slave? Was it to procreate or was it to humiliate her and her man or was it both? Did they really had legitimate rights that our ancestors became their slaves, because as they had stated it is written somewhere in the Biblical scriptures that we are the cursed descendant of Canaan whom was the son of Ham, one of the three sons of Noah?

As already stated several countries decided after the abolition of slavery that the Negroid race should be systematically maintained as being the last on the pyramid of achievements, by constantly creating obstacles for their advancement, locking them up in prison or killing them for every and no reason, sterilizing them without their consent, enforcing laws that they could not marry, experimenting viruses on them, using their body alive or dead for research without their knowledge or consent, making films or news denigrating them to influence public opinion, to despise them as a race that is categorized as lazy and corrupt in its core, that is only capable in indulging in criminal activities. As if we as a race had done something so wrong that has transcended in a deep seated hatred, disgust and an unexplainable fear in the white man for the black Negroid race, for generations and generations!

What could the Negroid race has possibly done to deserve that hatred and disgust or what threat could the Negroid race possibly possess, if the Negroid race was only a primitive race wondering around for thousands and thousands of years in the woods in Africa apparently far, yes very far away from them the white, a more intellectually and morally developed race and only mating with their own primitive kind, living a very primitive life and probably just waiting for the God abiding Christian white man to come and rescue them by taking them by force, to his land and teach them how to become a civilized and better human being, by giving them the Bible and at same time enslave, rape, kill and dehumanize them?

Why does the US call the enslavement of the Negroid race or the so called African Trans-Atlantic Slave Trade, 'the original sin' of their new established country? Is the original sin not the sin of Adam and Eve, the sin of the rebellion or disobedience of humans against God or their creator? Why do the enslavers or their descendants still keep referring to the Bible to justify their deeds of enslaving and dehumanizing another race? Why does it seem that they do not have any guilt feelings for these horrible deeds of enslavement? As if though they were entitled of doing just that. Why did the majority of groups of the white Caucasian involved in this whole enslavement belong primarily to very religious groups that came from Europe and had settled themselves in the various newly discovered territories of the Americas and the Caribbean? And why was there no enslavement of African Negroid black people in Europe?

It just did not make any sense at all, there must be some other reason out there that would explain the real reason behind the enslavement and the still existing deep seated hatred that keeps flaming up the passion to constantly suppressed, humiliate and or denigrate the Negroid black race. And why does it appear to be that this must definitely have something to do with the Bible? But what is it? Will we ever know what it is that keeps their torch of hatred towards us with so much passion from generation to generation? What do they know that we were not allowed to know of our ancestors the enslaved Negroid black race? Why are there so many loose ends in the explanations that the enslavers of our ancestors have provided to us? Is it there plan to keep us busy and preoccupied with the constant need for survival, to avoid that we stand still and questioned their motives? Should we just deny all these lose clues and carry on with our day to day lives? Or are we in one way or the other obligated to seek what really lays behind their actions and motivation of their selective treatment towards us the Negroid black race?

Chapter 2.

Our history and struggles as the 'Children of Curaçao'!

Our beautiful island Curaçao has about 160.000 inhabitants, is situated in the Caribbean Sea and is part of the Kingdom of the Netherlands. We call ourselves 'Dushi Hende' which means 'Sweet People' with a good and warm heart, whom always seems happy and willing to help or share. Nearly 80% of the inhabitants are in part descendant of The Transatlantic African Slave Trade, brought in as recorded by the Dutch West Indian Company. The African heritage is duly noted in our folkloric dances, dresses and the way we appreciate each and every day as a blessing of our creator the Almighty God. Our expression of gratitude towards God, our creator is mostly exhibited in making an effort to have each day the best time as possible on earth, sharing our happiness and good fortune with others and assisting others to reach their set goals in life. We are known as a nation that does not idolized famous people, and are also known to be very cordial, generous and caring to visitors and or total strangers. We are also perceived to be very proud but also humble people, which are a very rare combination, without any apparent reason for this proudness.

As a nation we also like to discuss various interesting and controversial topics, like politics, religion and other beliefs and also the history and advancement or struggles of our nation! This is maybe a common practice for all nations in development and in search of their destiny, I assume. It is also very important to us that we as a nation maintain our own culture, custom and our native language Papiamentu and to also be respected as a nation that is working towards the fulfillment and happiness of its people! But most unfortunate the vast majority of our nation is under the impression, that it's right to fulfillment and happiness is being constantly negatively impacted by its colonial oppressor, which oppression is exercised by the Dutch Government.

But still this same nation fears for the abandonment or the lack of protection and love from their former slave masters and colonial oppressors and are therefore as it seems unable to free themselves from their grip! Why is that? Are we in some way or the other suffering from the 'Stockholm Syndrome' as a nation? And why is the Dutch Government constantly claiming openly but most of the time subtlety that we as a nation are lazy and corruptive in our core? That we as a nation can also not do anything good or correct on our own, that we essentially need them to assist us as a nation in every step or decision that we need to take or must make? That they genuinely love us and that we must consider their actions as tough love? Because all that they do is in their effort to assist us to reach a higher level of citizenship and that the perception that we have that they are out to negatively impact our wellbeing and happiness, is incorrect or not founded in facts? And that to the contrary of what we believe that they are meddling in our democratic elections, they are really trying to assist us in choosing the right leaders to determine the right and better course for our country and our nation?

But if the Dutch Government is claiming that the perception of the vast community on the Island is incorrect, why is then the Dutch Government for example, more focused in imposing on our government to build a larger prison on the Island instead of investing in resocialization, education and job opportunities? Why do they sabotage all our economic pillars? Do they want to drive us all to the edge that the only solution that is optional to our community would be to join a drug or other criminal organization to provide food on the table? Is that the reason that they are so focused on enlarging the capacity of our prisons? Is that also the reason that they are constantly stating, as though they really want it to be a reality, that we as a community are a bunch of criminals that in one way or the other are involved in the dealing of drugs or other criminal activities? Is that also the reason that they have decided to take total control of our judiciary system? To be able to incarcerate all that are against their judgement and vision for us as a nation, in the yet to be enlarged prison on the island?

We know from history that the black Negroid enslaved men could be killed or imprisoned if he dared to look at a white woman! The black Negroid could also be killed or imprisoned if he tried to empower his own people! The black Negroid were not allowed to have an education, you could also be killed or imprisoned by authorities if they find you holding a book! And that after the abolition of slavery as a consequence only certain low income jobs could have been performed by us, the descendant of the enslaved Negroid black race. Bonding with a partner or marrying was also completely forbidden through harsh punishment in the time of slavery. Humiliating and denigrating the black Negroid woman, by passing her around various man, was also a tactic used to infuse in the black man's conscious, that the black woman is not worthy and cannot be trusted, which consequences are still felt in our community till this date! The numbers of families only existing of a mother or grandmother as caregiver is unusual high on the Island, which is exactly the same situation when our ancestors were officially freed in 1863. Grandmothers and mothers not parents, with their generations of children and grandchildren, most of the times not even their own biological children, but children of other slaves that were left in their care by the slave owners, were released without a support system, into poverty. But in those days the youth did not mind being poor, they were very happy not being slaves anymore, but now the mentality of the youth has changed and they have hardened their hart, reason why the youth delinquency figures are staggering high on our beloved island!

Another core problem is how to reach unity as a nation, are we as a nation ever going to surpass this group separation problem and really become one nation with one goal? This seems to be a very but very difficult and sensitive issue, due to the fact that our nation still consist of the same social separated groups as before the abolition of slavery, for the vast majority of the descendant of the enslaved black Negroid race, mostly the poor, lower and the upcoming middle class, the descendant of the Ashkenazy Dutch Jews which were the majority of the slave owners, the upper middle class and the rich, the descendant of the Dutch soldiers and Government officials and other new immigrants from The Netherlands and other countries which was a mix of the poor, lower to upper middle class to the rich. Acknowledging these groups of socially and historically diverse and adverse people, of which the two first established groups for sure did not really mix, other than the rich man having a secret black or mixed race mistress, of which the children out of wedlock were never accepted as family, unity would be only reached in each group separately, which was very noticeable in election years!

It is also noticeable from historical accounts, that in contrary to various other European nations, the Dutch slave owners refused to grant their slaves their freedom. Therefore the Dutch Government had to pay the slave owners a compensation of 300 Dutch Guilders for each slave for the slave owner to reluctantly set their slaves free. But did we as descendant then became slaves or property of the Dutch Government, through this buy-off transaction? Is that the reason that they as the Dutch Government are treating us as though we after the perceived abolition are now their property? The Dutch Government had actually planned to enforce a repayment by the former enslaved Negroid people of the compensation of 300 Dutch Guilders that was paid to the owners to free the slaves, but this plan was later dropped, due to criticism of other European countries.

The former Dutch slave owners next to the monetary compensation also demanded that in order to grant the Negroid slaves their freedom and a piece of 'their land' to live on, a piece of land that the slave owners actually had received for free from the Dutch Government went they came to established themselves on the colonized lands, that the former Negroid slaves would have to work free of payment for another extra 10 years, the so called 'Paga Tera' arrangement or 'Paid for your Land' agreement. So actually the abolition of the Dutch enslaved Negroid race was not in 1863 but factually in 1873!

There was a lot of segregation practices after the freedom was granted to the as recorded over 200 years enslaved Negroid race of generations of people of Curacao, which had led according to international critics to one of the darkest days of our nation, the 30th of May 1969. But for the vast majority of the population which was of the Negroid race, the 30th of May 1969 was a truly liberating day for our nation. It was the day that we demanded respect and being treated as equals, that we demanded equal pay for equal work and that we also demanded that children of our families not automatically had to be place in an education career path of only doing cleaning work for the girls or only carpenters or other manual low paying jobs for the boys! The change after May 30, 1969 has guaranteed a rapid increase from poverty stricken or very low income to a middle class income for a large group of the black Negroid community in our country.

But going back to the recorded over 200 of enslaved years, where our history, heritage, legacy and religious beliefs were taken from us, when our ancestors became slaves, because the children or young slaves were separated from their parents and brutal punishment was given to any slave trying to teach young slaves about their own history, heritage, religion and legacy. The only ones entitled to teach the children of the enslaved Negroid race, were the missionaries of the Dutch Roman Catholic Church. These children were then taught of the greatness of the Dutch Nation and forced to only speak Dutch, because according to their teachers these missionaries, their own language was garbage and that they should take over the superior culture of the Dutch nation and to only learn the history of the Dutch people, because they the previously black Negroid enslaved ones, had no history and no legacy! That they the children of our ancestors were of a dumb race running like wild animals in the jungle and doing nothing to reach spiritual awareness through the teachings of God and Christianity. There were also other black Negroid slaves that served as spy and keeper or 'bomba' of the other slaves. But why would a slave take a job to betray their own race? Was this normal behavior to obtain benefits or were there a significant separation of groups or different interest in the black Negroid race in the ancient past?

I also learned afterwards that the Vatican or the Catholic Church had prohibited the enslavement of the Indians in America and the Caribbean, but the Vatican did not plead for the prohibition of the enslavement of the Negroid black race as slaves. Why was that? And that these Indians were also not brought over from Curacao to the mainland of Venezuela, but that a sanctuary or reservation was created on our sister island Aruba, were all these so called Indians that were living on Curacao and the other islands were brought, to live secluded and in tranquility, where they were protected by the army of the Dutch colonist. But why were the Indians saved, secluded and protected? And protected or secluded from whom? Why were they not killed or in war with the white Europeans as is claimed by western history? Who were the ones that were killed then? Were the ones who were living on these lands and killed by these colonists, from the Negroid black race? That were living in harmony and forming families with also these so called Indians? Was this also the case in the USA and other claimed territories? But why was this done by the Dutch colonist arriving on these

34

territories and why was the history changed and adapted to depict a different scenario of the real situation and or happenings? Why was it important to proclaim that the enslaved Negroid race were brought over from the continent of Africa, instead of admitting that the Negroid black race were already living on these discovered new continent?

It is recorded that the Netherlands took possession of the Islands as their colony in 1634 from Spain, but after the Second World War in May 1945, there was suddenly a movement to eliminate colonization of countries in the world. This change of the European Nations point of view was apparently thanks to the by the Vatican or Roman Catholic Church acknowledged Anti Christo and mass killer ever existed, the Fuhrer of Germany Adolf Hitler! Because the plan of Adolf Hitler was to colonized all European nations and forced every nation to only speak German as the colonizer's language and to also adapt to their culture. A decision immediately after the Second World War was therefore taken by all attending countries in the newly established United Nations in October 1945, to become allies and to essentially forbid any attempt of a country to try to colonize another country on planet earth!

All the inhabitants of the already colonized countries by the Europeans needed to decide through their democratic chosen representative that they want to become completely independent or still be a part of that particular colonial country but with equal autonomous rights. It was forbidden that the former colonial country could force the inhabitants of the former colony to adapt to the language, culture and customs of the former colonizer.

In light of these developments our country signed in December 1954 the Statute of the Kingdom of the Netherlands. The Statute would have guaranteed that all the Islands of the Dutch Caribbean would have been recognized as autonomous countries under the protection of the King or Queen of the Netherlands. In 2010 however the judiciary system and the financial control of our country Curacao, was succeeded back to the Dutch Government under a concession Kingdom law, which actually means that we as a nation became a full colony back of the Netherlands! This was done under the pretends that we as a nation are essentially incapable to manage our finances and that our nation is filled with corruption, that only a Dutch control on our judiciary system will guarantee the elimination of corruption, making our democracy with this Kingdom Law a superficial one at best!

Many locals on the islands does wonder why the Dutch Government keeps crawling back in time and insisting on keeping a tight grip on the people of the island of Curacao? Why are they doing that at every opportunity that they get? What is there to gain which such a small economy that the island can gather? Is it really our great harbor that keeps them interested? Is it maybe our ideal location that can serve as a hub as was proven in the Trans-Atlantic African Trade Slave? Is it that we maybe have oil or gas in our territorial waters? And why did they need to take away the blooming offshore business of Curacao and make deals with the US to establish that same business in the Netherlands? Why is there a military US base in our country and we as a nation does not have any financial benefits of the use of our territory from this?

Why does it seems that the Dutch Government still feels the need to have monetary gain from the island and or its people and continues to impose power over our country and our people? Are we not being colonized again by these acts of the Dutch Government? Is the United Nation not a body that is supposed to prevent this from happening? Or is it a permissible act, if they the Dutch Government corrupt our own Government or politicians in doing exactly what they want or need to be done, to be able to through our own elected government, colonized our country and our people again?

That agonizing feeling of being oppressed constantly ripped off and not be understood and accepted by a foreign nation is very palpable amongst our people! Why do we feel that the Dutch Government does not want us as a community to have any windfall? Why do we feel that they are on a quest to create conflicts between our own people? Why do they not permit our government to enforce our own native language Papiamentu in our school system, instead of insisting that if we use the Dutch language to instruct in our school system, our children would be better off? Meanwhile our drop outs figures are through the roof due to the fact that our children begin the primary school with a deficit of at least 5.000 Dutch words in comparison with the Dutch children that speaks Dutch since birth at home! Why will they not accept our language Papiamentu as a legitimate instruction language to be used in our education system? And why will they not teach their children in the Netherlands also Papiamentu, at least the basics, as it is an official language existing in the Kingdom of the Netherlands? But instead they are treating our language which is a recognized language that is being taught at several universities in other parts of the world, like a language for only primitives? Do we not deserve that they respect our native language and give it its rightful place in the Kingdom?

Why do they not teach their children of our existence and our own history in their school system? Why do most Dutch people in Europe believe that in the Dutch Caribbean we as people are far, far behind in everything in comparison with them in Holland? Why do some of these Dutch people in Europe even think that we are still living like uncivilized bush men? Is it not the responsibility of the Dutch Government to ensure that all the Dutch children in Europe learned about the people of all the Dutch Caribbean Islands, our way of living, the same as we must learned about theirs? So that all in the Kingdom will have the knowledge and respect for the culture and customs of the other nations in the same Dutch Kingdom?

Why do they not accept our way of acknowledging that life is precious and that our souls really needs to express this in dance and joyfulness each and every single day that the Lord had bestow his blessings upon us! That we do not live to work, but work to live! Why do they feel the need to put us down as a nation and declare that we are a nation that is lazy, a nation that only wants to have fun and party? Why do they at any chance that they get, emphasize that we are also a corrupt and criminal nation? Why do they feel the need to punish us or regard everything we do as a criminal act, meanwhile if they do that same act it is not regarded as a criminal act, but a little misstep! Why does it seem that they are still trying to impose their life values and their culture and custom same way that were essentially done during the slave period to our ancestors? What do they actually need us to forget or to wipe out of our system, that seems to be inscribed in our DNA as a nation or as a race, the Negroid black race?

All these questions have tormented all of us as the descendant of the enslaved Negroid black race! Generations of my people however wanted to be accepted by the Dutch white society and changed their ways and tried in every sense of the word to become white! But a group still held very tight to their own values, culture and customs or what was left of it. That does mean however that they were and are still constantly in a fight to defend their own language, culture, customs and values, to be able to maintain these. While at the same time being criticized by others, that they are playing the victim role and holding themselves back by not adapting to a much bigger and more civilized language, culture, custom, and values as that of the Dutch European people!

Do they not understand that when you lose your essence of your own language, culture, customs and values, you lose part of your soul? That if you cannot accept yourself as what you perceive as your identity, you will never be able to receive fulfillment in life? Is that maybe actually their goal? Obstructing us the descendant of the enslaved Negroid black race to receive fulfillment in live? Using all their energy to keep us divided as a race or nation? But why, what is the passion that drives their need to do this? Do they know something of our core existence that we were denied to know? Is that the reason why we were cut off of our history, that children were separated from their parents? That various groups with different languages and adapted cultures were brought together to confuse the children even more? What is the reason that they cannot let us be? Why, why and again why?

Chapter 3.

The family gathering that revived my quest!

As a family tradition my eldest sister alive Dee, had always tried to maintain the family reunions of our family, the same way that these were organized at least three times a year, by our mother's family to encourage togetherness and family values of all the children and grandkids of my grandpa and grandma. These reunions also filled the gab of what to do in the school holidays, since most of the families did not have the funds to go on vacation abroad or stay on the island in a fancy hotel with a pool and this was then something that we as children could look forward to.

I remember in particular one trip that my aunts and my mother organized to go camping on the beach on the far west side of our beautiful island, for two or more nights. It was arranged that all the children and the woman would sleep in an old school bus that was abandoned and that was cleaned up by my uncles and younger aunts. My uncles removed the majority of the school bus chairs to make space for sleeping and left a few chairs at the far end, were we could put all our bags. My mother and the other older aunts were in charge of all our meals in a make shift kitchen. We just turned in after enjoying a great day at the beach and after eating a delicious barbeque, ready to go asleep! But there was a small beehive under one of the chairs that was apparently disturbed by one of my nephew's feet. I was very little but did never forget how we all ran out of the bus screaming and laughing. Thanks God no one got bitten by a bee! That night we decided to sleep under the open sky, which was very peaceful and very beautiful, while one of my aunts told old family stories.

When my sister Dee got older, I had tried to maintain these traditions of organizing big family reunions for all my siblings and their respective family, but with my career and afterwards own business, I could not keep up. Fortunately my youngest brother Ray, whom is actually older than me, decided that it was very important to maintain these family traditions that had begun as far as we know in an earlier generation of my mother's family and took over this task of organizing periodically family reunions to celebrate our family heritage.

At these reunions we would from time to time tell stories that our parents told us and their parents told them, play Domino or 'Bon Kune' which means 'be good to your fellow me', both very liked games in Curacao, dance or discussed politics and our economic situation on the island and also enjoyed delicious food. Most of the time these family reunions are held at the homes of one of us, at the beach, or another public space, but occasionally we do rent a space to celebrate a special event!

It was I think our 4th family gathering of that particular year, were all my siblings with their own family, are expected to be present. Although not everyone can be present at every family celebration, happening or reunion, we have always managed to obtain a core basic of at least sixty percent, whom was present at each and every gathering. As hoped, me, my husband and some of my kids and grandchildren, were again one of the last groups to arrive at this particular family get together, this time at my eldest sister's

Dee's home. I love arriving when nearly everyone is already present at the gathering and the mingling and socializing groups has already been formed. After making my way to each and every group, I decided to sit down at the table of my brother Ray. I love to discuss various topics and aspects of life with my brother because he has a unique point of view, that most of the time will derail you of the known tracks!

We started as always discussing the development of our country and our political turbulences. It was noted in the group of six at my table that for a small country we currently have an abnormal large quantity of political groups. With no scientific analysis done to explain the cause of this, everyone offer their own view and explanation of this defiant fact. According to Esther, a family friend, who was sitting just next to me, this was because of the distrust of our people in the politicians of our country, who seem to forget their promise to the people that voted for them, as soon as they are elected and take seat in the government!

"All politician change their view on issues when they enter the government and new parties emerges promising that they would be the exception on the rule. Which the people naïve as they are believe again and again in these empty promises" Said Esther.

"That certainly does make sense Esther, but we still keep believing in our politician and will not abstain of voting, that is actually a good thing for our democracy. The participation of the people has gone up at our last election. The growth of more parties is definitely inspired by the thought that we as the people would like to see some fundamental changes in the way our country is being governed. Do not forget that for some significant years we only had two parties, 'Partido Democrat' and 'Partido Nashonal', both essentially right wing parties. It was after the revolution in 1969 that a real left wing party was born, namely the "Partido Frente Obrero" I replied.

"I do not agree with you that the 'Partido Nashonal' was a right wing party, it is nowadays that their agenda has been changed to have a more right or capitalism view" My brother Ray replied.

"But how do you explain the distrust of our people in the government over and over again, going to new parties at the end of each term?" Esther replied.

"I think it is because our people are not convinced that the parties are serving their needs or are not really left wing parties. But they still have the hope for a party that they can rely on" I stated.

"The distrust is not in only our politicians but in general in all the people of our country, we simply do not trust our own people" Ray commented.

"We do not trust our own people in the government, because they only think of their own personal benefits as soon as they are elected they become corruptive. We should become a province of Holland and let the Dutch politicians governed our country, which would ensure our prosperity as a country. They do a good job with their country so they will make a better job, then our own politicians" My nephew Richey elaborated.

My nephew Richey went to live in Holland since he was a college student and just recently, after over 20 years in Holland decided to

44

return back to his homeland. He has visited his homeland Curaçao nearly each and every year though, sometimes more than once per year. And although he does complains about the various situations he would like to change in Curaçao, to make our country even more European, he does perceive and appreciate that we do have a different culture and way of living or appreciation of live then the European Dutch people in Holland.

"Richey do you forget that we have a party here in Curaçao that actually represents the Dutch Government! But nothing has changed for the better only for the worst, when this party wins the election!" Mani the husband of my sister Dee responded.

"Our own people, although they are very intelligent, are very lazy, not ambitious enough to pursue wealth, through hard honest work and also our politicians are not trustworthy or sometimes are flat out corrupt, because they want to get rich quick that is the main reason we cannot have prosperity in our country." My brother Ray stated.

"And Richey if we literally let the Dutch politicians governed our country, that would make us a colony again, which we were till 1954. In these colonial times, our people were only good enough to work as maids, bell boys and other low paying jobs. And the only education that we were allowed to receive was the basic knowledge of reading, writing and counting. I would not desire to see my country as a colony of another country again, that was the past and should forever stay in the past!" Said Mani.

"No, you do not understand Mani that would not make us a colony, we would be completely integrated in Holland, a very prosperous nation, with highly developed decent not corrupted politicians, who really care for the prosperity of their nation." Richey responded.

"You said it Richey, whatever they do it will not be to our benefit as a nation, but to the benefit of their own people and nation. Because you do believe that we are a nation, don't you? We would then have to integrate into their society and be a minority in our own country. But as proclaimed by the United Nations, every nation is unique and does have the right to express themselves in their own language and through their own culture, customs and value's. And you know as well as I do that there is a vast difference primarily of the skin color and most importantly in our way of living or experiencing life and the Dutch white people and their way of living or experiencing life. So the differences in appearances will be very obvious for a smooth integration and the culture difference are huge, that we might be secluded and targeted and encounter the same abuse as the black minority group that currently lives in the USA. And being a colony we will for sure be forced to adapt the Dutch lifestyle and culture, which will eventually make us I believe very unhappy. Do not forget the current developments in Bonaire, our sister island, that had to adopt the Dutch customs and culture and now are complaining that they do not even recognized their own country anymore" I replied.

"I do not think that race in this modern society is important, black or white, but it is obvious that the white race as the Chinese race has reached a vast development in their civilization. We as the black race must just accept that and take advantage of it and learn from them. There is nothing wrong with the fact that they were

46

here first and are therefore more intellectually developed as a nation then us, black people. That is the main reason that there are more white rich countries and their people than rich black countries and their people. Another problem is that we as a race are very religious and religion is definitely an obstruction to reach and maintain wealth." Richey said emphatically.

"We are not a very religious nation, religions create groups whom are very fanatic in believing their way of contemplating and glorifying their God is the only good way. There were and still are many wars in the name of religion and many people persecuted and executed because of their religion. Starting with the Catholic faith, the Jews and the Muslims, who killed or got killed in the name of religion. But I do believe that we are certainly a very spiritual nation and a nation that believes in an Almighty God, we as a nation also very much believe in sharing what we have with others and you cannot get very rich with that attitude. If I recall the United Nations made a comment in a report in 1950 or so, that the People of Curacao were one of the most generous and humble people on earth, who loves treating all visitors and or total strangers as though they are high regarded visitors like 'Kings and Queens'." I stated laughing.

"But we are not the same people as we were in 1950 Isa, currently everyone only believes in taking care of themselves, just like the Dutch people, *"ikke, ikke en de rest kan stikken"* or the me, me and only me, mentality." Ray replied.

"Yes we are definitely adapting the wrong values from the Dutch people. We should have adapted their being on time mentality, are more precisely being at least 10 to 15 minutes before the agreed timeframe! Also at social events, they are crazy people! " I shook my head and laughed together with the group.

"You definitely do not seem to like the Dutch people Aunt Isa!" Richey stated.

"It is not a matter of liking Richey! Because I did have Dutch European friends, Chinese friends, Hindu friends and also many local native friends, unfortunately since I had my third child, with my career, study and a husband I just did not have the time to put in those relationships and lost contact with most of them. But I can assure you that I can like, love or even adore someone, but if that person is wrong, I will give it to him or her straight, you can ask Den or my children about that! I am sorry but that is the way I am!" I responded.

"Yes Isa is very straight forwarded since she was little, I can tell you lots of stories about that! And don't even let me tell you how she gets when she gets mad, if I were you I would run or she would just ignore you and shot you out completely and that for a very long period of time! Fortunately she does not get mad very easy!" Ray said laughing!

"Yeah, I still can get very mad at times, but I learned a few tricks, count to a thousand and or do not say or do anything. And then talk it out and reach a suitable solution. But I do not get mad very easy and most of the time it has been building up in time and you must be very dear to my heart, for me to get mad and upset at you!" I said smiling at my brother Ray.

"And you are only telling me this now" Ray said while smiling back and shaking his head.

"Let it go Ray, you know, some time ago I was working at a big international Dutch company. When I just started working there, they were just going to organize a social gathering for all the employees. Arriving as always a little late at each and every party I noticed that there was a kind of segregation going on, the CEO and other management were sitting together at one table, the head of departments together at another table, high paid employees or staff together at different tables and the other employees of lower income or job together at also different tables. I went to the table of the management and asked if I could join them at their table, they were a little surprised but immediately pulled a chair for me. And the first thing that one of them commented, 'You are late Isa, we do not appreciate it when people are late!' and I responded 'Oh my sincere apologies. But could someone as an invitee really be late at a social get together?' And they all laughed and then I asked them flat out, 'But with all due respect, why is everyone sitting in their own workgroup, I thought this would be the opportunity for me to really intermingle, from the management till the coffee lady at one table and not tables with segregated, oh sorry for the word, I meant separated work related groups! Is that the way this company usually socialize in Holland everyone in their own group?' They looked at me first if the sky was going to fall, but then admitted that they never would do this in Holland but thought that we the locals preferred to stay together and in our own comfort zone? On which I responded that 'if that was indeed the case, is it not your task as management to change that, don't you think?' On which they admitted that I was right and the majority of them stood up in an eye blink that really scared the hell out of me and went to the other tables to mingle. The CEO looked at me and said 'You are something else Isa, I like you' and I said to him 'I like you to, sorry what is your name again?' and stood up and joined another table a little embarrassed that I always had trouble remembering names and everybody seemed to remember mine" I said laughing.

"Yeah Aunt Isa always had problem remembering names, but sometimes when you least expect it, she does remember your girlfriend's name. I remember ones Aunt Isa caught me on a date with a girl that was actually not my real girlfriend and she comes over and she said before I can introduce my date to her 'I know, you are Desire, nice name'. I had to spend the whole night explaining to that girl that my aunt was confused!" Dino was laughing while explaining this incident.

"Sorry for that. But you can say a lot about Dutch European people, but they are very inclined to change and adapt their behavior if you confront them with the truth are what they perceived to be a truth, hidden or not. They will wait for you to tell them that they are wrong, although they already know that they are wrong and will continue the wrong doing or abuse if you permit them to do so, before they correct their actions! But at least they are willing to correct their action when caught. In their world if you do not speak up, they will walk right over you, but that is their business world and as it seemed not their political world, because our politicians definitely in the past have told them their truth and wrong treatment of us, but that did not changed anything on the long run, they still gathered strength and came back with the same conviction" I commented while shaking my head.

"Yes these Dutch people are indeed crazy men, you never know if you are on their good side or on their bad side. But they do respect it when you speak out and defend yourself. And you are right they are very persistent about being not on time, but much earlier. A Dutch employer said once to me, when it is agreed upon that you should start to work at 8 o'clock, you should clock in at 7.40 a.m. and should be sitting at your desk to start your computer and prepare your work at the latest by 7.45 a.m. or we would consider that you are late. Well I told him flat out that if he wanted me to start working or be at my desk at 7.45 a.m. he should adapt my contract accordingly and I will comply as my contract demands" Esther said with a big smile.

"You have guts! Are you still working there? I like woman like that, I never thought you have it in you" Dino now single said, while giving Esther a wink!

"Oh no, I do not believe in working for people that you do not trust, so I quit and got a much better job. God is good. You know Dutch people are not credible people, they promise me a huge bonus and steady promotion if the job gets done right. But after two years, they just did not want to keep giving me a huge bonus and the promotion as agreed upon. They knew I was doing a great job and complying with all my duties and also stayed if needed, after hours without complaining or making a fuss of it or asking for extra payment. I think that they were just looking for a reason not to give me or to at least lower my end of the year performance bonus as is stated in my contract, because I was earning this with such an ease. From other colleagues I heard that my position was filled very soon afterwards by a younger Dutch girl, with less experience than mine, that was committing various serious mistakes but that they were very happy with her and gave her a salary and a bonus arrangement of 25% higher than the ones I had." Esther said with a serious face.

"I have heard this before you know, that Dutch people seems to think and believe that only their own kind have the right or deserves to earn good money. It does not matter that they do a good job or not. Or maybe they are comparing these with what they can earn in Holland and want to keep the salary and bonus the same as the ones in Holland for the European Dutch workers. At same workplace that I commented before they were also giving me high performance grades, but were coming up with various excuses that the regulations did not permit them to give me a higher reward or salary. But people in the human resources were informing me, without me asking for these information, that various Dutch employees were getting higher rewards and salary for the same job, that I according to mine recorded job performance stats was better at" I stated.

"It is normal practice I assume that a nation reserves certain good jobs and or good salary for only their own people. We must do the same, but we apparently don't. We on the other hand do not see race, but the quality of the work done! And on top of that there are not many businesses run by our own people, like you do Isa" Ray my brother commented.

"Yes but currently we are only operating a small consultancy company, were basically my own family works at, actually we had that company since after me and Den got married and our first daughter was born. But when I took over the factory of liqueurs as the sitting Managing Director to continue this as our own family business, we had over thirty employees working in the high season period. And I can guaranty you that all of them were local people, very disciplined and hard workers. Unfortunately the export possibilities of our product were shrinking and we had to close down the factory. But Ray do you not think that there should be equal pay for equal job and our people did not start off with any capital, the 300 guilders compensation was paid to the slave owners not the slaves. So it will take some time for us the locals as descendants of the enslaved ones, to be the employers let's hope of the majority of the companies on the island to create opportunities for our own people. Although we as a nation do not like to discriminate foreign workers, we just maybe need to! At least till we have uplifted our own people's chances of prosperity" I commented on Ray's statement.

"You got lucky Isa, but everyone else I know in the business world does complain of our people being not disciplined and lazy. Putting a burden on these companies to make a decent profit" Ray answered.

"Are you not disciplined or lazy Ray, anyone at this table not disciplined or lazy no, anyone at this get together? I know there are a few, but they are definitely not even 10%. But I can agree that running a business here on the island is very costly, because next to the fact that our wages are higher in comparison with the region, our electricity and water costs are also extremely high, which makes it nearly impossible to run a sound business and compete soundly in the region!" I explained.

"You are definitely right aunt Isa, water and electricity is very high, not at all what is paid in the region. Now that I started working on my own and have my own barbershop at home, friends who also had a barbershop on the other islands, they tell me that our water and electricity is too high. Reason why you cannot create a reserve to invest in equipment" Dino commented.

"Maybe you could apply for a loan Dino" Richey suggested.

"But Richey our local banks do not give loans to local people, because the local people are not trust worthy and therefore are a big risk for them!" Ray responded.

"Not even the Small Business Lending Institutions that are specially design to give small loans to local entrepreneurs do not really provide loans to local people. Frits our brother Ray, had a very good project some 15 years ago, they requested a Business Plan with a market research, that at first I was amazed that they would require that for a small company and I assisted Frits with the Business Plan and research. They took all his documentation and after a period of 3 months or so advised him that there were too many tourist busses. While our research implies that there were not enough small and more personalized tourist tours with busses of only 6 to 8 persons, which the tourist seems to loves, because these have a chauffeur and a guide that will give them a more personalized attention" I explained.

"They are just protecting the big tourist companies you know" Richey my nephew answered

"That was also our conclusion. And nearly all of these big companies our owned by the wealthy locals that are descendants of the Dutch Jewish community" I replied.

"No, not for that reason, but because if the big companies goes bankrupt, many people will lose their job" Richey commented.

"That is not a fair judgement, others have the right to also pursue a business and compete fair and square" Ray said.

"Richey your argument has no logic, a big tour bus that can carry 50 tourists or so, have only one chauffeur and one guide. But a small bus of 8 tourists has also one chauffeur and also one guide. You do the math!" Esther replied.

"But their head office has various administrative employees" Richey responded.

"What kind of work do you do Esther?" Dino asked.

"I am a legal assistant, but I am still working to finish my masters in law degree to have a better paying job or my own practice" Esther replied.

"Everyone wants to get a higher paying job. Our wants to own their own business. The world is becoming more materialistic and so is our youth. No one wants to work a simple job or work for someone else anymore! That is what is jeopardizing our economy!" Richey commented.

"I do not see anything wrong with improving your knowledge and getting more diplomas, which could guarantee you to get a better paying job or better yet start your own practice or business! Because you are vacating a job that creates job opportunity for others who are not so fortunate to get more education or a diploma" I replied to Richey's comments.

"Yes and I will definitely employed locals as Isa did, exactly what the current law offices on our island are not doing. Most of these offices have nearly only European Dutch employees working for them. And where I worked they even now have a Latin American young lady in charge of cleaning and serving coffee, they sent home a very nice not so young local lady, can you believe that?" Esther said in dismay.

"Maybe our people or too lazy to work at the pace of these law offices and our own young ladies just does not want to work as coffee or cleaning ladies anymore?" Richey offered as explanation of the employment of foreigners at these offices.

"Richey there are a lot of persons like yourselves that believes that because we do are work in silence, are witty and organized and get our work done in a shorter timeframe then they whom are making a complete scene of how much work they have, they are presumably the hard workers. And the European Dutch people are just like that, creating a complete illusion if though they have a much larger load of work then their local colleagues. And the Latin American cleaning lady definitely does not work better than the local one, she is just paid lesser, with no social securities to do the same job" Esther replied annoyed.

"She is right you know, we the locals are or should be paid according to the law, but these Latin Americans or others from other Caribbean islands, most of the time illegal workers are paid much more lesser than that and does not have any social securities! So it is not a question of not wanting to work, it is a question of the employer not willing to pay as is regulated by the law!" I stated on Esther's and Richey's comments.

"Yes this is a great problem, because our own people do not report all these illegal workers, because we pity them and also out of fear that the economy will get broken also not the employers that are breaking the law and taking away the place of many local workers" Ray added to the subject.

"But going back to what you said earlier Richey, white people were definitely not first, as I recall we learned at school that Adam and Eve were brown people from the Middle East in the Garden of Eden and that their children were the ones who went north to Europe or Asia and so on and got white or lost their tan and the ones who went more south like Africa got darker or black. That is what religious people and the scientist explained in mine youth about the races. Most recently though I read somewhere that the symbolic Adam and Eve were certainly not white, they were black or more precisely Negroid people from Africa, DNA has proven in the last decade or so, that the first woman or Eve and the first man or Adam were black and from Ethiopia in Africa" I explained.

"That is not correct, scientist are always changing their minds and developing new theories. But we on Curacao must certainly not forget, that it is due to the actions of the white Dutch people that we were brought into civilization, otherwise we would be still running butt naked in the African wilderness, hunting down wild animals, without any civilized upbringing. We should therefore be grateful to the Dutch people for saving us! Are you all aware that black people do not have any historical contribution to mankind? Adam and Eve, Jesus, Albert Einstein, Columbus and other important people of the civilized world all came from the white European civilization. They have a more higher degree of moral then us, reason why Jesus Christ is a white man that is what I have learned in my days at school. Otherwise Jesus could not have had blond hair and green or blue eyes as is painted in the Bible." My nephew Richey commented. I was just floored with his comments and was getting very upset and angry!

"First how could anyone know if Jesus had blond hair and green or blue eyes? Was it written or described in the Bible? There were no cameras in those days and lastly do you really mean to tell me Richey, that you think it is a blessing that our ancestors were forced out of their country in Africa, to endure slavery for over 200 years or in other words, we should consider it a blessing the horrific dehumanizing actions that were done to our ancestors? Do you really mean we should be grateful to the white Europeans for that? And what kind of moral did they have if they were the ones torturing and dehumanizing our ancestors?" I asked astonished.

"Slavery was a long time ago aunt Isa, we all should get over that, that was the past. Where do we go from here that is the question we should ask ourselves. And we should let the European Dutch people guide us and teach us how to become further developed, civilized and not corrupt" Richey my nephew said calmly.

"Do you really mean that we all are corrupt, all of us on the Island of Curaçao including you?" Esther asked.

"No not all of us, but for sure our own political leaders!" Richey answered.

"If you do not know where you came from, as a human being or your past as a nation, or your own history you cannot work to prevent a repetition of what went wrong in your past to learn from it and prevent it to repeat itself in your future!" I replied to Richey.

"You know I have always wonder, that if we all came from the same source or from the Biblical Adam and Eve, do we not supposed to have practically the same skin color, facial structure and hair texture? Why are there different races in the first place? I know that we from Curaçao are from more a mix of races like Africans, Indians and Europeans, but where did the white, the black and the Asiatic or Indian race really came from?" My brother Ray questioned.

"I still believe that the first race was white Uncle Ray. And from the white race came the black or African and the Asiatic or Indian race. It has to do as the scientist explained with sun exposure." Richey responded.

"I was also taught at school that it was sun exposure Ray and that the first Adam and Eve were more brownish and the ones that went north became white and the ones who went south black!" I said affirming that, sun exposure was the explanation offered at school to me also.

"But the sun could not have changed our facial structure, a wider nose, thicker lips, our coarse or afro hair and mostly a decent but! There is something not quite right with the whole different races thing, if we all came from the same source, it's definitely a mystery" Ray reacted.

"Yeah if we were from the same race then we all should have had a more beautiful light color and sleek long good hair. And we are definitely not as ambitious as they are, it is the white race that has all the money, if we were ambitious we would have all the money and the white race would have been our slaves. So I am definitely going to be more ambitious!" Said Esther laughing out loud.

"I too would have preferred to have a more light brown color, but definitely not white, then I would not have to worry about getting to dark when going to the beach or other outside activities or work. I stopped working as a builder you know, a good paying job actually, because the ladies did not liked the fact that I was getting so dark. They would prefer me not working outdoor as a builder, but to have an inside job. You have no problem auntie Isa, your color is light brown and your hair is in between" Said my nephew Dino.

"What, did they really said that to your face?" I reacted annoyed.

"Oh yes, they said they would still like me for my looks and charm, but that their parents and family would not appreciate the fact that I was so black, like 'Shaka Zulu'. And why did God not bless me a black man with a more decent butt?" Replied Dino laughing.

"Yeah I would have want a little more flesh on my butt too, it makes it easier when I am sitting" Ray replied laughing.

"I think your wife Iris was ahead of us in the row of getting butts and she took most of it for her and your two daughter's uncle Ray!" Dino replied, which made us all laugh hard! Still I was amazed that my nephew would accept that kind of discriminative treatment, since he always portrait himself as a very confident young men. Why would he not love his own color and be proud of his own race? And why do we woman of African descent, straightened our hair and would love to have very long straight hair? Were we trying to be more white, I first really thought that it was a trend or style, that changes through time, in the eighties afros, in the nineties more straight or curly hair and now all together the afro or braided hair and also straight hair, depending on our mood of the week? Or were we definitely trying to change our appearance? Like also the white people who put curls in their hair, lay for hours in the sun to get darker and get plastic surgery to lower the height of their nose, fill their lips and also enlarge their butt. Is it a human desire to try to have what the other race has? Can we not be content with ourselves with what we were born with?

"You know Esther going back to the topic of slavery, I really do not believe that our people would have liked to be slave owners. You would had to be very much of an evil person to do the things that they did in those days to ensure that your slaves obeyed you and feared you and would want to stay your slave" Mani said.

"Africans also enslaved other Africans Uncle Mani." Richey replied.

"But not for an indefinite period and they did it for another reason and you never became their property, but was pledged to servitude only for a certain period. As I understood they did not have a prison system to lock up prisoners of war, a thief or someone you owe but cannot pay back. So the system that they use was a system of servitude for a certain defined period, to enable the offender or the captive soldiers to pay back by working for the King that won the war or for the people that you had stolen or borrowed money from. Many of those slaves marry into their groups of servitude and became family to their past masters whom they served. There was definitely no discrimination due to your color or race! And for certain more heinous crimes you would be put to dead or lose a limb" I stated.

"I did not know that, even though I did hear of a claim that it was the Africans that were the ones that started with the whole slavery thing of their own people first and the Europeans just copied and joined the club of slave masters but only in Africa!" Esther responded.

"That is also not completely true because I read somewhere that the Slavic European nations and also the Irish people were also slaves of other European nations" I replied to Esther's assumptions.

"When was that?" Ray asked.

"That I would have to look up Ray and for your information Richey, I also believe at first that Adam and Eve were white or tanned people, because of the pictures and statues in the churches, but the Africans were first here on earth and in the Bible it is stated that God made Adam from dirt from the Garden of Eden, which definitely could not have been white. And if your theory is that our core color is white and not at least brown and that we got darker through sun exposure, then all our babies should be born white as snow and eventually they would get darker through sun exposure. And we still have as noticed by Ray, more curled hair, a more flat nose, thick lips and the bumps to explain" I replied.

"You know I am certain that scientist are proven wrong as time passed, Adam and Eve were white and from the Middle East, as stated in the Bible and not from Ethiopia Africa" Richey stated again.

"Richey, God did expelled Adam and Eve out of the Garden of Eden, due to their disobedience. So I supposed they travelled in the desert into Ethiopia Africa and there was where they finally nested and had their children and died where their bones were found, as confirmed by scientist I supposed. There should be a correlation of the Bible and scientific facts or assumptions" I stated.

"Yes I also do believe that science must prove that the Bible is wrong or confirmed at least some part of the Bible or the other way around also! And I still insist that there is something not quite right, because beside the color we still have as I said before, many physical differences in hair texture, lips, nose and bumps. How do you explain these differences Richey? Does the cold make your hair go straight and lighter of color and your nose pointier and does the cold also flatten your bumps? It is still a mystery Richey and Isa does have a point that Adam was made of dirt from the fruitful paradise, which definitely could not have been white, but very dark brown. Or the Bible does also do not have its facts straight" Ray stated.

"Our father always stated that the Bible is a story for only a certain nation, I believe that he meant the Jews or Hebrews, that was according to him adapted or changed by the Roman Catholic Church, maybe he was right?" I commented.

"The Bible consist of two parts the Old Testament and the New Testament which regards the life of Jesus Christ! It is definitely true that the Old Testament was only for the Jews or Hebrews, but the New Testament is for all nations!" Mani explained.

"I believe that there is a God! But I also believe that the Bible has nothing to do with that same God, it is a group of many people that put the Bible together, to terrorized humans not to do evil! But if you listen to your inner self you would never do evil! So if your knowledge is within, why would you then need a book called the Bible telling you what you should or should not do? The Bible is a story of a nation and also a plausible explanation of the creation of humans and maybe also the races! It probably is based on the truth, but it has also as I believe corrupted the truth!" Ray commented.

"Yes, I also believe that the truth is hidden or that maybe the Bible was not correctly translated or that some truths were maybe exaggerated or maybe soften? The facts were indeed changed by someone, but why?" I added.

"Ray and Isa there are very religious person at this family and friends get together, do not let them hear that you think that the Bible is wrong, you can start a war right here guy's!" Esther said smiling but looking cautiously around.

"The best known scientific theory that has a missing link is that of Darwin, stating that humans evolved from apes to hominoids standing up straight and afterwards to Homo sapiens. But also he with his bogus missing link theory had the black man before the white man. As if also implying that the black man had stopped evolving, while the white man reached the top of human development?" I pointed out shaking my head in disbelief of this nonsense.

"That is exactly my point aunt Isa, they are indeed more intellectual developed then we, now you have the scientific prove" Richey said with a grim, satisfied with himself.

"So actually there must be scientific evidence that something happened between the original black man and the European or Asian man or races. Or these races do not have any relation to each other at all and were created separately. Because we as black people Richey, are surely very intelligent without the study or use of books and or theoretic formula's. And this is a testament of my own experience with white people, that have stated that they are amazed that we without the proper higher education that they had to endure for years of studies to understand a certain subject, we know more than them with all their degrees of education. When they asked me how I possibly knew the solution and I answer them, 'it just seems logical to me', they are very impressed" Ray added with fierce conviction.

"Guys the Darwin Theory is the proof that they are more intellectual developed then us. Besides that, all depiction in the Bible and films has a white Adam and Eve and a white Mary and a white Jesus. The Bible is the word of God and that can never be wrong, scientist are always reinventing and correcting their findings. The Pope or the Vatican began with the religion of Christianity and they are white and they are established in Rome Italy a European white country, the Jews are the ones that God had chosen and they are white and are now living in their promise land of Israel. We as the black race are the underdogs, the latecomers to the world party, we do very well in sport and music which is contributed to the more basic instinctive elements of mankind. And yes I admit that we are born with a very innate or natural intelligence but for some reason we cannot further developed these as a collective group, to also invent more important stuff or become well known for our theories, because it is proven by history that all historical inventions and important theories are from white people. Moreover according to scientist it has been established that it is not possible that black people eventually can become white. But white people can become black due to sun exposure. So that DNA stuff are definitely mistakes, that eventually will be corrected, as explained the original people were white and did became darker or black and as I understood also lazy or used lesser energy and unintelligent through centuries due to excessive sun exposure and hunger in Africa." Richey replied, leaving everyone just starring at him in disbelief.

66

"So our brains got fried in Africa due to the sun? And we got lazy because of hunger?" I finally cried out.

"As I said before we should let the past be the past! Our past has only been hurtful to us and digging in it will only hurt us more! Hey guy's they just finished, Pancho and Tito won the Domino game, it is now our turn to play and see who wins" Richey stated, while standing up ready to go join the Domino playing table, taking along with him Ray, Mani and Dino.

I was just shocked and very much disappointed to hear my own family in this present time speaking about their own race in such a denigrating way, while simultaneously unconsciously acknowledging their adoration for the white race as a superior race. Why do we do that? Put ourselves and our own people down? Is this the consequence of letting our children in the age of 18 to 19 leave the island to pursue a higher education in Holland? Do they teach them something that we do not know off? Do they put something in their food or do they manipulate them in believing that they owe them gratitude by taking our ancestors out of the bush men life of Africa, so that they could have a civilized life? Or is this a consequence of the slave period, that we still see the white man, woman or child as more beautiful of higher moral and intelligent? Have we been branded for live? Is the image of the white man as our masters still in our subconscious? Has the Willie Lynch system as proclaimed in his letter, really had the success that was sought, to make the black Negroid race eternal slaves of the white man?

Do we believe that we deserve to be put down, not deserving of love and happiness? I know that the majority of our people are not 100% black or Negroid, due to mixtures of the various lineages of other races, like the Indians, the Dutch Europeans, the immigrants of Latin American and others. But one drop of Negroid thus makes you a Negroid as the white man has established. Nevertheless why do we, still see ourselves our color, our hair, our nose, our lips and our hips and big bumps as inferior to the white Caucasian race? And why do some of us consider ourselves as a dumb race or not intelligent enough group of people. Could there really be a race that is dumb as a complete race? Can scientist prove this?

But how come that we as a race are very content with less and even enjoy sharing the little that we have, why are we lacking the ambitious drive and the urge to only focus on our own personal wellbeing, that seems to drive the white race? And why are there still many of us adoring or so submissive to the white race ready to please them in whatever way? Is this due to the impose slave mentality? Or is this due to something else?

I always thought that time will bridge that inferiority feeling of my own people. But nearly 155 years has passed since our ancestors were declared free people and I personally can still recall discriminatory behavior and comments between my own people. Did the period of slavery impose for generations the feeling of being less than your master, which in fact the white Caucasian people.

Now I really started wondering what needed to be done if possible to give us, the descendants of the enslaved black Negroid people back our dignity and acceptance of who we are! But who are we really? Why do we have an underlying pride feeling? Why do we not idolize famous people like other races do? Why do others perceived us as a humble nation? Why were my grandparents and my mother really generous people with also complete strangers? Was this an African way of living? Who were we as a nation? What if no one knows who we really are or were?

Why where man, woman and child as recorded all separated from each other, when brought over from Africa? Why where we not permitted to pass our history to new generations? Was it a deliberate objective that we should forget our history of who we are or were? Was it a planned out method to let us believe that we have no history? To let us think that our history only began as being their slaves? That prior to that we were living in the wild jungle as primitives? But even primitives have a history that they tell generation to generation to their children? Why did we deserve as is apparent from the history of the Transatlantic Negroid Slavery, such a dehumanized treatment? Who are we as the descendants of the Negroid Transatlantic Slaves? Were we really brought over from Africa by these white Europeans?

Because I have started to doubt that we were really brought over from Africa, since I recall clearly statements from a book were the first settlers that came from Spain an European country to the Caribbean, recorded that they were really amazed how well build, agile and fast the children of the so called "Indians" of Curacao were when they were playing a game of throwing and catching a small ball? Yes a small ball, would primitives entertain themselves with sport of throwing a small ball to each other? And is it a

69

coincidence that we are currently the country with one of the most players per capita in the Mayor Baseball League in the USA!

But hold on, according to same documentation of same settlers the Negroid black race were brought later on from Africa to the Caribbean or America? But what if this was a lie and that since 1492 they the colonizers encounter black Negroid people already living on these lands together with the now called 'Indians' and they lied that the Negroid race was brought from Africa and changed our history? What if we were already here on the island of Curaçao and we were as a nation very humble and gracious to total strangers, the same strangers that came to our shores as Spanish 'conquistadores' or conquerors and encounter the kind of people that did not liked violence, so it was easy for them the Spanish that came in the name of their Queen but also the Roman Vatican Church, to take over these islands and murdered the grown up males in charge and captured the woman and the children and they the 'conquistadores' took over the islands from us. Because we were just the same kind of people that the UN reported in the 1950 that we were, kind not violent and very humble and generous people? And what does the denomination of Indians really means? Could it mean the ones that believe in God, in Spanish 'los indios' or 'los en Dios' or 'los que emponen la creencia en un Dios'? Translated in English the ones that came and imposed the believe in only one God? Because the Spanish were the first ones to travel and to conquer for the Vatican Pope and the Queen of Spain new lands in the Caribbean and the complete Americas as recorded since 1492.

Although I was very upset of these claims by my own family members and friends of the acclaimed white supremacy, I was also very intrigued by the center question of my brother of the other races. He does have a point, how did these other races came to be? I never bother to stand still to that particular question. I always assume that since we all as humans has the same basic anatomy or a head, mouth, two ears, one nose, a torso with two arms and two feet with 5 fingers on each of them and that we all are capable to speak, we all came from the same source. But my brother was right the differences were too pronounced to come out of only one source, like the color of skin and eyes, wooly or sleek hair, tin or thick lips, steep or flat nose, flat face or forward jawline, more or lesser muscles and big or flat bumps!

If we really did evolved from apes as explained by scientist, we should compare the common features with the existing races. For example apes has straight hair, thin lips, flat nose, forward jawline and flat bumps, the underlying skin color under their hair on their body is mostly pale and their body is lean and not muscular. So if the Negroid race came through the evolution of apes to humans, how come then that there is only two common features with apes, which is the flat nose and the forward jawline? While for sure the Caucasian race has more common features with the apes, like straight hair, thin lips, flat butt, lean or not a muscular natural body and pale skin. This simply did not make any sense or maybe the entire human race simply has nothing in common with the evolution of apes to humans as is described in the theory of Darwin? But why did Darwin believed that humans, particularly his own race, the Caucasian race ultimately came from the apes?

What is the information that Darwin had on which he based his evolution theory? Did he also acknowledge the common features of apes with that of the Caucasian race? But why are not more apes turning into humans in these present times? Why can only humans speak and communicate on very intelligent and philosophical levels? And primarily, if the Negroid race was the first race and had wooly hair, how did the other races with straight hair emerged?

At that precise moment, sitting in deep thoughts at my table at our family gathering I decided that I needed to search for the answers to all these very disturbing questions. And would this has anything to do with the real reason, that was bugging me all my life, why my ancestors were enslaved as a race and many of them still living a primitive life? I felt in my gut that there is some kind of mystery or cover up in all of this? But cover up of what? What is it that some group of people are trying to keep a secret? It seems definitely to have something to do with the Roman Catholic Church or the Vatican, as it seems that they played together with the Queen of Spain a very active role in the conquering of the Caribbean and American continent and they had also depicted in the Bible a white Adam and Eve and also the role as missionaries to induce the captured young Negroid African slaves to accept their fate and to succumb to their white masters dehumanized treatments.

My father ones told me not to trust the Vatican, their church and their records or as he described, made up history. One early Saturday morning when I was in the 6th grade, I was sitting in my favorite spot in a large three just aside the front of our house, enjoying a cool breeze and the silence while learning history for a test the next Monday. My father came home from a night out drinking since Friday night with his friends. I was mumbling away my test to memorize this. He looked up and saw me in the three.

"What are you learning Isa?" He asked.

"West European history, dad!" I answered.

"Do not believe what you learn from their history!" My dad said.

"Why dad?" I asked astonished.

"Because Europeans are a bunch of liars and the Vatican and their Roman Catholic Church are the biggest liar of them all" My dad answered while he continued walking, struggling to climb the stairs at the front door of our house. It really shocked me why he would say that of the Catholic Church, which were regarded as holy, by nearly everyone else I knew at that young age. My father was the son of a real Arawakan Indian mother, the believed original natives of our country and a black Negroid father. He had stated that they as Indians knew various secrets and he always seem to be angry or disturbed about something. I had always thought that maybe that was the reason that he or they as Indians drank so much, maybe to forget something that was eating him or them alive. But is there a way to find out the truth, the truth that had concealed a secret for such a long time? My husband came to my table.

"Want to dance babe?" He asked.

"Sure honey, let me just finish my drink" I answered standing up.

Chapter 4.

In pursuit of the undeniable truth!

It was a very beautiful sunny Sunday, so I decided to go to a fair with mine two grandsons and a friend of the oldest grandson. My grandsons were 13 and 8 and the friend was 12 years old. After a few hours I asked if they would like to stay a little bit longer at the fair or go home and was very much startled by the answers of the friend of mine grandson.

"Let's go home auntie, I am getting too dark!" The friend replied.

"Yep, you are all getting very handsome and cute!" I said smiling.

"Handsome?? No way Aunty, I am getting black and black is ugly!" The friend commented.

"What? Do you believe that black is ugly?" I asked surprised and a little annoyed.

"Yes aunty, everyone says black is ugly!" He replied a little confused of mine attitude.

"Besides that, the more light colored or white kids are always treated better!" The friend stated with a very sincere face.

"Oh yes, where do they get better treatment?" I asked.

"Everywhere, at school by the other kids and the teachers, at the Bike Club, at the Parks, everywhere" The friend replied laughing, and looking at me as though he was thinking come on now, are you not aware of the fact that we live in a world of white or lighter color privilege. I turned and asked my youngest grandson, who was very light colored and had straight hair. He was the son of my daughter Rona and her ex-partner a Latin American man that came to Curacao at the age of 3 and considered himself as a genuine local!

"Are you treated differently at school because of your color and your hair?" He turned to me and said with a grunt on his face.

"I don't know Nanna, there are some girls in my classroom that loves to play with my hair, and wants to be my girlfriend they are annoying Nanna. I do not like that!" My youngest grandson answered.

"I wish I was white and had nice straight hair like you" The friend said sadly. I turned to my oldest grandson and asked him.

"Do you wish you were born white too, with straight hair?"

"Nope!" answered my oldest grandson, who had a very dark skin color and naturally curled hair.

"I would say, despite the fact that I do not have any more my long braided hair I am still a very handsome chap, with some baby fat, that I need to lose before I am 14. Just like my uncle Andrew" My eldest grandson said laughing.

"You sure?" I insisted.

"Yeah, but I really do wish that I would lost a few pounds tomorrow, then I could be better in all the sports that I love" My eldest grandson said smiling.

"Stop eating so much then" I said.

"No Nanna first you should stop cooking so delicious" He said laughing.

As we walked to the car to go home, I kept thinking, how many more of our people do feel not accepted or neglected because according to them, it is because they are black and do not have straight hair? Did I failed to acknowledge that my kids maybe also had this problem of not being fully accepted due to their dark skin color and curled hair. Was I now living in a fantasy world trying to ignore, that a majority of my people still does have an inferiority complex in connection with their Negroid features. Was this because I was married to Den that I have adapted myself to his life views that there are no differences in the races or should not be any differences in the races?

Suddenly I remember the time that I was finishing the 8th grade, in my time there was a separate girls and a separate boy's school. But at High School all boys and girls will be together at the same school. So my teacher told all of us girls with braided hair, that we should really try to iron or chemically straighten our hair, before we start at our High school. 'I had the same type of hair as you guys and the boys only made fun of me and made me cry, because I was stubborn and did not listen to my mother. Because my mother told me that when you straighten your hair and powdered your nose and face with white powder, you have accepted and are now working on becoming an attractive young woman' My teacher said. I thought she was crazy, I love my braided curly hair and what does straight or curly hair and white powdered face or nose has to do with becoming an attractive woman? Besides straightening hair with an iron or chemicals smells very bad and I am definitely not going to do that. Furthermore I was not allowed to use powder due to my asthmatic condition. But after a week nearly all of the girls with curly hair got their hair straightened. And when I started high school nearly all the girls attending high school had their hair straighten and powdered their nose with white powder!

After a few years at high school I fell in love with Den, he was a cute black young men with very curly hair, there were many family and friends who stated 'You could have done much better Isa' when I decided to marry him. And I immediately knew that since my husband to be was a lovely, very intelligent and ambitious man, that they were referring to his skin color, since I have a lighter skin tone and not so curly hair, I should have chosen a partner with my same tone of color or a bit lighter then myself. Which was a practice commonly called white washing your family tree. Which according to me, was a ridiculous point of view. You should marry the person that you love and feel that can fulfill you, even if he or she is green. Although I could not see myself choosing a person from another race in particular the white race, I just did not trust them as a race.

At same time I also recalled an incident some 20 years ago, with an assistant of mine when I was working as a financial controller at an international company. This assistant was a local dark colored married lady with chemical straightened hair, who did not yet had any kids of her own. Her husband was also a very dark local. She revealed to me that she nearly daily saw a group of little kids wondering bare foot with dirty close in her neighborhood and that there were in particular two of them, a boy and a girl, that she wanted eagerly to adopt, because they deserved a better life.

77

"That is very noble of you, racing kids is very hard and you would have to make various sacrifices. And if you cannot have kids, adopting one is certainly an option. Are those two kids orphans?" I asked.

"Oh I do not believe that we cannot have kids and I do not know if they are orphans, I just think that those two kids would make me very happy" She said.

"Why would those two kids make you happy?" I curiously asked her.

"Because they are so beautiful white and have pretty blond curls and gorgeous blue eyes, they certainly do not deserve to be poor, don't you think? I would love to wash them, dressed them with new nice clean expensive clothes and also buy for them a lot of toys to play with" She replied.

"What? Were the other little kids black?" I asked astonished.

"Oh yes, black and dirty with running noses, not a pretty sight at all!" She stated, pulling up her nose and rolling her eyes.

"So the white children were not as dirty and did not have running noses?" I asked trying to understand her point of view.

"You know, I really only noticed that they had blue eyes and beautiful sleek blond hair!" She said as though she was daydreaming and then went on finishing her task at hand.

I could not believe what she just said with such a conviction of being a good person, without realizing that she is putting her own Negroid black race down and not being deserving of a good,

78

decent and happy live. I will never forget the feeling of betrayal that had overcome me when this happened. Being a mother it really hurts you more if you witness discriminatory behavior of your own Negroid black race, towards Negroid black children.

In a flashback I also remembered the day that I took my little granddaughter to a party of a friend's grandchild. At same party arrived also a little white girl with blond hair and light blue eyes, with her mother. My little granddaughter was immediately attracted to this child as soon as she noticed her and stood up and went to stand next to this child looking at her as being amazed of her appearance and began to delicately strike the little girls hair. I stood up and went to get her.

"Oh, I don't mind, many little other girls on the Island do that to her hair" The mother said. I smiled and nodded at her and took my granddaughter back to where we were sitting.

"Always stay next to Nanna ok?" I reprimanded her.

"Ok Nanna. Is that a big doll?" My granddaughter asked.

"What is a big doll darling? I asked and looked around.

"Her!" My granddaughter pointed out to the little girl with the blond hair.

"No honey, she is not a doll!" I answered smiling and thought why does she thinks that she is a doll!

"But she looks the same as my dolls Nanna, the ones that you and mom bought for me, but much much bigger! Can I please have a big pretty doll like that Nanna!" She asked me with her big innocent eyes. Do we as Negroid black people without knowing it, are subconsciously teaching our children by giving them white dolls with blond hair and blue eyes, to be the protector of and to essentially adore and take care of white people, as if they were their own baby's? The next day I decided to buy a black big doll for my granddaughter, the price of the black doll was more than two times the price of that same doll with a white color, which according to the attending salesgirl was due to lesser demands and subsequent production of black dolls! 'That is very expensive! Do you have smaller black dolls?' I asked.

After the comments of my grandson's friend at the fair and the recollection of memories long forgotten I decided that I should not postponed my investigation and research on the subject of all the races and their origin, in the hope that I could find some answers to put a correlation together of all these outstanding mysteries. If the black Negroid race really is the first existing race as stated by scientist then how come the Bible or to be more exact the Vatican depicts Adam and Eve as white people or as the first human race! Why the contradiction? Is there a reasonable explanation for this? Or did the Vatican in Rome manipulated this fact and depicted the first humans in their image, but why?

So I began the next evening at home doing my research on the internet. Although I am a Roman Catholic, I am not a very religious person, but I do believe in God as our creator and consider the Bible when correctly translated or interpreted and not manipulated to be a book with deep factual insight of the past, present and our future as humans on earth. The timeline of the events as described in the Bible, does not always in my point of view has to correlate with scientific evidence, but as in the Theory of Relativity as presented by Einstein is explained and simply put, time in space is not the same as time on earth. And God, the creator of the Universe and mankind, as declared in the Bible, does not dwell on earth but in heaven, or the universe or actually in space! So some consideration of the disparity of time should be taken in consideration!

Now that I have established that the different timelines of the Bible and scientific evidence can deviate but basically what is declared in the Bible should be able to be established by scientist through hard scientific evidence or theories, I could move forward with my research. Because in conclusion, more attention must be sought at the correlation or the chronological order of the events in the Bible or other ancient documentation and backed up by scientific and or archeological find proof of evidence.

Researching I establish that the scientist has actually various theories but the most accepted ones are only two theories, the most popular one is the 'Evolution Theory', that states that humans evolved from hominoids or apelike beings to humans and the other more recent theory the 'Out of Africa Theory' of which they have DNA evidence that proves this last theory, the Mitochondrial DNA, that establish that life on earth as Homo sapiens began in Ethiopia Africa! Both theories actually acknowledge that the Negroid race came before the other races! The Bible however contradict this information, since according to the Bible Adam and Eve were white Caucasians with a tan!

DNA research also proves that the original black Negroid race has only one DNA in their system while the other later on emerged races has two DNA in their system, the DNA of the Negroid race and DNA of the hominoids or ape like beings or that the other races have the monkey gene! Which means that the first race or the Negroid race does not have the hominoid or the monkey gene in their system? Which also means that the Negroid race has a negative rhesus blood or a blood without the hominoid gene and does, due to this fact not fit in 'The Evolution Theory'? Is that the reason upon which scientist acknowledged that 'The Evolution Theory' has a missing link and or chain of evidence? Also the fact that the Negroid race does not have hominoid DNA in their system, indicates that the Negroid race did not actually evolved on earth, and if that is the case where did they then evolved from? But that the other races has the Negroid DNA and the hominoid DNA, hominoid or apelike being DNA. Is that also the reason that the Negroid race has wooly or very curly hair, while the hominoids or apelike beings has straight hair, as also the other races have as a recognition point of having the hominoid or apelike gene or DNA?

Scientist also acknowledges four races, the Caucasian, the Mongoloid, the Australoid and the first race the Negroid race. And that the Negroid race is at least 200.000 years on earth and the other races not more than 30.000 to 10.000 years ago! So a difference of at least 170.000 years! The Bible mentions that God created Adam and Eve no more than 10.000 years ago or less and that from this Adam and Eve all the other races apparently emerged. So the Bible apparently does seem to refer to the younger races as the created humans, taken in consideration the estimated existence of these races on earth! So who were the Negroid race, that were on earth at least some 200.000 years ago, whom apparently did not evolved on earth, could that also be deducted from the Bible?

In the Bible it is also stated that the Angels or the watchers of God were attracted to the woman humans and mated with them, because they found them to be so fair. Does fair stands for light or white color? Does the Bible implies that the Negroid black race were not created by God as humans, but that they were the Angels or the watchers of God, that are not from earth but came from the sky or heaven? And could this be the mating of the two species the children of the created first humans the Caucasian Adam and Eve and the Negroid race that created the Mongolian and the Australoid race? But wait the Caucasian race as a race also already has both DNA as established by scientist in their system! So that is a dead end, because how come then that the white race also have two DNA as from the beginning in their system?

But there is definitely some correlation in the Bible and the scientific findings of the mixing of the races if the Negroid race is thrown in the equation as the Angels of watchers of God! Because all the other races have as scientifically is proven, Negroid DNA and hominoid or apelike beings DNA! But neither sources have any explanation of were the Negroid race came from? No, the Bible does mention that the Angels or the watchers of God, if they were referring to the Negroid race, came from the sky or the heavens!

But how did the DNA of the hominoids got in the system of the new races that emerged some 30.000 to 10.000 years ago?

According to scientist this was through interbreeding of the Negroid race with the hominoids, but this could scientifically not have been possible. Just like as a donkey with its own DNA and a horse with also its own DNA born a mule, that mule is born 99.9% sterile! Apparently nature has its own build in prevention of mixing of species! The only possible explanation would be through divine intervention or genetic engineering, but that last one would have been impossible some 30.000 to 10.000 years ago or not? So was it God that did the divine intervention of the hominoid or apelike man with the Negroid race or the angels or watchers, to create the new races? But why would God do that? No that is a dead end, because it is stated that God created the Humans in his image!

Digging deeper for more possible explanation of the emergence of the new races, I found out that very ancient documentation were found some decades ago called the Sumerian Tablets, that also explained the creation of humans. According to these writings, that were very much older than the books used to compile the Bible, these tablets described that technological more advanced beings that called themselves the Anunnaki, came from another solar system and planet to mind gold on planet earth. What? Are they explaining the visit of aliens to planet earth? The Bible mentions that God and the Angels and watchers came from heaven or the sky is there some correlation here?

The depiction of these beings on the tablets has them looking the same as male humans. It seems that their hair and their beard were braided with beads in them and they were wearing also earrings, just like the Egyptians and other African black nations are accustomed to! The Egyptians claimed that they or to be accurate their ancestors came from the sky or the Orion Belt Constellation! Could they the Anunnaki then have been the Negroid race that existed on earth for about 200.000 years? They sure look like the Negroid black race!

The earth was void or useless as described in these writings and they came with a system to replenish the earth for them to have food and drinking water! This seems also to have some correlation with the Bible! The Anunnaki needed the gold to restore the atmosphere of their planet, but their own people just abandoned their work because of the heavy turmoil and escaped and hid themselves on planet earth! Hide themselves on planet earth, were did they hide themselves? The Anunnaki in charge then decided to create slave workers that they apparently called Adapa to mind the gold that they needed to restore their planet! It is also stated that they used their own DNA to genetically engineered slave workers to mind the gold and do other chores for them! So these tablets also described as the Bible does, the creation of beings by God or God's, but that these beings were essentially created to serve as slave workers?

"Oh my God, Oooooh my God!" I exclaimed sitting at my breakfast table while working on my research of the different races in the early morning hours.

"What is it mom?" My youngest daughter Sue asked.

"Oh you're up?" I asked, without taking my eyes off my laptop, still processing the information gathered in front of me.

"No I just got in, my friends just dropped me off!" She said.

"I thought you were not going out anymore, because you were too tired!" I said.

"They just kept bugging me that I am a party pooper and that I should go out more and offer to pick me up, so I decided to go have fun and we also decided to go to Denny's for an early breakfast were we also discussed some interesting topics!" Sue responded with a smile.

"Good for you!" I replied.

"But why were you saying, Oh my God, Oooooh my God?" Sue asked again.

"I have just discovered something unbelievable!" I answered.

"What?" Sue asked.

"I don't know how to say this" I answered.

"Seriously mom what is it?" Sue asked again, pulling her face forward as she had done when she was a little child and was demanding an explanation of me.

"Oh this is troublesome!" I answered, rubbing on my forehead and eyes.

"What are you working on? Financial Statements or another Business Plan for a company?" My daughter Sue kept asking, glaring at my laptop notes. She knows I liked to work at night till the early morning hours at home. Working on business plans or difficult financial statements at night does provide me the opportunity to work less hours and concentrate better.

"No, this is just a hobby research of why there are different races on earth" I answered.

"What, why are you working on that? I really thought that you have uncovered a big fraud or something!" Sue said laughing.

"Oh but I think that I did stumble on a potential big and worldly fraud or something!" I answered.

"What, seriously mom?" Sue asked.

"Yes, your uncle Ray got me thinking why there are indeed a lot of different races on earth?" I answered.

"Mom having differences is great, otherwise live would be to boring!" She replied rolling up her eyes.

"O yes sure, but how come, that is the question!" I said laughing.

"And what have you uncovered, that is so devastating?" She said laughing.

"That there seems to be a mystery in connection with the Negroid race!" I replied carefully.

"Is there a mystery with our race?" She asked puzzled.

"It sure seems like that!" I answered in slow pace and thinking, do I tell her or sweep her off and dig into this a little more. Although she was the daughter that had the most courage and was not afraid of anything.

"What is it mom?" She asked again, intrigued with my silence.

"Well do you believe in extra-terrestrials?" I asked hesitant, still not sure of my findings.

"Yes, you know I saw a UFO when I was very young remember?" She replied.

"Oh yes, you with a group of 2 other kids when we stayed in a hotel on the beach for a Convention. And you guys as children stayed in a room together to keep each other company, while we the grown-ups were enjoying a dinner ball. Good old times" I answered.

"Yes and we saw the space ship when we went outside our room to see if the Pizza guy had arrived with our Pizza yet, but came immediately running back into our room to get the other guys, to tell them that we saw a big space ship with a lot of lights hanging above the sea" Sue responded.

"That should have been very scary or not?" I said.

"Actually it was not really scary but rather amazing and exciting" She said.

"Yes, you are definitely the daughter born with a truck load of courage." I said laughing.

"Definitely, no one believed us at first, but I got a good look and was able to discharge all of the claims of the grown-ups, that it probably was a helicopter or a big boat or a tourist ship! Sure a noiseless helicopter that does not disturb the water and a big boat or ship that can vanish in less than one or maybe two minutes.

Because when we came back with the other guys it was mysteriously gone" She commented, again rolling up her eyes.

"Ok, hold your breath, it seems that maybe the Negroid black race are extra-terrestrials that came from another planet to planet earth to mind gold. Gold that their planet needed to restore their atmosphere" I said to Sue in one breath!

"Ok" Sue answered calmly if we were discussing the baking of cookies or cupcakes.

"That is all you have, ok?" I laughed nervously.

"Well I am processing, but if that was the case, were the other races already on earth?" Sue asked calmly.

"Apparently it seems that the Negroid black race, are the ones that created the other races or humans." I replied.

"What?" Sue asked astonished.

"I do not know yet if this is water tight information I will have to do more research and look into more sources" I replied hesitantly.

"But wait a moment where is God in all of this mom? You do believe that God created the world and the humans or maybe also us the aliens do you not mom?" Sue asked frantically.

"Well, it seems that they, the ones who came from another solar system and planet, came with the knowledge of One God or one supreme being. I personally believe, regardless of any information of existence of aliens that there is a God that created the Universe with everything on it!" I replied to Sue.

89

"I am with you on that mom, God is the almighty creator! But where did you then get the information that the Negroid black race created the humans? Was it not God that created us maybe the aliens and the humans" She asked.

"Well that is my conclusion with the information that I have just gathered" I said.

"What information do you have mom, to draw that conclusion" Sue asked.

"According to some ancient tablets called the Sumerian Tablets, it is stated that technological advanced beings that came from a planet from another solar system, some hundreds of thousands of years ago, called the Anunnaki created the humans, using their own DNA, to work as slaves for them to mind gold. The reason why they created the humans is because some of their own people got fed up with the work of mining gold and abandoned their duties and run off and hid themselves on earth" I responded.

"Ok, so you concluded that the Negroid race are or were the Annunaki, the beings or aliens that came from another planet, but why do you conclude that?" Sue asked.

"Because of DNA evidence and all the other facts seems to be leading in that direction Sue. The fact that the Negroid race is the first Homo Sapiens on earth since at least 200.000 years. The fact that scientist have confirmed that all the other races are hybrids, which means that they have DNA from the Negroid race and DNA from the Hominoids or manlike apes our presumed predecessors, that existed for millions of years on planet earth. The fact that the other races only have seemed to exist for about 10.000 to not more than 30.000 years ago, according to scientific evidence. And all the various evidence found all over the world of a technological more advanced civilization that lived on earth for definitely more then 50.000 to 100.000 years ago. The fact that there are also various ancient very large stones with carved Negroid faces found all over the world, when it was technological not feasible to travel to other continents, nor make these impressive carvings or structures like the pyramids. And that these were apparently depictions of an advanced civilization that were called Gods by the humans. The word God in ancient times actually meant my Master or my Lord the one that protects me, gives me knowledge and guides me. And the last but very important fact that I have been wondering about my whole life, that the other races took revenge and made the enslaver the slave in the African slave trade!" I replied.

"That is crazy!" Sue said laughing nervously.

"Yes very crazy, I have to cross check and keep digging for more information, since it does not seem that the black Negroid race were ever regarded as Gods or the Masters on planet earth!" I replied also laughing nervously.

"No I did not mean it that way, what I meant is that if your research is correct and knowing you I do believe it is, that this is then the world upside down" Sue said still laughing nervously.

"Yes the history of the world is then a big fat lie!" I replied.

"Mom you should make a report or better a video of your findings and make a presentation to all our people, maybe also abroad. Maybe you can charge for attendance to cover your cost" Sue said enthusiastically.

"No are you kidding, I started this research just because I promised that I will sort this mystery of the different races out that we discussed at our latest family gathering, in which uncle Ray stated that it seemed impossible that all the races came from the same created Adam and Eve or the Negroid race. And Richey stated that white people are the intelligent ones and that we had to be grateful that the white Dutch people captured us and saved us from being savages and brought us over from Africa to the Caribbean and the Americas to be their slaves, can you believe that? But I think now that it would be great if I could write a book of these findings or revelations! That is what I feel in my gut that I should do." I replied in deep thoughts.

"Revelations? Is that not a word that is used in the Bible?" Sue asked slowly.

"Yes indeed, maybe these are indeed the revelations that the Bible is referring to. The revelation of who we are as a race and our significance for the other races on earth!" I answered.

"But why was our race the Negroid race, that were regarded as God's then forced into slavery?" Sue asked!

"That is just what had hit me with a force you cannot imagine, that is the reason that I was saying Ooooh God! It must have been payback, for creating the humans or the other races with the sole purpose to be the slave workers of the Negroid race or the Anunnaki! And that was the question that I was always looking for the reason for their hatred that was expressed in the enslavement and cruel treatment of our ancestors." I said in astonishment.

"Definitely payback!" Sue confirmed.

"Their history also begin as being slave workers, is it for that reason that they wanted that the descendant of the Negroid race also have only the history of being their slave workers?" I asked myself.

"Probably they were just mimicking all that was done to them or better yet making it worse to try to feed their hate and anger of their true beginning!" Sue suggested.

"I definitely need to write a book of these findings!" I mumbled.

"But mom black people or surely the people of Curaçao do not read books, so you are wasting your time!" Sue said rolling again her eyes and laughing out loud.

"Ok, you're right the majority of the people of Curaçao do indeed not like reading books. Why is that actually?" I replied.

"Only God knows" Sue responded with a smile.

"But I still believe I need to write a book and not in Papiamentu but in English, to go on the international market" I said in deep thoughts.

"An international book is a great idea mom" Sue nodded.

"There is another interesting fact of the first Negroid race on earth. Which is in regards to their blood, they all seemed to have had a negative rhesus factor blood!" I continued.

"Is that the same rare blood that dad has?" Sue asked.

"Yes, it seems that the original Negroid race all had a negative rhesus factor blood. You know why?" I asked.

"No I don't" Sue answered.

"Because this blood has a direct link to the Anunnaki, it is as scientist has call it as a joke, a not earthly blood type!" I answered.

"Do explain" Sue said with a flat face.

"Well the hominoid that existed on our planet for millions of years had monkey gene which has a direct link to the positive rhesus factor blood, which blood also would be the blood that could be explained in an evolution process. Did you know that the word rhesus actually comes from a specific monkey, the rhesus monkey? And that if you are rhesus positive you have monkey gene in your system and your existence or the existence of your base race, could easy be explained as evolution on earth. But the apelike man or the hominoid had a little help from the Anunnaki or the Negroid race, whom injected their DNA into the apelike man or hominoid to essentially upgrade the hominoid specie to humans." I explained.

"Come again, explain further please!" Sue asked.

"Well according to me there is definitely a scientific connection, with the monkey gene and the positive rhesus monkey blood in

94

the evolution process. The evolution process is based on man developing from apes to humans. But the evolution theory as explained by scientist has a missing link, the jump from hominoid or apelike man to humans. And there is also no scientific explanation for the existence on earth of the negative or no monkey gene blood being in our system. " I said with satisfaction of the reception of my preliminary findings by my daughter Sue.

"When are you going to tell Dad?" Sue asked with a grin.

"Tomorrow, I mean today, it is already tomorrow" I said laughing!

"Good luck with that" Sue said laughing and leaving the room. My husband is a very down to earth person that definitely does not believe in aliens and all that science fiction stuff! Although he believes in certain mystic aspect of life like reincarnation and the afterlife he also believes that it is best not to ponder about these and just accept these for what they are and move on. For this same reason he had also suggested to me when I was very young to let the whole enslaving of our ancestors thing rest, because no good can come out of it, it will only hurt me and restrict my ability to interact with white people. His way of seeing life is to concentrate what is now your present life and opportunities and forgive and forget the ones that has done you wrong in the past or your prior life and try to make the best of your present life!

There must be a good reason he says that we are created to forget our prior lives, so that we can have each time a clean start! But how can we learn of our mistakes if every time we start without the prior knowledge I would ask him? And he would answer, 'I believe that deep in our subconscious we know what we need to know and learn or do in each and every life opportunity!'

My oldest son when he was little used to ask for his father, but he did not meant my husband but strangely enough my brother Ray and he also refers to my sister Dee as being his Grandma or Nanna. Always when we are going to visit my sister Dee he would make comments if like my sister was his Grandma!

"My Nanna always makes me hungry because she makes delicious bread just for me!" Den Junior would say.

"It's your Aunty Dee and not your Nana Junior and she does not make bread, we buy a special bread at a place near her house" I would again and again tried to correct him!

"No mom she is my Nanna and she makes special bread for me!" But as observed earlier he also referred as a small child to my brother Ray as being his father and not his uncle, he would also call my brothers home his home and our home the new house where he is staying.

"Mom could we go visit my father?" Den Junior would asked.

"Your dad is working honey, I know it's a Saturday but he needs to catch up with some work and we cannot go visit him!" I answered.

"No, not my dad, but my father!" He said.

"It's the same Junior!" I laughed.

"No it is not!" He persisted.

"Who is your father then Junior?" I asked.

"My father is Ray, but he had another name then and his home was my home!" He said with a smile. And Den would say don't argue with him let him be, he will grow out of it, we all have it when we were little! And I said to him 'I am pretty sure that I did not have that when I was little!' And he answered, 'Maybe you just do not remember, which is probably better, because you cannot live in a past life, you have to live in this life and make the best of each life given to you!' It was a little different with my youngest son Andrew, Andrew would inform everyone that his mother is a Queen, his father a King and his three sisters and he would be princesses! And that we all live in a huge castle, with a river with plenty of fish and with a garden with large trees with fruits. I found it very cute that he had such a vivid fantasy and thought that he was maybe confused due to his young age that he was a boy or a girl. The other thing was that he never mentioned his brother Junior in his fantasy!

"You're a cute and strong prince not a princess Andrew!" I told him.

"I am a prince and not a princess, are you sure?" He would asked. Both of them when they got older stopped claiming that they had another life or had great fantasy of another life! Another interesting note that happened with Junior was, that he asked us when he was just 4 years old, why Saint Nicolas was here on the Island on his birthdate, giving local kids gifts and not in Spain where he lived giving the kids there a gift!

"Mom are all the kids in Spain naughty children?" Junior asked.

"Well no, I think there are naughty and good children everywhere Junior!" I answered.

"Then why is Saint Nicolas not in Spain but here in Curaçao giving the good children gifts?" I was perplexed and did not know what to give him as an adequate answer.

"And why are his Pete's black? I do not remember them of being of different colors? Are also all the white Pete's from Spain naughty?" He kept on asking me. I just panicked and did not know what to answer him, as he kept staring at me with his big eyes, waiting for an answer. And what did he meant that he did not remember them of being of different colors, was he again referring to a past life?

"Saint Nicolas is a saint Junior and God allows him to be at various places at the same time!" I finally answered him.

"And the black Pete's?" He persisted.

"Well the white Pete's from Spain could not make it, because they had the flu!" I continued making it up and trying not to tell him too much!

"All of them?" He asked with his innocent big eyes.

"Yep, sadly all of them!" I replied and was really relieved that he just smiled, turned and run into the garden to play.

I never recalled my daughters telling me of such experiences of a prior live, but their conduct seems to imply that there also was a mystery there! When my eldest daughter was very little she used to prepare whenever someone comes to visit us, a bag with goodies for them! As soon as she noticed that the visitor is about to leave she would run to the kitchen cabinets and pick a plastic bag in which she would put a bag of beans, a can of tuna and other stuff. Then she would run to the leaving visitor and hand her or him the bag saying 'Here you go, now you have food to share with your family!' Most visitors found it cute but some were really wondering if it was not me that had stated to her that their family is poor or in need of food or something! But she also eventually grew out of it, but the first time that I told her that she cannot give our food away, she cried the whole day and was very sad and I decided that she may do it and that we together will prepare the bag with goodies for the visitors.

My youngest daughter Sue when she was little had commented also that she was actually not meant to live in such a big house in such a fancy neighborhood! That when she looked down she saw me and her sisters, living in a small house in a neighborhood that was considered a ghetto! We were enlarging our home from two bedrooms to five bedrooms, when I was pregnant of her and I did went to live for three to four months before I gave birth to her at my sister's Dee's home that was a small house in a government housing project! So that was also very strange that she said that 'when she looked down' she saw us living elsewhere! Looked down from where? When I asked her about it, she said 'You know!' And seemed very perplex when I told her I did not know and repeated 'No, you do know mom!'

Rona on the other hand was a mystery on her own! Everyone commented that she had an old soul! A soul of an old aristocrat lady I guess, she as a little child commented on the value of crystal glasses and porcelain set of cups for drinking tea, a very fancy old cute soul! But they all grew out of it as it seems as soon as they turn 4 or 5 and I really thought that it is best as Den suggested not to ponder or question them about this!

Den was told that he had a blood that is a mystery to scientist, he definitely would not believe me that this meant that maybe he has an alien blood. He just believes that the mystery of his blood will be uncovered soon, nothing to put much attention to. He does not like to discuss or go in depth about the mystics, spirits and or other mysteries in the world, for sure nothing to do with UFO's or extraterrestrials. He had a saying that 'If you do not bother them, they will definitely not bother you!' I decided after a while to go to bed and to inform my husband of my findings later on in the day. But when I got to our room I noticed that he was watching a film. He tends to go to bed very early at night and go for a run and a swim very early in the morning.

"Hey babe are you already awake?" I asked my husband Den, since it only was four in the morning! And normally he would wake up at a bit before five in the morning!

"Just got up, I think I went too early to bed last night!" Den said smiling.

"You would not believe what I have just discovered. You got a minute or two?" I said exited and decided not to give him the long but the very short version, with a twist.

"Sure hon, what is it?" Den replied, turning down the television.

"You know I have been searching for some answers of the why of all the differences between the races, primarily the differences in the hair texture on earth as Ray brought up! Well I just discovered that maybe the Negroid black race, your race are actually aliens from another planet!" I said smiling.

"Oh is the Negroid race now only my race because they are scary aliens?" He smiled back, trying to grab me to tickle me.

"No stop it! I am actually dead serious, it's not a joke, our race are supposed to be aliens that came from a distant planet, most probably, from the Orion Belt Constellation!" I added.

"Same Orion Belt that you and Den Junior are chasing for years in the sky? But aliens that is nonsense honey, how did you ever came to that conclusion?" My hubby asked laughing.

"Don't be like that, it's not nonsense, scientist had discovered tablets of an ancient civilization called the Sumerians on which was written that a far more technical advanced civilization called the Anunnaki, came to earth to mind gold to correct the atmosphere of their planet. Their own kind had enough of the hard work of mining gold and decided to run away. The Anunnaki which seemed to be the Negroid race, then decided to create humans, or the other races, yes you heard it right, they decided to create humans as slave workers to do the mining of gold for them!" I told Den.

"Isa these are all myths of ancient people believing that they are Gods or what not!" Den replied.

"These are not myths, but to the fact documentations of a civilization that seems to have existed or lived on earth at same time of the appearance of the first Homo sapiens or the first race the Negroid race! By the way do you know what the word Homo sapiens means?" I rebutted his objections and added another peace to the puzzle.

"So you then assume that they are then the same group or the same civilization?" Den asked.

"First let me answer you this, Homo sapiens means 'the wise man' I mean this has always puzzled me, that the first humans that were just starting to come out of the 'ape life' are suddenly considered 'wise'? And to your question, most certainly I assumed that, because there is no scientific evidence of any other intelligent being on earth, for sure 200.000 years ago, so the Anunnaki are the black Negroid or African race. Another fact is that according to scientist, the black Negroid race does not have hominoid or monkey gene in their system and therefore they would have a negative rhesus blood type. That according to them is a blood of not earthly origin. Do you hear me, not earthly origin! The same blood you have! So definitely your race" I said laughing, thinking that he would probably still not believe me.

"You think it has something to do with my blood?" He asked seriously, pulling his body in a more upright position.

"Well, all other base races on earth have next to the Negroid DNA also the rhesus monkey gene or DNA in their system, because that positive rhesus monkey blood has a direct connection with the hominoids or apelike man that were living on earth for millions of years, which should have confirmed in part the evolution theory!

Or an explanation by scientist for intelligent beings or humans on earth!" I explained to him.

"People always teased me that I have blue blood at the donor station, now you think that I have alien blood?" He asked laughing like he had toothache.

"That is what it seems like!' I answered.

"And what about the AB blood type?" Den asked.

"Well I have not exactly find out anything about that yet. But I have a theory, you want to hear it?" I asked.

"Shoot" He answered.

"The AB type is about 5% of the entire population on earth. And I bet that they did not count all the Africans running wild in Africa! And your blood AB negative is under 1%! So it is my theory that the rarest is also the alien blood, because they would have definitely been in the minority! So your blood the negative AB blood is the Anunnaki or alien blood. By the way for you to have AB negative blood it is also my theory that your dad and your mom both must have had AB negative blood too. Ok, than the positive O blood the blood with the highest percentage is the blood of the created other races by them the Anunnaki or aliens! Now here comes the interesting part, the mating of the Negroid black race or the Anunnaki, with the created other races then resulted in the existing of the A or B blood as a standing on its own blood! Because when an AB blood mix with an O blood, the child of these two races like in my case would be or A blood or B blood, never O, because O blood is recessive or in simple terms the AB or A or B blood is more dominant! And the positive blood type is more dominant, it vanishes out the negative blood type. So you are definitely a direct pure blood lineage of the aliens that came to earth, Den" I explained my theory to Den. Den laughed and replied.

"Ok! So according to you I definitively have alien blood and not blue blood!" Den said still smiling and shaking his head.

"Maybe the alien Negroid blood is the blue blood!" I answered.

"What do you mean?" Den asked a little startled.

"Well it seemed that these black Negroid beings were called 'The Gods' because they were spiritually guiding the other races and were also living a life as leaders or as the Kings and Queens, with the other races at their servitude. And that these races were first as I already said, created with the only purpose to serve as slave workers. And I believe that this is the real reason that are ancestors were enslaved in the new discovered territories, it was a plan of pay back or vengeance leaded by the Vatican, to be executed far away from the society in Europe that had adored these black Negroid as religious icons or leaders or as King and Queens. And you know something else lots of the depictions of this religious icons and King and Queens had, that you also have, is your eyes" I blurted out.

"My eyes?" Den asked.

"Yes your mysterious almond formed eyes, it was then that it hit me, like some sort of 'déjà vu', that I felt the connection to our past, our ancestor's life, the Anunnaki. I have always wondered why your eyes are formed that way and that all our girls seem to have these same eyes like yours" I answered.

"I must have inherit this from one of my parents. You know my grandparents has always told us that our ancestors came from Spain and that we are Hebrews. We do not talk about it much, because people tend to ridicule us because we are not white as the Jews are!" Den commented.

"Oh yes now I remember that you had mentioned that ones to me, I was also puzzled of that being correct" I replied.

"What do you intend to do with this info Isa? You know that people can get crazy or paranoid with this information! It could be very hard on the other races to learn that they were created with the only purpose to serve as slaves and that they are half hominoid or apelike man" Den said.

"Yes I know, count me in I am also half and half, your own special ape monkey" I said to Den smiling. He grabbed me in his arms and said.

"Indeed my own special monkey, I love you, you do not even know how much Isa!" He said and sighed while holding me tighter.

"I do not feel any lesser because I have DNA of both species in me, but I can relate to others who have not loved but hated the Negroid black race and now have to live with this fact, that they cannot shake it out of them, that they actually are hating themselves, because they are in fact Negroid to, as of the beginning. But you know I deeply believe that the truth is a sacred thing, nothing can be built on lies! And they have already had their

105

vengeance and enough is enough, our people the ones that were shamed and harmed, deserves to know who they are and whom their ancestors were, to understand why they were hated!" I answered.

"Ok, so you believe Isa that it is better to know the truth, although the truth can sometimes break something beautiful?" Den asked with his head down.

"There is nothing beautiful in a world where we as a race are being constantly discriminated and humiliated Den, without knowing why or believing that we are an inferior race. I do not want that for my kids and my grandchildren" I said shaking my head not understanding his comment.

"Forget what I said! How are you going to tackle this? Can I be of any help?" Den asked.

"Well first I need to share this on our family app as soon as I have put together more information! And afterwards I think I will definitely write a book, I think that the truth needs to be told, as ugly as it may be! And if people are going to get crazy or more crazy than they already are, others deserve to know this dark secret to help them understand why all the discrimination and the hatred. And to help our race get their dignity and confidence back, by knowing whom their ancestors were. With this knowledge comes also a greater responsibility for our race and I know that we are certainly up to it" I answered with a big smile on my face.

"You know babe, you have finally got your answer on the reason of the hatred and enslavement of our ancestors by the white man. I am very proud of you!" He said while giving me a kiss and pulling me again into his arms.

My oldest sister alive Dee called me that same day and asked me if I can come over to pick up the rent money that was distributed as part of a deal of an inheritance of a great uncle and aunt that did not have any children. I confirmed to her that I will be at her house the next day just after working hours. Me and my older sister were very close, due to the fact that when I was just a young teenager we had together a very traumatic experience. One night very late just some minutes before 1 am, when I was supposed to be in bed but pleaded to Dee that I will do the dishes for her if she let me stay awake and finish watching a scary movie that had just started at 11.30 pm and that I really needed to see! Sitting in the living room enjoying the climax of the movie that was about to reach its end, my sister Dee yelled at me from the bedroom, that we all were sharing as girls, to get the door for my other sister Mitta, who had gone out with her boyfriend. The film was just so intense and at a culminating point, so I decided out of an impulse to walk with my back towards the door to be able to still to follow the amazing ending and opened the door without taking my eyes from the television or my movie! It seemed eerily still and suddenly I felt very but very, very cold and all the hairs on my back and my head stood up and it was like someone screamed very loud through my mouth, while I was slowly turning my head around to face the door! Our house was very small, so everyone got up and ran to save me, my father with a huge baseball bat, ready to strike at any one that was hurting me, as I was still standing at the door as in shock still screaming my lungs out. My mother shook me and ask me what is wrong, but I was numb and could not speak! My sister Dee responded that she had heard clearly that my sister Mitta got home with her boyfriend and that she could see a silhouette at the door, through the bedroom windows. And that she heard that they also knocked at the door and that she had then asked me to open the door since she was already in her night gown and did not want Mitta's boyfriend to see her in her nightgown! But when I opened the door there was clearly no one standing at the door, at least no living person!

Before a week had passed it seemed that the same incident had occurred at a house in the neighborhood, but this time much earlier just after midnight. Freddy and Musa were living with their niece Rosa in a cute little house in the neighborhood. In that same week Rosa got really sick just when she opened the door after waking Musa and telling her that it seems that someone was knocking at the front door and although it was very late she wanted to go see who it is, because she thought that there could be a neighbor that needed their help and she told Musa that she is going to see who it is. Musa decided that it was best to follow her, and as soon as Rosa opened the door she fell on the floor and was having a kind of an epileptic shock, her whole body was shaken, her eyes were rolling and she was just getting blue, while she was spuming out saliva. An ambulance with high sirens came driving in our street and all the neighbors got up to see what was happening. Rosa stayed for days at the hospital, but when she was released she was never the same person again after that day! My mother told us what Musa has told her of the incident of Rosa and she told us that we were blessed that nothing happened to us, the same week. And that it all had according to her, to do with the tearing down of an old tree in our neighborhood by the electricity company. It seems that, that huge tree was housing an evil spirit that needed another space to call home and that that evil spirit was probably now in Musa's house or worst maybe in the body of Rosa? After acknowledging what had happened to Rosa, my older sister and I created a very tight bond of mutual protection and togetherness. Because whatever came first to our house it was definitely intended for my older sister Dee, because she was the one in charge to open the door for Mitta, since I was although it was on a Saturday night, already supposed to be in bed and asleep before midnight as required by my parents!

So I thought maybe I could address this issue of the Anunnaki or we the Negroid race being aliens with her and her family to see what their thoughts are.

"Hi Dee" I said giving her a kiss on both her cheeks.

"How is Mani?" I asked.

"He is at his sister and should be arriving soon" Dee answered.

"OK! And how is it going with Tony and Dino, are they here?" I asked.

"They are fine, Tony is at work and Dino went out to cut some hair at the house of a client. Do you need them?" Dee asked.

"Oh I just wanted to talk to you all to get to know your opinion on a somewhat complicated subject. So I can also get a feeling on the title of a presentation and later a book that I would like to write " I said.

"You finally decided to write a book, good for you" My sister Dee said. I was indeed for a long time walking around with the idea to maybe write a book over us the descendants of the Negroid race, but it just seemed that there were so many unanswered questions that I never started writing, but now it is entirely another story!

"Maybe I can pick only your brain?" I said to Dee smiling.

"Sure, what is it about?" Dee asked.

"It is about the creation of humans, religion and aliens!" I stated.

"What, is it a science fiction book? I do not believe in aliens Isa!" Dee replied laughing.

"But you do believe in the mystic as do I! What if I told you that I have maybe discovered that Jesus and the Virgin Mary, Moses, Saint Nicolas and various others named in the Bible are black or Negroid people. That the Bible is a book of their history, their present and the future faith of the Negroid race and that they actually came with their religion of one God from another planet, because they are or more correctly, we are actually aliens living now casually on planet earth. And that they our Ancestors decided to create humans as slave workers to mind gold for them that they needed to save their own planet? And that, that is maybe the reason that our black Negroid ancestors were enslaved and dehumanized in the African Trade Slave?" I informed Dee. But Dee my sister was obviously upset.

"Ohhh no, no, no, I believe that it is God that created us the humans!" Dee answered a little annoyed.

"Ok! Put that just for a minute aside, what would you think? You and I both believe in the existence of things and secrets beyond of what we see and can possibly understand. So what would you think if it was the truth?" I asked Dee again.

"Isa I am not at an age that I could began to doubt in the beliefs that I have established for decades and which had given me peace of mind. So I do not want to discuss or change my personal believes, but if you believe in this new and yet unknown truth then you must pursue this and write your book" My sister Dee said to me. I was a little disappointed though and knew that more people are going to have same reaction of not being able to open themselves for a new believe system, although this belief system would primarily replace the players from being white people to being our own black or Negroid race people! But it will never replace the belief in God our Father and his son Jesus Christ!

After a few weeks of compiling some more information and cross checking all the information gathered I decided that I was ready to start sending all available information to our Happy Family Group app, where all my siblings and their kids and some other family members and friends communicate with each other. I decided it would be best if I spill it all out, since my daughter Sue, my husband Den and my sister Dee did not react as shocking as I first thought they would! And my husband only request was, to put it all out there, but step by step as different theories or findings the same way that I have discovered them and not to lead them as of the beginning to the end to my own conclusion or my findings, but to let them also take each step as I have also taken each step and let each of them decide at the end what to believe or not. He also cautioned me not to bestow any feelings of hate or revenge by our own people.

So I had to be very clear as per my findings that it was indeed the black Negroid race that actually started with the enslavement, by creating humans to be in their servitude, but that they later repented and were not sure how to solve this problem, either by erasing their creation or to embrace their creation, that they later learned to love, perfectly aware that their creation will eventually take revenge on their own descendants. That would have been a very difficult decision for our ancestors to take, nevertheless they decided to ow their responsibility and protected, saved and guided the by them created humans.

When I opened the family app I noticed that there was a discussion of the possibility to organize a family and friends bus trip to the Beaches of the west side the first Saturday of the summer vacation in July, before the ones who are leaving the island for a vacation abroad so that they also could participate. And of course there is the usual staying of all of us, some 30 to 40 persons, at one large beach house for five to six days in the summer vacation which is more in the middle of the summer vacation period. The amount of children and adults, sleeping on matrasses next to each other on the floor on the large veranda in the open air always amazed me. Because these same adults and children will definitely not sleep at home on a matrass on the floor and in the open air!

Swimming and playing games all day at the beach and in the evening by acclamation by all present the request for me to tell the same ghost stories my parents, aunts and uncles had told me and a few experiences of myself year in year out, without the audience getting bored! But I do switch it, playing guess the artist or the film or a group quiz or a karaoke or dance competition! Another of our favorite events is the camping in tents at Santa Cruz, another one of our great beaches at the west end, for 3 to 4 days, beginning Thursday in the afternoon before Good Friday and celebrating Eastern Sunday on the Beach! Santa Cruz will be packed with a lot of tents of many other families that also came to celebrate this holiday in their tents! This great experience of living for a few days in tents does give you more appreciation of the comfort and luxuries at home, since we need to share a bathroom with all those present at the beach to take a bath, sometimes standing in lines for more than an hour! And also everyone gets to do their business in the same four to five toilets that are available to all that are enjoying the camping on the beach! But other events are also organized during the year so that all the nephews and nieces can be together and appreciate each other's company.

"A bus trip is a great idea on the first Saturday Nelly! Our last bus trip was three years ago" I commented.

"Are you going abroad on vacation this summer aunt Isa?" My niece Nelly asked.

"Not this year love! You know I have travelled a lot for vacation or business and the best place for a vacation is on the beach of my beautiful island, Curacao. So I am also on the list of Nani, for going to the beach house with my grandkids!" I wrote while smiling.

"That is great aunt Isa, but you would not know and appreciate that if you have not travel! Are Sue, Ella and Rona going abroad with their kids?" Nelly asked.

"Yes, they are going to Bonaire for a few days at the end of July and we are all going to spent a week at the Kunuku Resort, in the first week of the summer vacation!" I replied.

"But then you are not able to participate in the bus trip, aunt Isa!" Nelly commented.

"Why not?" I asked.

"Because you would be at the Kununku Resort!" Nelly answered.

"The Kunuku Resort is at the west side, so we can easily participate in the Bus trip! No problem at all! This would get the kids also out of the swimming pool for a day. I cannot make any commitments for the grown-ups, but me and my grandchildren will be joining you guys for the bus trip" I answered.

"Ok! So I can put you aunt Isa and your 3 grandkids, 4 in total!" Nelly asked.

"Yes please!" I confirmed.

"Ok! Dad and Mom and my little sis, total 3!" Nelly kept counting.

"You know, since uncle Ray is going put also uncle Den on my list, for a total of 5!" I requested. Nelly kept counting who are the ones who are interested in going on the bus trip, so she can confirm the arrangements! I decided that I will wait a few hours before sending my app with the information that I have prepared, avoiding that my piece of info would get lost in the turmoil of reservations and preparations of the bus road trip!

"Hey guy's a few of us had some very interesting discussion at our last family get together at aunt's Dee's home, that had inspired me to start an investigation or research on the creation or the evolution of humans and the different races. The reason is that as observed by uncle Ray, how come if we all came from the same source there are so many differences, like our nose and the European nose, our mostly wooly hair and the European straight hair, our mostly decent behind and the mostly flat behind of the Europeans! Most of us believe in God and also the creation by God of humans as explained by the Bible. But there is also some scientific theories, like the 'Evolution Theory', which states that human beings, came from apes or monkeys, evolve to hominoids or apelike men to homo sapiens or the modern humans. Another Theory is the 'Out of Africa Theory', which states that the first homo sapiens or humans were Africans or the Negroid black race! There is also a lot of ancient documentation of also the creation of humans. Both uncle Ray and I also believe that in the end all scientific evidence must in some way or other tie in with the Bible or other existing documentation on the creation of humans.

The theory of evolution by natural selection of the scientist Charles Darwin, published in 1859 is based on the notion that mankind evolved from ape like man or hominoids to Homo Sapiens or humans. But without transitional life form being found however, this theory of the evolution of mankind has a "missing link" or a

115

missing chain of evidence and is therefore considered by many as a bogus theory. This theory also seems to subtlety imply that the black Negroid race has stopped to evolved or that the white race evolved further or that maybe the black Negroid race does not even belong in this theory of evolution! Reason why I am now only going to concentrate on the possibility of the out of Africa Theory and the creation of men, as reported in the Bible and also other creation myths, like the ones mentioned by the Sumerians on their tablets. All of this must also tie in with scientific available facts or scientific assumptions or theories.

I personally always believed that the Bible is a history book of accounts that happened or is happening and accounts that needs to happen in the future, as many other people I guess. But the main reason of my quest is as pointed out by uncle Ray, the differences between the black and the white race. Because seriously I had never stood still and questioned the differences in regards to the black and in particular the white race. But as noticed by uncle Ray there are really great differences that cannot be explained away as coming from the same ancestors, like still the color of skin, the hair texture, face and body structure. So I have decided to start at the beginning when it all started and dug up information of the Bible, when it was written by whom and what is written in it. Here are my first findings" I wrote on WhatsApp.

The first information that I send to them was about the creation as stated in the Bible.

"The Bible is divided in the Old Testament, which could also be described as the Torah and the New Testament. The Bible is a

116

bundling of books in which the word of God is proclaimed and consist of a collection of 66 books written as recorded by about 40 authors in three different languages, Hebrew (the Old Testament), Aramaic (the Old Testament) and the Greek language (the New Testament), on three different continents, African (Egypt, the Old Testament), Asian (Middle East, the Old Testament) and European (Greece or all over Europe, the New Testament). There is also some interesting discussion that the Middle East is actually part of the African continent and not a continent of Asia! It was actually in the 1850 that this land called now the Middle East was redefined as not being from the African continent but from the Asian and European continent by the Europeans!

The Bible is spread over approximately 1.600 years. The first writings, or what is called The Old Testament, were from 3.500 years ago or about 1.400 years before the birth of Jesus Christ. The Old Testament regards the creation of earth and men and some predictions in the future! The New Testament regards the period since the birth of Christ his life and his death and after his death! The first 5 books, were written by Moses in Hebrew and the books are named Genesis, Exodus, Leviticus, Numbers and Deuteronomy. And as you all should recall Moses was raised since being a baby as an Egyptian by the daughter of a Pharaoh! So it seems that the Egyptians also spoke Hebrew! The Hebrew Old Testament was translated into Greek approximately 250 BC or before the time of Christ. In the book of Genesis or the Book of The Beginnings, which was written as stated by Moses is revealed the creation of earth and of humans by God. 'Let us make men in our image, after our likeness and let them have dominion over the fish in the sea and the birds in the sky, over the life stock and all the wild animals and over all the creatures that move along the ground'. And the Lord God formed man out of dust of the ground and breathe into his nostrils the breath of life. And God put the man, which he named Adam in the Garden of Eden. Then God saw that it is not good for the man to be alone and he took a rib from the man and formed the female, which he named Eve.

Ray and Richey, out of these scriptures one could ask which color does the "dust of the ground" of the fertile Garden of Eden have to be to comprise the skin color of Adam. A white color complex as is the allegation of the white West Europeans or the Vatican, who claims that God is white and therefore created Adam and Eve in his white image, is certainly very doubtful. I have also learned from scientific evidence that out of completely white parents can never be born a black child. Completely black parents however can bare a white child or a child without sufficient pigmentation or melanin, which is due to a genetic disorder, called Albinism. Which could explain why there was a migration to the north of a large group of the ancient Africans or Ethiopians or the Negroid race or the Negroid Albinos to get away of the sun and very hot condition that has caused various diseases for this group of Africans.

That also concludes that if Adam and Eve were created white, as the first and only human's race on earth, the black human race could not have ever existed. Modern scientist had also proven that not even constant exposure to sunlight for generations and generations could darken the skin of white people and make them black people. It is the quantity and the quality of melanin, which is internally produced by the pineal gland that determines the skin color of a person. Which means that of the original white Caucasian race of Adam and Eve, can never be born a black or dark skinned child. The child would then be born white as is his parents and would then be exposed to sun to obtain a tan or reddish, but not a black color. And all of this without even taken in consideration all the differences in the facial and body features and the hair texture of the Negroid and the white race!

As the story in the Bible goes, Adam and Eve had everything they would have wished for, but disobeyed God by eating from the forbidden tree. Could God have been so cruel to create Adam and Eve as white people or people without pigmentation or melanin and literally expose them nude due to their disobedience, out of the "Garden of Eden" unto the harsh, bare and very sunny and hot condition in the northern part of the African continent or the nowadays called Middle East area?" I stated.

"Before you go further Isa, I have never read the Bible, but does it really mention, 'Let us create or make men' and not 'I God created men', who is the 'us'?" Berna a friend on our family app asked.

"According to explanation given by our priest when I was attending Catholic school as a child the three together, The Father, The Son and The Holy Spirit are supposed to be the us" I answered.

"But the son did not exist as yet, he came later!" Berna replied.

"Yes your right, but time and space are concepts that we as humans do not really comprehend as yet. And that maybe the Son Jesus always existed besides his father God. My mother always stated that the Bible is sometimes too complicated to follow and understand, that it is better to follow your natural instinct or gut or your spiritual guidance" I replied.

"And what does your natural instinct and your gut tells you Isa?" Berna asked.

"That there is definitely an Almighty Creator of the Universe that we call God and that the Bible does have glances of the truth in it" I answered Berna.

"You are really a firm believer that God really exist, aren't you?" Berna asked.

"Oh yes definitely, I just feel the goodness and greatness of him in my soul. And I also do believe that he has sent his son to earth to teach us how we can free our spirit and live a more spiritual and happy life. And that he permitted himself to be sacrificed for the sins of our forefathers! What I never believed is what the religions are creating as reality for us and using the bible to misinformed, make us scare of God, with a thousand and one rules and mislead us, because loving and appreciating God is supposed to be loving, respecting and appreciating your fellow man and following your gut instinct, but that is my personal opinion" I answered.

"Another thing the Middle East is definitely not in Africa Isa!" Berna commented.

"Well it seems that what we now called the Middle East was named that way in the 1850 or so by the British people when they colonized that part of Africa, then named North Africa! The Middle East is as I understood, on the tectonic plates of Africa and is part of that continent and not a standalone continent or on the tectonic plate of Asia. But there are still some discussion what the truth is on that issue!" I answered Berna's question.

"And I always thought that it was on its own tectonic plate, Arabic plate or something like that!" Berna replied.

"Berna there are only 7 tectonic plates, Africa, North America, South America, Europe, Asia, Australia and Antarctica! I have also noted that there seems to be an effort for whatever reason by the West not to include the area called the Middle East to the African continent" I explained to Berna.

"Isa you mean to tell me that if Adam and Eve were white, we as the black race would have never existed?" My sister Ann asked.

"Well it is scientifically impossible for the first two people if they were white to have a black child" I answered Ann my sister.

"So Adam and Eve must have been black then. What about Jesus and the Virgin Mary? And if Adam and Eve were black, from where did the white race came from?" My sister Ann asked.

"But two black persons can have a white or pale child, a child that is an Albino. But still if whites are in fact Albino's, a genetically imperfection to their skin color, they should actually still have the same features as the black people, but without the skin, hair and eye color. An Albino is a person that has a deficit in the production of melanin and therefore has partial or complete absence of pigment in the skin, hair and eyes, thus making their color white, their eyes blue or green and their hair blond. Which could have somewhat explained the emergence of the white color race out of a genetic disorder of the originally black Negroid race. But that still does not answer the question Ray our brother had in regards of the other changes, for example the hair texture, lips, nose and butt!" I tried to explain to my sister.

"Oh yes, I saw a girl like that with white blond afro hair, she looked very special and beautiful. But she had indeed a flat nose, thick lips and a nice but. So the one race excludes the other race? But do you know what race Adam and Eve were, I want to know that" My sister Ann kept on asking.

"I will get there soon, but this is all that I have for today, but I will continue tomorrow!" I responded to my sister.

"No don't do that, I do not want to wait Isa!" My sister Ann reacted as if she seemed very disappointed.

"I will come by today late in the afternoon and explained it all to you personally if you are too eager to wait, because my fingers are getting numb!" I replied.

"Perfect, I will be awaiting your visit!" Ann responded and closed also for me the conversation on the subject on our family app.

My sister lived just a few minutes from my house and I decided to visit her more early in the evening. But when I got there Marla, one of her daughters informed me that she forgot that she had a 'Bon Kune' game to attend to and left a message for me on my phone and I forgot to look at my phone before I drove to her house.

"No problem Marla! How is it going with Drick your hubby, is he at home?" I asked. I loved to talk with Drick, we both have interest in the mystics of the world and always seemed to have same point of view and it would be interesting to hear his point of view on the subject of the different races and the possible origin of the Negroid black race.

"Yes, he just got home aunt Isa! I'll call him for you!" Marla responded. Marla and her hubby and their two children lived in an extension of my sister's home. It was very common on Curacao, for grown up children with their own children to live together with their parents, due to the very high rent prizes.

"Hi aunt Isa!" Drick said while entering the main sitting room.

"Hi Drick!" I said while given him the usual kisses on his cheeks.

"We owe you a visit aunt Isa, but time is short I am now working two jobs, one full time and the other one on a part time basis" Drick felt the need to explain why I did not see them anymore visiting me at home. We loved to watch very scary movies together or other mysterious plots of murder to identify who the murder is, before the film reveals it.

"Life is a hustle, I know, I have been there" I said smiling.

"Definitely a hustle! But we have plans to start a business and we need some capital to invest in some equipment and materials, reason why we are working extra hard to obtain extra money" Marla replied.

"Great, I am very happy for you guy's. Any help or advice you need I am here for you! But the reason I needed to talk to you is because I have a mystery that needs to be solved Drick" I said.

"Tell me aunt Isa, what is the mystery?" Drick asked.

"Well, what if I would tell you that the black Negroid race, our race are maybe descendants of aliens that came from another planet in a complete other solar system!" I said.

"What?" Drick asked looking at me as, 'are you losing it aunt Isa?'

But Marla looked at me as saying, 'whatever you say aunt Isa I know it is the truth!'

Marla and me had some very interesting experiences in which I had my mother whom was then already deceased, visit me in my dreams and asking me with desperation to ask Marla as a young lady to come to my home the next morning and to spent the whole day with us. Just before leaving her home to come to our home, Marla was visited by her boyfriend that invited her for a road trip together with his friends all on motorcycles as a surprise. But she told her boyfriend that she already made plans to go spent a day at her favorite aunt's house and that she cannot disappoint her aunt, because it was going to be a special making cookies day! Marla was very good in making delicious butter cookies!

That same day her boyfriend who was leading the group of bikers, was hit on his bike by a car, of which the driver claims that he did not even saw him on the road. He was brought to the hospital in an ambulance in a very critical condition with a broken rib a broken hip and a broken arm. His parents informed Marla that the doctors said that he was lucky to be alive and that he thanked God that she was not his back rider, as he had originally planned. Because if that was the case he or she would have died since he only had one helmet to wear on the bike!

A few years later Marla was engaged to a much older boyfriend that seems very obsessed with the whereabouts of Marla. My mother began visiting me in my dreams again informing me that Marla's boyfriend was dangerous and pleaded with me to convince Marla to leave his boyfriend and come live with us for a period of time. Marla did came to live with us, which her boyfriend did not appreciate, because he could not exercise all his control on her the way that he wanted. I tried to convince Marla that he was emotionally abusing her and that maybe it was better to leave this older obsessed guy, but without success. Because although she told the boyfriend that she had enough of his obsessive behavior, he would bring her gifts and ask her out to dine and talk and she would be charmed again by him and forgave him. But then again he would threaten her and be out of his mind if she did not immediately picked up the phone when he calls her, as in a vicious cycle. But one day I had a terrible feeling that Marla was in great danger that led me to inform the boyfriend that just came at my house to offer Marla another reconciliation gift, that he was stalking Marla, because she has already decided not to be his girlfriend anymore, and that he needs to accept this and move on and that if he persist, then I will call the police if I see or hear from him again! On same occasion I also handed him back his phone or the phone that he had given to Marla!

But Marla was upset that I was so harsh on him, she argued that she could have gone with him and explain to him in a private setting at his home as he had requested, that she really does not have any more romantic feelings for him, but that they could still be friends, because he was very good to her and helped her when she was having trouble at home! And I heard myself saying to her: 'I know that it is his plan to have you come to his home so that he can kill you and afterwards commit suicide! Because he believes that if he cannot have you, not as a friend but as his lover no one else should have you!' I was completely shocked when I uttered these words, it just did not seemed that they came out of my own mouth! Marla was also shocked and then I decided to tell her about my dreams of my mother or her grandmother, the first one some 5 to 6 years ago when she was 15 or 16 and that it was her that persisted me in inviting her to spend a day with us the same day that her boyfriend asked her to go cruising on his bike and had a terrible accident in which case if she was with him as his back rider she would probably have been killed! And that it is again her grandmother that has warned me in my dreams this time also of an impendent danger if she remains with this particular boyfriend! After hearing this she decided to definitely cut all contacts with this older obsessed boyfriend. Just a few days later the ex-boyfriend, after constantly and desperately trying to contact her through her mother and other family members or friends, committed suicide and left a letter for Marla in which he states that they belong together and that it was his wish to be with her forever, but if that cannot be the case, he does not have any reason to live!

The next day late in the afternoon I decided to continue sending more information on our family app. This time I use my hubby's phone app to first prepare and write the basic information and forward them to myself, piece by piece to be able to later forward them to the family app.

"Hey guy's, here is part 2. In the book of Genesis, it is also stated a precise description of the location of the 'Garden of Eden'. There should be 4 rivers that originated from the Garden of Eden. The first one Pishon, who also passes through the region of Havila, the second one Gihon, who passes through the entire land of Cush/ Ethiopia, the third one Tigris who passes on the east of Ashur and the fourth one Euphrates. And that in these areas there should be an abundance of gold and other precious metals and stones. It is well known that Africa is one of the richest continents of precious metals and stones. Scientist has also discovered that there was a sudden movement from the ancient people out of Ethiopia Africa to the north, or to Europe and Asia" I forwarded to the family app.

"Isa hi! Sorry that I missed an opportunity yesterday to discuss this, but I understood that you already told Marla and Drick everything but asked them not to brief me yet! And now you are again explaining all of this, it is too much info, just get to the point please!" Ann my always impatient not so more little sister commented.

"Well there are many people on this family and friends app that maybe need to have the complete information Ann! Me, Drick and Marla have a history of discussing mystic things. And I know that with them I do not really need a lot of explaining, because it is a complicated subject, if you do not have any base information. I have to cover various areas so that at the end it all will come together" I tried to explain to my sister Ann.

"Ok! Continue then!" My sister replied.

"According to scientist the first race existing on earth are the Negroid race, some 200.000 years ago! And Ray, I have found the explanations by scientist to the questions of the different features of the Negroid or black race and the Caucasian race. It has been scientifically established through DNA, that the emergence of the European white race was due to mixing or interbreeding with hominoids or ape like man named Neanderthals and the Asian and Australoid race due to interbreeding with also ape like man named Denisovans. Which interbreeding according to scientist has changed permanently the features of the Caucasian race from the Negroid or black race. The permanent maintaining of the white or fair color by the Europeans, a much more thicker skin as the Neanderthal, to adapt to the cold and the change of the structure of the hair from coarse to sleek hair, a more pointed and larger nose, tinnier lips and no bumps, which are very common with apes and other animals on earth, would have developed due to this interbreeding with these apelike man or hominoids" I kept on sending as explanation to the family app.

"Why do you call them apes aunt Isa, or they not other people? There is mention of other people in the bible. Because Adam and Eve had two sons and they would have intermarried or interbreed with the daughters of these other humans, not apes?" My niece Nelly asked.

"Well Nelly, if Adam and Eve were the first created humans, then their cannot be other humans or it would be the siblings or sisters of the sons of Adam and Eve! The only other beings were the watchers and or the Angels of God and the hominoids are described by scientist as apelike man, named the Neanderthals and the Denisovans. These apelike man the Neanderthal and the Denisovans could not speak, but only grunt, which fact limited their further intellectual development. Because the difference according to scientist in a human and a man like ape is that humans have the ability to speak, write, create music and art. And I never before read the Bible myself Nelly and have now only read the Genesis part of the beginning. But indeed it was always a mystery for me also, to as with whom the sons of Adam and Eve procreated, when I was attending Catholic lessons at school. But maybe you are right and the Neanderthals and the Denisovans were really regarded by God as another kind of humans with whom the sons of Adam and Eve interbreed with? I do not know. But that also means that humans were not the only intelligent beings on planet earth. Who created then the other beings on earth? And of what and how did they live if the earth was void before God created Adam and Eve? I will have to owe you these answers for now. But let me continue with I have already prepared" I wrote as an answer to Nelly.

"The proportion of the human body also varies of that of the manlike apes. The Human or Homo Sapiens should have a 'sacred geometry', the 'Vitruvian man' proportions by Leonardo Da Vinci or what the scientist nowadays called the Phi in the human body or the 'golden ratio' which was documented since 6.000 years ago in Mesopotamia, the land of Summer by the Sumerians. With this golden ratio of the body, it would be very easy to have great achievements in various sport activities" I forwarded to the family and friends app.

"So you did some research I see aunt Isa" Richey finally joined the conversation on the family app.

"I do definitely believe that they were not apes but other humans, it was forbidden by God to lay with animals" Nelly commented.

"Well maybe there were other beings on earth Nelly" I replied to my niece.

"Yes definitely there were more beings on earth, but they were certainly not apes or apelike man!" Nelly stated.

"But in regards to our earlier conversation Richey, if the white race emerged as a genetic disorder, that we now call Albinism out of the black Negroid people as originally created by God in his own image, that went to the North were they mate with the Neanderthals or apelike man what did the white race as a race lost as the perfect creation of humankind by God, due to this interbreeding with the Neanderthals? Because the white race certainly would have lost some God given potentials by the interbreeding with Neanderthals, which were not humankind but manlike apes as presented by the nowadays scientist? Does not that fact implies that they could never be the Superior Race if that denomination even exists?" I asked Richey.

"Aunt Isa, if that was the truth they did not lose anything, they gained something as far as I see it, because the facts according to written history is that the white Europeans had the greatest achievements and they are the ones that have the best developments for their countries and they are the rulers of the world" Replied Richey.

"Yes they certainly are the current rulers of the world. But it is also known that in ancient days the Sumerians, the Nubians, the Ethiopians and the Egyptians all acknowledged black races were the powerful ones in the world. The European white races were as documented by themselves, in the stone ages when the Ethiopians, Egyptians and Sumerians all black races were already in their golden ages. Which is perfectly explainable due to the theory of the interbreeding of the first specie with hominoids, which would had sat the white race back in their development" I stated.

"But the Egyptians were not black, but white" Richey pointed out.

"Richey Egypt is in Africa, all ancient people of Africa were black and the paintings on the wall of the Egyptians are all depicted as black or brown colored people, with braided hair" I replied.

"Yes Richey, everyone knows that the Egyptians were not white but as we are, some very dark and some more brownish, but definitely not white" My niece Nelly commented.

"No you are both wrong, they painted their faces and body black or brown. I saw a documentary were the nowadays Egyptians explained why their ancestors painted their faces and body black, which is a sign of fertility, before they let the painters and sculptures make a depiction of them. And that they had straight hair but wore wigs with a lot of braided hair. That is also why all the films of Egyptians are of the original white people" Richie mentioned.

"Richey there is historical documentation that Egyptians are the same people from the first nation the Ethiopian Negroid nation that decided to migrate and lived at different territories. But that afterwards Egypt decided that they wanted to be an independent state, the same which occurred with England and North America" I replied.

"Have you ever seen pictures of ancient Egyptians Richey, they are black or dark brown and their hair are curly or braided as is currently done in our and other African black cultures. Google images of Egyptians, Richey" Nelly mentioned.

"Yes I know that, but as I mentioned before it is because they paint their skin dark as a sign of being fertile and they were braided wigs to look more prominent" Richey repeated.

"Does that imply that black people are more fertile or has lesser problems getting a woman pregnant and had a more prominent life and was therefore the black color and the braided look copied to belong to an elite group of that period? And who was that elite group that they decided to copy, was it the black Negroid race?" I asked Richey.

"Well they did not explain it in that way, they just stated that their skin was colored black to emphasized their fertility and that the Egyptians did not have braided hair, but straight hair and wore wigs of braided hair to look more prominent. These evidence are supposed to proof that the Egyptians just were not black" Richey wrote.

"Well I think they certainly failed in doing that. Maybe the current Egyptians whom are not black, but are now in Egypt due to conquer and migration of foreigners, mainly Arabs, did not want to acknowledge that the history and legacy of the Egyptians are not theirs, because the ancient original Egyptians, were for sure black. They had a forward jawline, thick lips, a more flat nose and nice butts! I think I will continue tomorrow guys" I ended the app.

I was exhausted, my nephew Richey's comments on this topic always brings up mixed emotions in me. It was for me impossible to comprehend how a person can have such denigrating opinions of his own race and people. It almost seems that he in fact hates himself or he did not accept or believe that he belongs to the Negroid race! At that point and time I decided that I was not going to waste more time convincing him of my findings, he would never be open to believe in the fact's that I would present. In his mind it is the white race that is the superior race that has dominated the world in ancient times and that has always dominated the world. He had already made his mind with the white race being the ones that are not corrupt and holy and the best ones to be in charge of bringing happiness to the people on earth!

A few days afterwards at the office my husband asked me if I wanted to join him, his cousin Fred and another friend Lilo for a 'Jambo' lunch. 'Jambo' is one of our delicious local foods, but it also can make you very sleepy afterwards, not a good idea when you have a lot of work to finish. Normally I would also decline to join him in his manly friend's lunches or other events, since they would go on rambling about football and other men talk, but I began an interesting conversation on the black Hebrews yesterday with his cousin and I knew that my hubby also liked the subject. A good plate of 'Jambo' was also irresistible, although I had to lose

133

some pounds that I gain, by snacking while doing my research on the races at late night or early morning hours.

We went in one car since they were also coming back to the office to wrap up a deal that Den was helping them finalize. When we got there and were seated, his cousin started talking about his blooming business at St. Martin and why it was very difficult for him to start a business in Curacao.

"You know here in Curacao there is a constant battle to avoid black people, to start a business and to be successful, you guys are very lucky!" Fred said.

"Well we are counting our blessings" My husband answered.

"So it is not the same in St. Martin?" I asked curiously.

"No it was very easy for me to start my business in St. Martin, after struggling for years to start in Curacao some 20 years ago, I went to live on St. Martin and started in a nick of time" Fred replied.

"Why do you think there is that difference of approach in St. Martin in comparison with Curacao?" I asked.

"Well Isa I believe that in Curacao they look at from which family you come and in St. Martin they look at what is your project and what it can mean for St. Martin's economy!" Fred replied.

"I never thought of that, now I understand why many in the field, first thought that I was the illegitimate daughter or granddaughter of the founder of the company that we took over" I said laughing.

"Don't worry about it, it's a let's keep it in the family or groups that are already wealthy thing, no wannabe rich, but currently poor black intruders allowed" Fred replied laughing.

"Yes many local and young entrepreneurs are experiencing the same treatment on the island and then the Government is putting their head in the sand and claiming that no discrimination is taken place at the established financial institutions. These financial institutions even deny your petition and then give your idea to the same group that already has it all, to be executed!" Lilo replied, he was also born and was living on Curacao but decided to migrate and start a business in St. Maarten also.

"Fred yesterday you were just beginning to explain about the fact that you believe that the real Hebrews are black and not the white Jews and that you are now in a group that are currently investigating this! Who are the black people that you believe are the real Hebrews exactly?" I asked.

"Well we have a group that is also corresponding internationally and we believe that the Hebrews are us the ones that their ancestors were brought over as slaves to the Caribbean and the Americas but not only from Africa but also from Europe!" Fred responded.

"I have also heard that, but I still think it is very far fetch, don't you think Den?" Lilo the friend asked Den. Den my husband only shrug his shoulders, not wanting to go much in debt.

"Actually I think I have living proof of the black Negroid race being the ones that brought religion and science to planet earth! Tell him about your blood Den!" I said, encouraging Den, knowing that he does not really like talking about these things. World politics, world economics, history and its consequences, important world happenings he was very good discussing these issues but other more mystic or conspiracy theories was not really his kind of topic.

"What is there to tell, I have a blood type that is considered not to have an earthly origin and some people say that I have royal blood or Hebrew blood!" Den replied a little uncomfortable.

"But how can that be possible?" Lilo asked.

"Well they stole our religion and our history" Fred answered.

"Who is they?" Lilo asked Fred.

"The Vatican or the Roman Catholic Church and the white Jews" Fred answered.

"And also the Arabs" I added.

"That is ludicrous, why would they do that?" Lilo asked.

"Lilo, the Hebrews, Jesus, the Virgin Mary, John the Baptist, Moses, Saint Nicolas all were black Negroid people!" Fred answered.

"I heard a lot of conspiracy of that also, that all these people were Negroid, but it does not make any sense! You cannot buy anything with religion, so why would they steal it?" Lilo asked.

"It is all about power and control Lilo! Power that the misuse of religion can give you to have control over people!" Fred answered.

"You mean to tell me that the Arabs, the white Jews and the Vatican Church stole the religion of the Negroid people, so that they could use the religion to gain power over their own people?" Lilo asked in astonishment.

"Well I am not so sure about the Arabs, but surely the Vatican and the white Jews!" Fred answered.

"Oh definitely the Arabs too!" I commented.

"So the Catholic faith, the Jewish faith and the Muslim faith all mainly different white peoples religion, are according to you stolen religions from the Negroid black people?" Lilo asked in disbelief.

"Yep! But Den what is there special about your blood?" Fred asked curiously.

"Well my blood is AB rhesus negative blood. Only 15% of the population has a rhesus negative blood. And scientist just do not understand why there are people with this blood, because it just does not fit the evolution theory that we evolved from apes. The combination AB negative blood is only represented by a percentage less than 1%. I have been teased to have blue, Hebrew and now on top of it all, alien blood!" Den answered with a weary smile, since he was not at all comfortable with this topic.

"And having AB negative blood according to my theory means that you have a direct blood legacy to the Anunnaki or the alien blood" I further explained.

"Why alien blood?" Fred asked.

"That is very interesting and creepy, I do not even know what kind of blood I have, but I sure got to find out now!" Lilo said smiling.

"And how did you find out Den?" Fred asked Den.

"I am a blood donor!" Den replied.

"You know I have read something about the DNA of the Hebrews being identified, but I never thought it would be so easy to check your blood, I really thought that it was an expensive thing to do, researching your DNA. But I still do not understand the alien thing!" Fred commented.

"What about if I informed you that according to ancient documentation named the Sumerian Tablets, it seems that the Negroid race came from another planet and a complete other constellation. That the Negroid race are the descendent of technical very advanced beings called the Anunnaki that came to earth to mind gold! And that they created the humans as slave workers using the hominoid DNA and upgrade this with their own DNA! Modern scientist has established that all the other races have two DNA, one of the Negroid and one of the hominoid! Which means that the Negroid race, is the Anunnaki and that all the other races are hybrids, of two species!" I said. Fred was just staring at me in silence with his mouth open, then he finally spoke.

"I heard of the Anunnaki, but I never made the connection. So the plot maybe bigger than I thought!" Fred said slowly shaking his head.

"Maybe I am slow, but did you just said mam that the Negroid race are essentially descendants from extra-terrestrials?" Lilo asked.

"That's exactly what I said!" I responded.

Two days after this lunch I decided to forward the last prepared information to the family app.

"Hi guys, this is the last part of the first package of information that I have prepared for you in regards of the differences of the races and the creation of humans. Sorry for the delay, I needed to finish some work to get food on the table, ha ha ha!" I wrote. And forwarded the prepared info to the family and friends app.

"So next to the documentation of creation of humans in the Bible and the Evolution and the out of Africa and mating with hominoid's theory of scientist, there is also documentation of another ancient black or African civilization called the Sumerians tablets. According to these writings of this civilization which writings were between 8.000 to maybe 20.000 years old, the Sumerians claimed that, human beings were genetically engineered by more technological advanced beings that came from another solar system and planet to mind gold to restore the atmosphere of their own planet!

The humans were created because the group in charge of doing the mining of gold, decided to abandon their mission and hide themselves on earth. The humans were created in their image, just as is stated in the Bible. They called the created men Adapa which is more than one man of flesh, which stands for hu-man! Adap is one and Adapa is plural! Also just as nearly as is stated in the Bible, in the Bible it is stated Adam! They committed mistakes when making the male humans but decided to, as I understood, cloned them to make groups of them for specific tasks and to speed up

139

the process, because they did not have any time to lose to get the job done and return back to their own planet to restore it! After some time they saw that the male humans were unhappy or depressed and decided to create a mate for them and created a female out of the DNA of the created males, for all the male humans of the different groups! In the Bible there is also the mention of creating Eve from a rib of Adam! Which is what we now scientifically call the cloning of people!

Ray are you there, this is getting very interesting! So the reason to create the humans was to have sufficient intelligent beings to work as slaves, because the hominoid that were on earth were not intelligent enough to follow instructions. The gold was needed to correct the atmosphere of their own planet, that was deteriorating. Their own people as stated abandoned the work of mining and other exhausting work that they were doing for thousands and thousands of years it seems. Their own people that abandoned the mission of mining gold and other duties, were considered deserters or fugitives by the ones in charge. In the Bible there is also mention of fugitives or the land of the fugitives! It was their intention to destroy the deserters or fugitives and the created humans that they considered imperfect, through a big earthly flood, just as described in the Bible, before they returned back to their planet with the mined gold. But some of their own people, primarily the group of the Anunnaki under the scientist that was in charge to create the humans, were against this and decided to save the humans and stayed behind with the created humans, to protect, guide and give them knowledge!" As soon as I sent this I was keeping my fingers cross for the reactions.

"That is scary stuff aunt Isa, if some of them stayed behind who are they?" Another niece named Linet asked.

"Well according to the Sumerians they were called the Anunaki, the beings that came and created humans as their work slaves on earth to primarily mined gold for them" I replied.

"Do you know were exactly did they came from?" Linet asked.

"Apparently they came from a planet in the Orion Belt Constellation, the same constellation which the Giza Pyramids of Egypt mimics" I stated.

"The Giza Pyramids that the Egyptians build? Did they mention how they look like? And if they stay behind do we have any idea where they are now? Were the Egyptians the Anunaki?" Linet asked.

"As I understood the humans were created in their own image, just as stated in the Bible, but apparently it seems like they sealed off some DNA capabilities of the humans, which our scientist currently regards as garbage DNA. So they had to look the same way as we do, I assume. I saw some images of the Anunnaki were they also had braided hairs, earrings and other ornaments on their body, same as the Egyptians and in the African culture. So it seems that they are the original race or the Negroid Black race. Which is established by scientist to be the first existing race on earth since at least 200.000 years ago and this without belonging to the evolution of hominoid or apelike men theory. So maybe the ancient Negroid people or the Ethiopians and the Egyptians were indeed the Anunnaki that came from the sky or another planet.

What I also have discovered is that these beings had a special blood, which seems to be the Rhesus negative blood. Because if you are Rhesus positive it means that there is Rhesus monkey blood in you. But the negative Rhesus blood, is a blood that cannot be explained by scientist as being from earth! Which is the same blood that uncle Den my hubby has!" I wrote!

"O no, is uncle Den an extra-terrestrial?!" My niece Linet asked.

"Apparently he is a genuine one, which means that I am married to a real alien, and my children are half aliens" I wrote, trying to lighten up the intensity of the subject.

"Aunt Isa are you still there, it is getting very creepy and I am alone at home, I think I am seeing shadows?" Linet commented.

"Creepy? This is making my head spin Isa! And my fingers are trembling. Do you mean to say that aliens really exist and they look just like us?" Said a friend named Mili on the voice app.

"Yeah aunt Isa, who are the ones they call the Greyes?" Linet asked.

"I do not have any idea! But if the Anunnaki could have made humans, maybe the ones that first left made the 'Greyes' also, to monitor the left behind Anunnaki and the in their eyes imperfect created humans? Or maybe the 'Greyes' are a complete other species in the Universe? I do not have any clue" I replied.

"You mean to tell me that there could be several aliens walking around on earth and that they are really abducting people as are mentioned in some films? I thought that the whole alien thing was science fiction?" Mili responded again on the voice app.

"Apparently not! But if our ancestors were the Anunnaki, why do they not come and take us back with them aunt Isa?" My niece Linet asked.

"Yeah why do they not come and bring us the descendant of their kind to their more advanced planet? I would be glad to leave the earth, were life is a constant struggle!" Mili voiced on the app repeating the question of Linet.

"I don't know, the first group of these Anunnaki just betrayed their kind and abandoned their work to save their own planet and the second group also chose to fight against their own kind to stay behind and save the life of the created humans. So I assume that both groups were considered traitors of their own kind at the end and the 'sin of the father is definitely also the sin of his children or our sin'!" I replied.

"Then we are definitely f*ck!" Mili replied on the voice app laughing out loud, making me also laugh nervously. Because she is right if we are not on the good side of our own ancient kind and are also not on the good side of the created humans side, we were trapped and definitely f*ck up!

"It is interesting to know, that scientist do not understand why there are humans with a Rhesus negative bloodline, which makes it a not earthly or unexplained bloodline on earth according to scientist. All humans are supposed to have a positive Rhesus factor bloodline! According to published information only 15% of humans

143

on earth has a Rhesus negative bloodline. Which if I understood correctly means that 85% of us do have a monkey gene or came from hominoids, Neanderthal, Denosivans or another hominoid and have this in our DNA system, reason why the majority of us have a positive rhesus factor. The hominoids or manlike apes that existed and had the monkey gene in their system and we adapted this also in our system, due to interbreeding of the first Negroid Black race and these hominoids as explained by scientist. Or through mating of Angels and the Watchers of God mating with the created humans! Or through genetic engineering as explained on the Sumerian Tablets. But it is definitely a fact that the original first black Negroid race only have one DNA and also a negative rhesus factor blood in their system. The majority of also the descendant from the black Negroid slaves on Curaçao, the other Caribbean islands or the Americas are as I presume in these modern days mostly a mixture with other races" I forwarded from my app.

"So are we aliens or not?" Mili wrote.

"Seriously I thought that you guys are grown-ups! Do you guys really believe this alien nonsense? There are no aliens and no one is coming to save you and take you to another planet Linet!" Richey reacted.

"Well I believe what I have presented and have tried to provide all the possibilities out there of the creation of humans and who the Negroid race might be! You should make out for yourselves what to believe! Do not be afraid to be ridiculed if you believe that we

144

the Negroid race are indeed aliens! Although most of us are mixed with Indian and European blood also!" I answered.

"But uncle Den is most certainly 100% from the Negroid black race, as you said aunt Isa, most of us are more a mixed race with other different races and maybe for that reason we all have a positive rhesus factor, but still we are more Negroid. So maybe there is a real possibility that the Negroid race, are the left behind Anunaki people or the advanced aliens that came to earth, aunt Isa and I am happy to belong to that race!" Linet wrote.

"Yes Linet! It sure seems that way, the evidence is too compelling! I have also discovered that maybe we are also the real Hebrews or the Israelites. The nation of God's children and it is also stated in the Bible in Deuteronomy, that the 'Children of God' will be brought into slavery!" I answered.

"What, but how can that be possible, the Hebrews or the Jews have as common a rare religion and they are all white people! And they were gassed and killed in the holocaust!" Nelly commented.

"It seemed that the Virgin Mary was Negroid, Jesus was Negroid, Saint Nicolas was Negroid, Moses was Negroid and many more Biblical persons were Negroid people" I replied.

"But if all of these information are true, which I am not saying they are, because I believe in the Bible and the creation of humans by God and not some technical advanced beings, that would be the Negroid race, why would there be an effort to cover this up and who would have the money to do it?" My niece Nelly asked.

"The truth can sometimes be very ugly Nelly. And there seems to be some cover up of the history of the Negroid black race by three groups according to my research, which part I have not yet completely concluded, but it seems that the Vatican or the Roman Catholic Church, the Arabs or Muslims and also the white Jews or the Ashkenazy Jews played important roles in the execution and cover up of this! And these are the three largest religions on earth" I responded.

"That is crazy, the Arabs and the Jews are enemies, but the Vatican that is another story, they are very well known in cover ups so that does not surprise me at all! But why?" Nelly replied.

"I also believe that they wanted to take revenge of the Negroid race that created them essentially to be only their slave workers and to afterwards destroy them in an earthly flood as is stated in the Bible! It went gradually in time beginning with the Roman empire by their Emperor Constantine that was out to have a religion that he can use to control and bring his people together! So they took over the religion of the Negroid race and adapted it to make it their own religion, as a tool to dominate or have power on their own people, through fear mongering since 400 AD. Then the Arabs started ransacking Africa and also took the religion from the Negroid over in 600 AD and adapted this to suit their needs! The white Jews were just converted Jews that also joined in about the 1.000 AD or so to also claim the religion of the Negroid as their own religion! The Anunnaki, the ancient Ethiopians, the ancient Egyptians and the Hebrews all believed in one Almighty God that created the Universe and everything in it! In those days before 400

AD the Romans believed in many Gods as did the Greeks, both Caucasian races!" I responded.

"So you believe aunt Isa that the Bible is written by the Anunnaki? Nelly asked.

"It seems that the persons who wrote the books that are incorporated in the Bible used the same information of the Sumerian tablets, because this was a much older document. So the basic of this knowledge is on the Sumerian Tablets! The Egyptians had their own Bible which is called the Kolbrin Bible, they also had their own 10 commandments. Moses was essentially raised by the daughter of an Egyptian Pharaoh! The Egyptians had also their own Jesus and his virgin mother and all of this over more than 7.000 years ago! The whole story of the Garden of Eden was also already known thousands and thousands of years before the writing of these books that were used when putting the Bible together, as originating from the Ethiopians. Also the story of a virgin and her son originated from Ethiopia, whom we now call Mary and Jesus! So it seems that each group just copied the knowledge of the ancient Ethiopians, the first nation on earth, dressed it up a little, changed names and dates and named the bundle the Bible, the Torah and the Quran!" I answered. It was really silent for quite some time and I decided to let it sink in. If all your life you have been told that the color of the sky is blue and now you see that it maybe is pink, it will take some time for you to process that the sky is still the sky and will forever be the sky, but that it is not the color that you thought it was or named it to be!

"So the Bible can still be used as useful information?" Nelly asked.

"Definitely, the basic information is in there, it is mostly the interpretation that is doubtful and when it really happened is also not very important and what names are used is also not important, because important is that it did happened!" I answered.

"So the information that is in the Bible was prepared by our race, the Negroid black people?" Linet asked.

"But the creation of the humans was not by the real God but by advanced beings the Anunnaki or the Negroid race?" Nelly asked.

"Yes Nelly that is what it seems like! They found on earth hominoids or apelike man and decided to upgrade their capabilities with their own DNA! So they used both DNA to create a new specie that they called humans or man of hu and hu is flesh! The Africans or Negroid race calls themselves man of soul! This was done due to an apparently 'force majeure' circumstance of their own people quitting the job! But since they did believe in God as the primary creator they also knew that they have messed up and decided to make another mistake to try to destroy the created humans. But a group decided that they were going to save the humans and this same group or their descendants was later brought into slavery. That is what I believe, at least the basic information and the knowledge and the prediction of the future is presented in the Bible! It also seems that the Bible needs to be taken literally, the description of places is very precise, what the person is experiencing and describing, should then be accepted as being very precise also. Very ancient people had for thousands of years painted on walls or described flying beings in small or big objects. There are also ancient paintings of all of these objects that looks like flying vehicles or UFO's. So everyone with a Bible should go and interpreted the Bible as though there were very advanced technological equipment and technology used than maybe we are aware of now and see if you can give another meaning to different happenings and descriptions in the Bible" I explained.

As I was explaining that, I suddenly remember that I once got invited to a special mass of a colleague that was a Jehovah witness. I decided to go and experience what are the differences in the Roman Catholic Church and the Jehovah Church. At the moment of the ceremony of receiving a piece of the bread that represented Jesus Christ and if I am not mistaken a glass of wine, that represented his blood, my colleague Dasia asked me not to take the bread or drink from the glass, but just to pass it along. At the end of the mass I asked my colleague Dasia why we were not allowed to have the piece of bread and drink of the wine, but just one or two persons in the entire Church.

"Dasia why can't everybody participate fully in the reception of the body and blood of Christ?" I asked.

"Because not everyone is worthy of it" Dasia answered.

"I don't understand" I said.

"Well it is stated in the Bible that only 144.000 people on earth will be taken up to heaven to the Kingdom of God and our congregation has only two persons, that has been chosen" Dasia replied.

"So according to your religion it is already precisely decided that only 144.000 people are going to heaven and the chosen ones already know that they are the chosen ones?" I asked perplexed.

"Oh yes, only 144.000 people, it is not only my religion it is written in the Bible, the Bible that is also used by Catholics!" Dasia answered.

"That is strange, it seems just like there are precise available seats on a big plane or on a space ship or various of them to take the chosen ones to the Kingdom of God in heaven!" I replied laughing.

"Do not joke about that" Dasia replied annoyed.

"I am sorry, but what happens to the rest of the good and devoted people of your religion then?" I asked.

"When Jesus Christ comes to earth for the second time, the earth will become a better place, because all the evil people will be destroyed and we will all live in peace and love one another. And God will put only his people in charge of the world" Dasia replied.

"O.k. I understand, it will be than like heaven on earth" I replied.

"Yes, just as it was supposed to be as from the beginning" Dasia confirmed. Looking back at this, was I correct, could there be a promise that they would come back with their spaceship to take 144.000 people from earth to live on their planet in the solar system of the Orion Belt Constellation? And were these 144.000 people primarily their descendants that had their pure blood, the rhesus factor negative blood? Were they still genuinely concern with the imperfection of the created human or hybrid race, or the mixed races, which is nearly the complete population of the whole world or the planet earth?

"But going back to the Sumerian Tablets, the Anunnaki purpose to mined gold, is that they were going to use the gold to correct their atmosphere that was deteriorating to save their planet. There were hominoids living on earth but it seems that the Anunnaki decided to upgrade these hominoids with their own DNA, to make a kind of slave workers. Scientist has established that the 3 new other base races had traces of two DNA or species in their system, the Negroid or homo sapiens DNA and also the hominoid or apelike man DNA. Essentially these other races are then considered a hybrid, by scientist. And the common factor of these races and the hominoid is for sure the straight hair" I continue writing on the family app.

"So the beautiful straight hair that we all want to have is the one thing that is inherited from the monkey? Then maybe I should not straight my hair anymore?" Linet asked.

"You can still do that Linet, if you want to! You can do whatever you think that will make you more attractive! The straight hair is just a scientific recognition point to consider when evaluating the differences of the other races with the original Negroid black race" I replied.

"I was just thinking now of going back all natural, so that they would recognize me when they come back, ha ha ha " Linet replied.

"I do not think they will recognize who you are only by your hair Linet, but by your nose and big hips and but, ha ha ha" I replied.

"You never know aunt Isa, they are coming from above!" Linet replied.

"I will get more information on the Anunnaki, the Sumerians, the Egyptians and the Ethiopians, which were all as it seems black African or Negroid nations. That is also established by scientist to be the first nations on earth. I will want to dig more in these ancient nation's history and religion. Because at school, which was a Roman Catholic school I have learned that the Egyptians and all the Africans adored various Gods and also the sun as their God and were therefore considered pagans!" I continue writing on the app.

"What is a pagan, aunt Isa? Linet asked.

"Someone that has other religious belief, such as the belief in more than one God" I answered.

But why did the Catholic Church claimed that the Egyptians and the African nations are pagans, was that an unintended or an intended lie? It seemed very important that I now can find out who we really are as the black Negroid race to understand why we are being treated or to be precise mistreated, in particular by the white Caucasian race. Could it really be that the African Trade Slave was an act of revenge for their origin or creation as slave workers as is stated on the Sumerian Tablets? A revenge that they were created by our ancestors, solely to serve as their slave workers? Did they wiped out our history because they also did not have any history before being a slave worker? Did they invented the whole storage of gold at Central Banks to have a bargaining tool if the left Anunnaki returned back to earth because they need more gold?

At the end I was exhausted but very satisfied with the information that I have gathered, and already provided to my family, although due to the devotion in some religions and the mixed colored or variations of races from very light brown to very dark brown skin color, also sleek hair or curly or afro hair of some members of my family, I was not sure how these info would be perceived by all of them. But I had to continue my search for the truth, because I was very intrigued how this will finally turn out. If my conclusion were on point then what I am discovering could have a major impact for the entire world. The history of the world will need to be rewritten and religious believes and interpretation will have to be adapted, although the core existence of one Almighty God and his begotten son known now to us as Jesus Christ will remain the same.

I was definitely very interested in the comments of my brother Ray, the one who brought up the differences of the races and concluded rightfully that it did not add up that we all came from the same original parents as described in the Bible, Adam and Eve! The one that had intrigued me to find out what was going on! The one that same as me believe that science and the Bible must cross same roads. The one that provided me the insight to dig deeper, so that I could also discover what has been bothering me for so long, which is the reason why our ancestors were enslaved and nearly wiped out of the surface of planet earth. Days has passed and I was still not getting any comments from him on what I wrote, so I called my brother Ray, to find out if he had read what I wrote to hear his comments!

"Ray hi, its Isa!" I said.

"Isa hi, how are you? How are the kids and Den?" He replied.

"We are fine! You know I called you to ask if you read what I wrote on our family and friends app about the origin of the different races?" I asked him impatient.

"Oh no Isa, it was too much to read! You know I do not like to read so much information I began reading the first part, but then I got lost and decided that it would not have any relevance to read the second part or the third part! You should have kept it simple and shorter or send photo's to break up the monotony! Why don't you be yourself and give it to us straight as you have always done!" He said laughing.

"You know it was you that asked the right question, to make me revive my old quest of why our ancestors were enslaved. And I was really hoping to hear your comments! Besides it is a really complicated topic, which touches various religious believes, so I had to go with the necessary caution and explanations on the family and friends app. You know that there are various deeply religious people on that app, your wife included!" I commented.

"Nothing is complicated and me and religion do not go together, it is best to just hit us with the truth as you always have done and if this is not possible to at least break it up in several days not only three days! Or better yet make a presentation, I can organize a reunion were we can really interact and see pictures, pictures speaks a thousand words! Maybe we can do it in the summer vacation at the beach house Isa?" Ray suggested while laughing. Yes my brother Ray likes laughing or making jokes a lot.

"Sue also suggested that I need to make a video or a power point presentation! But I do not think it would be wise to have it at our vacation at the beach house, it is not PG 13! The group will also be too big and there will be also young teenage children present!" I responded.

"Why may our kids not know what the truth is Isa?" Ray asked.

"Ray the implication of my findings can be very devastating for young teenagers, I do not think that you understand the magnitude of what I have uncovered!" I answered.

"Isa maybe our teenagers needs this to feed upon to be able to establish a better understanding of the complications and the burdens of their lives and to ultimately free themselves of any and all things that are keeping them enslaved in their minds!" Ray answered.

"Oh I do believe that teenagers need to know, but I do not know if I have the capability to put this on a level of their understanding!" I responded.

"I am sure you can do it Isa! You are the aunt that all the kids loves when you tell stories, because you put the story at their level but still interesting that even the old ones would like to listen in!" Ray responded.

"Let me first start with the grown-ups and figure afterwards a way to incorporate the young ones!" I replied.

"Isa I got to go pick up the kids, maybe although now we only have one car, the other one is at the garage being repaired, I will try to get a chance to drop by your house today, to discuss how we can do this, see you soon" Ray finished our conversation.

Although I was a little disappointed that he did not read my apps sent on the topic, I still decided that it is very important for me to pass on this knowledge and if I needed to make a video or a power point presentation I definitely will! Maybe I really could put a little group of adults together to discuss this also at the beach house? No it is definitely not a good idea, because you cannot forbid others, mainly young curious teenagers to be present! So I would need to have a private setting to present these findings.

But if I wanted to be prepared I had to keep digging for more collaborating information of these facts, of the Negroid race being a technical more advance civilization that came to earth to mind gold to fix their planet. I will have to put all of these information in a chronologic order, which will lead to the logical conclusion that the only viable option would be that there were technological advanced beings living on earth that created the humans or the other races. These technical advanced beings also build impressive structures and monuments, like pyramids all over the world. And these same beings used their own DNA and the DNA from the existing hominoid or apelike man living on earth to genetically engineered the humans and also cloned them creating also 3 groups or what we now call 3 races with different features, the

Caucasian race, the Mongolian race and the Australoid race, some 30.000 to 10.000 years ago. And that these technological advanced beings called Anunnaki were in fact the black Negroid race or the first homo sapiens which means wise man in Latin, that were on earth at least 200.000 years.

This would definitely also explain the reason that the Negroid race were nearly completely eradicated, which was later converted in an intention for an eternal enslavement of the Negroid race on earth, through the so called "Transatlantic African Slave Trade"? As a sort of payback or revenge of the other races that were created as slave workers to be later disposed of in an earthly flood? This certainly could be the reason of the so called Transatlantic African Slave Trade and the dehumanizing efforts that were establish by law to treat these Negroid black slaves, also after the abolishment of the slavery of the Negroid race! Of which the government of some nations are still till today are treating or are trying to treat or put the Negroid race down, every chance that they get! It also seems that the behavior of some of their citizens also reflects the aim of their government mainly to keep oppressing or not give the people of the Negroid race a fair chance to excel!

I recall a couple of years ago when on a hot afternoon my brother Frits came to visit me at home. I prepared some cool drinks and we sat on the balcony on the side of the house, enjoying a cool breeze and started discussing the opportunities and complication of life, work and the opportunity of a career or a small business.

"Frits I cannot believe that you are still planning to pursue your own business, of a Tour Bus company for tourist! I commented.

"Oh yes, I am old but not dead yet!" Frits said laughing.

"I could make your business plan for you to get financing" I reminded him. He had already applied at the small business agency for a loan to buy a bus to have his own tour bus some 14 to 15 years ago. He was denied the finance by the agency because there were too many tour busses on the island according to the agency. Which he regarded as a very strange reason, because there were indeed very large tour bus companies, but not many small groups tour busses. The small tour busses would have more success in getting 90% of occupancy due to the more personal attention, visiting of various local places and the folkloristic cozy design of this bus, as described in the by me prepared business plan.

"Oh no there is no need for a business plan, I am planning to rent a bus with a capacity of 9 passengers, from a friend and old colleague" He answered.

"That is a good set up! But why do you want to quit your job now at this age and start a business" I asked.

"I am just fed up with the treatment at my work" He responded in a sad voice.

"Do not let them get you down Frits, they are just not worth it" I responded, putting my hand on his shoulder.

"Isa, how come we love our job but do not get the opportunity to be able to excel as other groups of people or races on our Island. Why are we constantly as locals put down, by other races as though they are better than us" Frits said. He was a good tourist guide but did lately mostly only receive work by his new employers to primarily drive the bus. It was mostly the European Dutch people or the Hindu Surinam tourist guides that were allowed to do the guiding part of the job. And most of the time he observed that their knowledge of our country and culture to act as tourist guide was not up to par. According to Frits, they could speak Dutch fluently, but there English and Spanish were deplorable. He had guided tourist at his former job, were a local was the owner and was also a good driver of big and small tourist buses. But when the business of his prior local employer went bankrupt he applied at the vacancy position of driver of tourist busses at another company that was owned by European Dutch people. He did also informed the new company that he is also a certified tourist guide. But they decided to only use him as tourist guide when there is really no one else available to do the job, otherwise he is the driver of the tour bus.

"Frits I have worked for Dutch companies and can inform you that their own people will always come first, what I assume is a normal impulse, you have to be very damned good to be recognized and promoted by Dutch people, over their own kind. Because they rather promote their own people, even if they are not so good at their job, I guess that this is a support system to their own race. The way I tried to keep my career moving up, was to encourage them that we must think big and be an international company and score high points by always communicating in English in order to have them keep up with me, because English is a second language for both them and me! And the Dutch language although I am pretty good in that language also, it is still as acknowledge by them

159

a very difficult language to write and express your thoughts in!" I replied laughing.

"If that is the case then they would never recognize me as a guide, because they insist that every meeting is in Dutch and my Dutch is good in the field of chit chatting and telling our story to tourist, but not in technical terms which they love to use in meetings, but my English and Spanish are way better than theirs in telling and answering questions of our stories to tourist! And most tourists are English or Spanish speaking. My colleagues are also always looking down on us the locals as though, they are more or superior than us" Frits stated in frustration.

"Do not worry about that, it is a need that certain people have to put other people down, due to their own minority complex" I replied.

"Once, the tour guide was very busy explaining on such a boring tone and some tourist decided to come to me asking me if I am a local and started asking me questions and all of a sudden a large group is surrounding me and I am in my element explaining about the historic site that we are visiting and its importance. You know what the guide did, he just entered the circle, stood with his back towards me and said to the tourist: 'Folks he is just the driver, could we move on and join me for the explanation of the site that we are visiting' and moved on just like that!' Frits said bowing his head. I felt his humiliation and it hurt me pretty bad, I did not even want to know how much it must have hurt him!

"What, is he crazy and that in front of the guests that is unacceptable and also unbelievable" I said shaking my head.

"Yes that was very rude and some tourist reprimanded him that they are free to listen to whom they choose! That was a very odd and uncomfortable moment" Frits said sadly.

"What happened when the tour was over?" I asked.

"At the end of the day, various of the tourist gave me a big tip and the guide got very angry and some tourist decided that they will deliver a complained to the company" Frits explained.

"Well he learned his lesson, did they kept him as employee or did he just receive a warning? I asked.

"Nope neither! The next day at the office the supervisor called me to his office to inform me that I should remember my place and be a silent driver and not to speak with the tourist during the tour, because that could have a negative impact on the reputation of the entire company!" Frits replied.

"What? Did they seriously reprimand you and not the tour guide?" I asked astonished.

"Oh yes they did, I asked to speak to the Manager who is also the owner and the supervisor informed me that this message to me was personally redacted by the Manager! I have after a few months asked the supervisor why I was not requested anymore to replace any of the tour guides and he replied that the Manager has establish that it is prohibited to ask me or any driver ever again to replace a tour guide! Because only he the Manager has the authority to pick out the tour guides for the company and that the tour guides should cooperate and replace each other, as is and always was demanded by him the Manager of the company!" Frits replied with a melancholic face.

His dream of being able to work as a tour guide, at which he was really good at, at that particular company maybe not fulltime but at least part time was shattered by a foreign tour guide who could not bear to stand beside someone with more charm and knowledge of its work then he could ever accomplish. Whom foreign tour guide despite of his despicable behavior was supported by the Dutch European owner of the company! And my brother was now forced out of pride to start at a late age with an adventure of his own tour bus company to receive fulfillment in his life of being a tour guide! It just make me sad and mad that various of my people are broken by Dutch or other foreign employers not willing to accept their talent to the benefit of their own company, why do they do that?

It just did not make any sense if they really want their company to succeed! What is the reason that seems that all the existing other races decided that they are going to make the life of the Negroid black race difficult? Are we seeing ghost or really playing the victim role here? Is this all in our heads? Are the majority of us really very lazy, not competent or not intelligent enough to get the job of our dreams and are incapable to maintain or find the job of our dreams? Why do we think that opportunities are not shared on an equal level when it comes to the Negroid black race? Is there another more sinister reason for this constant discrimination and or trying to keep the Negroid black race down? Why and with what purpose? Do they know something that we do not know? Why does this keep coming up again and again, the efforts of the other races to keep the Negroid race people down? Is it really all in our heads? Or is there a real reason for their discriminatory or mysterious behavior or actions, this does not seem natural to me! It seems like an imposed behavior but imposed by whom and why? What are they afraid of if they give us a decent chance to prevail?

The Dutch Government has established a distinction in citizenship one could be 'autochthone' or 'allochthone' or in English an indigenous or allochthone' citizen, the last one meaning those that were formed elsewhere! But even the ones that were born and 'formed their' were not categorized as autochthone, because they were not of white Dutch European parents! The Dutch Government had also an entrepreneurship funding program that only the autochthone or the European Dutch can get free funds, up to 100k guilders to migrate and start a business in Curacao or one of the other islands in the Dutch Caribbean, if they went to live on these islands for a minimum stated years! All these state sponsored Dutch entrepreneurs should have attended a business course! Do they teach these entrepreneurs at these sessions the truth about our origin and to assist them to avoid that the descendants of the Negroid race reach financial progress or job satisfaction as a condition to receive the free funding? Or was I now getting really crazy, because it really seemed like a coordinated effort or some kind! Again and again in the past I have brushed off the feeling that there must be a conspiracy by the Dutch Government to dupe or oppressed us the descendants of the enslaved Negroid race as a whole! But there did not seem to be an important or powerful enough reason to sustain the suspicions of myself and others on the island!

But with the secret that I have now uncovered I was very certain of my conclusion of were the facts are now leading me! And my vision of how it all is intertwined really came together when I realize that this was payback! The so called Trans-Atlantic African Trade Slave was their revenge! Yes the revenge of the created humans as slave workers on the creators themselves the Negroid race, it just seemed logical to me! And we as Negroid race are a race that really needs everything to be logical, otherwise we cannot accept it as a truth! So do I need to start preparing a presentation to receive more feedback to polish the to be taken track of actions? Do I have time to invest in putting it all together with all relevant pictures and in an order that will be easy and not too complicated to follow but with sufficient power to tear down the walls of false truths that was induced to us through the received education at our mostly Roman Catholic schools!

After weeks of careful consideration I decided that I needed to start preparing a presentation for only selected groups of people. To evaluate their reaction and to adapt were it is needed to be adapted for maybe much larger groups! But I still needed to have more information and definitely pictures to have a water tight presentation or to at least motivate some people to raise some questions! Sitting on my front veranda were I have a marvelous view, I was researching on my laptop for more information and or correlation of the Bible, the Tablets of the Ancient Sumerians, other ancient documentation and the scientific already established evidence on the subject, to prepare my presentation. My oldest grandson Amon came to sit next to me drinking a cup of hot herbs.

"That smells delicious, what kind of tea is that? I asked.

"This is not pre-made tea Nanna, my other Nanna Chela gave me this natural fresh herb to drink before I go to bed" Amon said.

"Is there more of that?" I asked.

"Yes, but this tea does makes you sleepy Nanna" Amon said.

"I think I will call it a day and the tea will help me fall asleep, since I have all these questions running in my mind" I replied.

"I'll get you some Nanna. In a small or a big mug Nanna?" Amon asked.

"A big one please, but finish yours first, I am in no hurry" I said. After finishing his tea he went to the kitchen to prepare my cup of tea.

"Here you go Nanna, be careful it is a little hot" Mine grandson said.

"Thank you dear!" I answered.

"Nanna you know, we have to do a group project at school of a country. And we do not know which country we are going to choose yet. Do you have any ideas of interesting countries?" Amon asked.

"Can I recommend a country in Africa?" I asked.

"I suppose so, could you also please help me with this assignment?" Amon requested.

"Sure, I will research Africa for one of its interesting countries. But it is getting late you should really go to bed now. Tomorrow is

Friday the last school day of the week. And you also have a test tomorrow" I said to my grandson.

"Nanna look your Orion Belt is right above our house" Amon said enthusiastic. Amon knows that since many years, since he was 4 or 5 I have a telescope and was very interested in looking at the stars in particular the Orion Belt.

It was my eldest son Den Junior that got me interested in stars and other planets in the universe. Junior my son was always since very little studying the stars and planets, reading about the stars and planets and researching the stars and planets. He also could draw various buildings, cars, trains and planes, with remarkable details of their supposed mechanism of driving or control, since he was about 5 to 6 years old. And the teacher wanted me to take him to a psychiatrist because he never was interested in drawing people. One day there was news of a plane crash and he suddenly looked up and said to me because I hate flying and get very upset, when there is a plane crash.

"Don't worry mom I will make a plane that does not fall out of the sky!" He said looking at me with his big smile.

"That is not possible, egg head" My eldest daughter Ella replied teasing him.

"Stop that Ella! You never know maybe he is going to be an inventor of new planes!" I replied.

"Sure it's possible this plane will land and take off vertically!" Junior said very certain of himself.

"That is a helicopter, not a plane. And a helicopter cannot fly very far and can only transport a few people!" Ella replied shaking her head.

"No it will be a plane that can carry over thousands of people, can take off vertically, that will fly on very, very high speed in all direction can hold itself still in the air and will also land very smoothly vertically" Junior answered very confident of his future invention, while demonstrating with his hand how the plane will work, Junior was then only 8 or 9 years old when this happened. We all laughed because it seemed very sweet but something completely impossible! But when he got older his greatest passion was a career in astronomy, but my husband and me did not agree with his career choice, because of the low possibility of getting a job and after finishing high school, he decided to change his career choice, for a career with more job opportunities. Now as I look back what he was describing it looked more like the technology that is claimed that alien spaceships have rather than our own planes that we are using to fly around in. How could Junior had this knowledge of air dynamics or more specific alien space dynamics at that age?

"Where is it?" I asked.

"Look right there" Amon replied.

"Oh yes, I always get the chills when I see those stars, you know" I said.

"Me too. Remember Nanna a few years ago when you suddenly decided to go camping at night at the beach at Caracas bay in the hope to be able to spot the Orion Belt" He asked.

"Yes I remember. It is your uncle Den junior that since he was a little boy had a passion for the stars and other planets and he told me all about the Orion Belt Constellation and I got hooked also! Especially when I learned that the Egyptians build their pyramids in the same angle as the Orion Belt and that they had stated that their ancestors came from those stars! " I said.

"Yeah Nanna and it was really by chance that we saw it. You just said the day before Nanna: Hey guys let's go camping overnight at Caracas bay, I have a feeling that we would be able to see the Orion Belt! And we did" Amon said enthusiastic.

"Yes that was like magic, because you do not get to see it every night. But it is really getting late and you would have to get up early to go to school. So go to bed" I said smiling.

"Goodnight Nanna" Amon said, standing up ready to go to bed.

"Sweet dreams love" I wished him.

The following Sunday after preparing and enjoying our traditional weekly family big breakfast of eggs, fruits and cake and our also traditional made hearty soup for lunch, with all my kids, grand kids and my hubby, I started researching a country in Africa that was interesting enough for my grandson to give a group presentation at school. I called him to explain to him why I thought that giving a presentation of the complete continent of Africa and afterwards concentrate on one of its diverse countries.

"Amon I thought that due to not much is known by us living on Curaçao of all the countries in Africa, I thought that you guys should start first with a general presentation of Africa and all its countries and then concentrate on Egypt" I said to Amon.

"Nanna, you know I said to the group that you are going to help us prepare about one country in Africa and they said that a presentation of wild life and running hunting Africans is boring" Amon said disappointed.

"The presentation that I want to prepare is going to show the other side of Africa next to its wildlife, its beautiful beaches, its diverse and ancient countries and also a look of some metropolitan cities in some of its countries" I said to Amon.

"What is metropolitan? Amon asked.

"A very large vibrant and modern city, with skyscrapers, metro trains and other amenities" I responded.

"Does Africa has that?" Amon asked with big widened eyes.

"See, many people think of Africa as a continent with only wildlife and safaris and people walking around bare foot with spears to hunt" I said laughing.

"I 'm siked" Amon said clapping his hands.

"Ok. Listen to what I already have as information and if you understand everything: Africa is the world's second largest continent, where also the world's second most quantity of people are living. Africa has also the youngest population of the world" I kept on explaining to Amon.

169

"The youngest population? I thought you said Nanna that Africa was the oldest population?" Amon asked confused.

"Youngest population means that there are more children then old people living in Africa. Oldest population means were there are more older people living then children, Amon!"I said.

"Ok!" Amon answered smiling.

"What I said was that Africa is the oldest existing civilization of the world, the cradle of humanity, it is the place were the first humans or what they called homo sapiens, which means 'wise man' in Latin arose about 200.000 years ago, in the first established country of the world Ethiopia. Ethiopia means burnt face or black Negroid people in Greeks. Negroid people are people who has very curly and sturdy hair, a more flat or not high nose, thicker lips, a more muscular body and a decent behind. The Ethiopians were very religious people that believed in one God. The Ethiopians had a governing system with a High Priest as the ruler of the nation. Same way as now the Vatican nation and country has, with the Pope as the ruler. But this system was first practiced in Ethiopia. The first African Ethiopians were living in large buildings or castle, they also build various pyramids and obelisks, not as big as the ones that the Egyptians later build, but still the first ones.

Africa is also the continent that has all the climate areas, from tropical to northern and southern temperature zones. Africa is also the continent that has all kind of precious gems and various precious stones, like diamonds, ruby, emerald, silver, gold and also crude oil. The continent of Africa, has 54 countries, as you can see, ranging from worldly metropolitans till deserts, safari land and the most beautiful beaches.

But we will be concentrating on the most historic and ancient country that has shaped the world, Egypt. Egypt is one of the oldest existing countries in the world, after Ethiopia. Egypt first had also a High Priest that ruled, just like Ethiopia, but changed that later on in Kingdoms that were ruled by Pharaohs. The High Priest was demoted to adviser to the Pharaoh.

The Egyptians build the pyramids of Giza that till today is a mystery for modern man of how these were build. The Egyptians had written laws and rules for all their citizens. And they wrote hieroglyphs on their concrete walls and also carved or painted their own images on their walls. Egyptians liked to wore their hair in braids to tame their wooly hair. They also wore earrings and various other ornaments and painted their eyes with lines to accentuate their eyes. Painting faces and wearing ear or nose rings is very common in the African culture. The Pharaohs also build other impressive buildings and great large sculpture of themselves.

The Egyptians were very advanced in their technological knowledge. Because till this day modern man cannot understand how they managed to build all these structures. That in our time will need thousands of large and heavy equipment and also a lot of manpower and many, yes many years to build. Some people even belief that aliens helped the Egyptians build their pyramid, because they do not believe that such an old civilization could have achieved to build these structures. And that seems really interesting because the Egyptians also claim that their ancestors came from another planet in another solar system, namely the constellation of the Orion Belt. The Giza Pyramids were actually build with the same angle as the Orion belt. So the Egyptians do claim that they are indeed aliens that came from another planet, far far away! But we can still see this constellation in the sky as stars from planet earth!

The Egyptians had advanced knowledge of the universe and its planets and the stars or the suns. Some of the planets that they mentioned on their walls that has thousands of years, are only discovered now by modern man in the Western societies, whom are claiming that they had discovered these. Same way that the Western society claims that they have discovered a new world, when Columbus went to the Caribbean and the Americas. But the Indians had already discovered these lands and were living on these lands for thousands and thousands of years! It was also discovered that the Negroid Egyptians and or the Ethiopians were also already in the Americas and the Caribbean also way before Columbus! Massive head statues were found everywhere in the world of the Negroid Ethiopians and the Egyptians. Even the Australian Aborigines claims that the Egyptians had lived with them and had gave them great knowledge! Various writings on mountain walls were found with the same system of writings that the Egyptians used on their walls on mountains in Australia!

The Egyptians had knowledge of healing with various kind of herbs and also how to prevent certain sicknesses. They had knowledge of various herbs that modern man are now using to cure various sicknesses. They also performed various difficult surgery to cure their people." I briefed Amon and also showed him the various pictures that could be presented in their presentation at school.

"This is very cool Nanna, you remember when I also had long braided hair. And you cut it off because it was against school policy when I started Kinder Garden at 4 years old" Amon said with sadness in his voice.

"Yes I remember, I still have your locks and also those of Junior and Andrew I said to him. The schools just does not permit boys to have long hair" I said.

"That is not true Nanna! If a boy has straight hair he can keep it, as long as it is a little above their shoulders" Amon replied.

"Oh my God no! Did they did that at your school also? Why do they with straight hair always get to keep their hair long? Did the teacher explained that?" I asked.

"Yeah she said it is because the type of hair!" Amon said annoyed.

"Unbelievable the same stupid reply again!" I said annoyed.

"But this was since primary school, when I was in the 6th or 7th grade, when I started again letting my hair grow. The teachers at primary school were annoying, the teachers at high school are cool. Do you think it would be possible Nanna for me to put earrings and maybe also a nose ring?" Amon was asking!

"Well you should ask your mother or your father or better yet wait till you are eighteen" I suggested laughing.

"What would you say Nanna if I was your son?" Amon kept asking.

"Well I personally do not think that something that will let you feel empowered should be denied to you, as long that it does not offend anyone else and it does also not hurt your health!" I answered.

"Girls get to keep long hair and wear earrings and it does not hurt their health Nanna!" Amon said.

"Yep your right! But we are living and trying to copy a culture that is not our culture and the schools and all the offices are imposing that same culture upon our people! Our culture is actually the African, or the Ethiopian or the Egyptian culture! Many boys have dropped out of school when the schools have forced them to choose, or you cut your hair that our in braids or locked or you get suspended or thrown out of school! Your uncle Andrew nearly also had to cut his long braided hair at high school or get expelled! He was modeling and the long braided hair was one of the features that the modeling agency liked! The day his school called me to talk to me about a possible suspension because he refuses to cut his hair, when I arrived, there was just a white Portuguese boy walking by, with long blond brownish hair. I stopped and asked him if he was attending this same school and he said yes. So I asked him if he could do me a big favor and accompany me to the head office, he was startle but I assured him that he was not in trouble! When we arrived I introduced myself to the superintendent as the mother of Andrew and also introduced the boy as going to the same school and thanked the boy for his kindness and sat down. The superintendent asked if I was aware of the situation with Andrew that he was not complying with the rules of the school by cutting his hair 2cm or less, as is stated in the school rules. And that both I and Andrew had signed the school rules as approval and acceptance. I explained to the super intendent that Andrew got a job as a model at an agency and that they really wanted him to keep growing his hair and also the braided hair look! And that I always encourage my kids to be unique and if they can maintain a hobby or a job without jeopardizing their education they have our blessings, to learn the value of money and also the sweet sweat to earn money! But the superintendent insisted that rules are rules and that Andrew needs to comply and cut his hair! And then I asked him 'Does these rules only apply to Andrew?', 'No, definitely not, these rules apply to all students he claimed!' And I said, 'I just came in with a student, you know the one that I introduced, Rodrigues was his name, he has long hair, but was never asked to cut his hair!', 'No because he has straight hair we do not ask boys with straight hair to cut their hair at the required base length! They can keep it till above their shoulder', he replied. 'You mean to inform me, in my face, that you are discriminating black boys I asked astonished! That the rules only applies to black boys with curled hair? Do black boys need to straighten their hair to be able to keep their hair long or at shoulder length? If that white boy can keep his hair long then surely Andrew can keep his curled hair long and in braided form above his shoulders! And if you suspend him I will drag you and your school in court and will write these discrimination practices of your school in newspapers, will give interviews to radio and television' And then I stood up and left the head office. Andrew did not get suspended and we never heard about his hair being braided or long again!" I told Amon.

"But you did not fought for me to keep my braided hair at primary school Nanna, I was very sad when I had to cut my hair, it felt just like they were taking part of me away!" Amon commented.

"I am so sorry love, but pinky swear I will fight for you now!" I promised.

"It's alright Nanna, I don't think I will wear my hair long again, it will take years to grow my hair back again! I will tell the guys to come over so they can see what you have prepared and we can also start to practice" Amon replied.

"Great, I will see what I can include to make it longer, so all of you can have a decent presentation" I replied.

"Ok Nanna but do not make it too long or to complicated and please more pictures" Amon said smiling. I gave him a thumbs up and continued to sort for more information on Africa and its ancient civilization.

A few days afterwards while working at the office I decided on my lunch break to continue my search for the preparation of my presentation. But first I needed a title and description that will capture as from the beginning the attention of the people interested in this topic! 'Why are there different races?', 'The different races that emerged from the Negroid race?, 'The Mystery of the Different Races?' Yes, that sounds great and it is where it all began, with the observations of my brother that pointed out that it is nearly impossible that all of the races had one and the same origin and the misguided theory that only the influence of the sun, had created these differences! Seems like a good and interesting title and as under title I could include something like the first race on earth as from at least 200.000 years ago the Negroid race, the first homo sapiens or the first Ethiopian nation on earth? Maybe a little shorter?

I decided to figure this out later and focus now on the Egyptians, since most of the documentations on the Ethiopians were destroyed by the Arabs in the 1300 or so. The only information that prevailed from the Ethiopians were information and documentation provided by other nations and also the fact of the ruins in Ethiopia, which indicates that they were the first nation with Pyramids, Obelisk, castle, churches, although they were not so big or grand of that of the Egyptians. It was known by renowned anthropologists that the myth of the Garden of Eden originated from Ethiopia. Ethiopia was regarded as the cradle of mankind before scientist had established through Mitochondrial DNA that the first Homo sapiens, which actually means wise man in Latin, were from Ethiopia Africa.

Ethiopia was a very religious nation that had a High Priest in charge of the nation, this same system was copied by the Vatican. Their wardrobe and also their headdress were also copied by the Vatican. The Ethiopian had rituals using a cross and beads that was also copied by the Vatican or the Catholic Church. It was also known by other races or nations that the Ethiopians could predict the future and had mystical knowledge, which were regarded as performing black magic. These information were mainly gathered from documentation other ancient nations as description of who the Ethiopians were as a nation.

The Egyptians however wrote or engraved and painted many of their accomplishments, religious beliefs and others on their very thick walls, which was a little bit more difficult to destroy all of them. On the walls of the Egyptians it is written that their ancestors had created humans, next to a wall were there are depictions of various rhesus monkeys. They also stated that their ancestors created dogs, men best friend out of wild wolfs and cats out of tigers, lions and panthers to make them domesticated pets. Is this what we now call genetic engineering of a specie, to create another specie? On their walls it is also written that they used various mystic rituals to accomplish certain goals, which was also considered black magic by the other races or nations. I also discovered that the Egyptians did not regard the Sun as their God, they would indeed stand in the sun and pray or chant to recharge their internal battery with energy and rejoice!

It is a fact that the Negroid black race or the African nations attitude is of always demonstrating their joy or gratitude to the Creator of the Universe of whatever they received from Mother Nature. But this was interpreted by other races as adoring the Sun, or adoring the rain or whatever, instead of being grateful to the sun to provide to them energy and joy in life. As discovered by scientist the Negroid black race actually does not need energy drinks or other excessive food to increase their energy level, they could use the sun to load up energy, and used it when needed in a time span of a day. It is interesting to know that solar panels are essentially build upon the same concept of black or dark skin cells absorbing the energy of the sun. But to be able to receive and absorb the energy without damage to the skin, the skin should be black or of a dark color!

The Egyptians and other African Negroid nations consider highly the symbol of the Nagar or the Negus!! The word Nagar is written and pronounced without the word A of which later on, the name Nigger or now the more accepted word Negroid is derived from!! The Nagar or the Negus is depicted as a snake that stands for Wisdom, Power and Protection. The Egyptian royalty or pharaohs also used this symbol on their crown. A Snake is also depicted in the Bible as the one who influenced Eve to eat of the fruit of Knowledge and Wisdom to also achieve power in the Garden of Eden! So both sources have in common, that a snake has something to do with knowledge, power and wisdom.

But why would the Bible imply that it was incorrect of Eve to eat and also encourage Adam to eat from the tree of knowledge and wisdom to gain power? Is it not a positive thing to have more knowledge, power or wisdom? Could it be a hidden sign that the in a haste created imperfect humans to serve a certain purpose, were later on further perfected through genetic corrected engineering by the Anunnaki or the Negroid race that stayed behind, to be able to have more knowledge, power and wisdom? And that after this perfection and receiving of guidance by the Anunnaki or Negroid race, the created humans were ready to be freed out of slavery or bondage, which was named the Garden of Eden, where they were originally created as slave workers?

The Sumerian tablets also described that the Anunnaki or the Negroid race regretted that they had created the humans because the humans were imperfect and wanted to annihilate the humans! Just as also is stated in the Bible! Now the question is did they regret because the humans were imperfect? Or did they regret because they were playing God and wanted to erase their mistake of creating intelligent beings, the humans or hybrids on planet earth? Were there certain boundaries crossed when did was done, although the ultimate goal was to save their own planet? Because they with the ability to see the future knew that if the created humans remained alive, they were going to eventually take revenge of their descendants! This also means that the group of the Anunnaki that decided to stay behind on earth with the created humans knew what was awaiting their future generations! Is that what is stated in the Bible in the books of Deuteronomy? Was this actually a punishment for the creation of the humans? Is that why the group of the Anunnaki that created and also saved the humans were cursed as according to some religions is stated in the Bible? And needed to repent to receive redemption?

Did the first Negroid are Anunnaki group that abandoned their duties and fled and hid themselves on earth, did they also participate and assisted in identifying the group of Negroid or Anunnaki that first created and later also saved the humans? Is that the reason why there are also Africans from the Negroid black race that are stating that the Negroid race which are the descendant of the enslaved Negroid race are the cursed ones? Is that why these Africans are also stating that the Negroid race are essentially man of soul and that the created humans are man of flesh? Meaning that the hu of hu-man that stands for the flesh? Does that mean that the Anunnaki or Negroid race men had created intelligent beings without souls? If this was the truth, what have our ancestors done? Is that what they are referring to as the imperfectness of the humans?

According to the Egyptians you need to have a pineal gland with a liquid called melanin in it, which they believe is the soul, to be able to descent to the heavens when you die! Scientist has established that when a person dies, at exact that moment the person loses some grams of weight! The reason for this is not known to scientist, but Egyptians and Africans believe that it is your soul that resides in the pineal gland as liquid melanin that is leaving your body, to commence its journey in the afterlife. But that same pineal gland seems to be galvanized in white or pale humans. Which was maybe a crossing of a line, because creation of intelligent beings was not something to mess with, because only God can create and provide them with a soul?

In a flash back I remembered a friend telling me of a book that he had read, in which a white lady that was abducted by grey aliens was hypnotized and stated under hypnoses that the grey aliens told her that they were studying the humans because they were amazed that the humans had an immortal soul? Could that be the reason of the sacrificed of Jesus Christ? Was it through his sacrificed that he opened a kind of gateway or something, so that the created humans could also have an immortal soul? An immortal soul that will be able to travel to the afterlife as stated by the Egyptians on their walls, despite of them not having melanin in their pineal gland? And by sacrificing himself at the same time Jesus Christ lifted also the curse of the descendants of the Anunnaki that created the humans and stayed on earth?

It seemed logical that if the humans were not a creation by the Almighty or as we called the Father our God they would initially not have a soul. Only God can provide a soul to the by him created beings! The Anunnaki or the Negroid race that also believe in the existence of an Universal God knew that they would not have been able to create or genetically engineered a being with also a soul! So what they created was an intelligent body but without a soul and that is the reason why they named them men of flesh or humans? Could not having a soul means that you are evil or wicked? As stated in the Bible? Or could not having a soul means that you are more vulnerable to be possessed by evil or by demons? Or could not having a soul means not being immortal or having an afterlife or going to heaven, but just to stop existing?

My son in law came into my office to ask me some advised in connection with the office expansion and improvement project that we were working on.

"Hi Nanna, see you are working on your presentation of the different races, I hope it is coming along as you expected! Can I disturb you for a moment?" Sidney asked. He called me Nanna since his daughter my granddaughter was born.

"Sure, with what can I help you? I replied.

"If we are going to expand that part of the office, would it not be better to put a bigger air unit?" He asked, showing me some drawings of the expansion plans.

"How much is that going to cost?" I asked.

"Well we can use the freed unit to put it in another office space that we were going to replace anyway. The additional cost will be 800 guilders" Sidney replied.

"Ok! What are till now the total additional cost in comparison with the first budget? I asked.

After deliberating with him what would be the best possible cost saving scenario to continue with this project, I resume my thoughts of the possibility of Jesus Christ coming to earth to open a gateway for the created humans to have a soul, an afterlife and the possibility to also go to heaven and also to lift the curse of the descendants of the group of the Anunnaki or the Negroid race that had created humans! That had decided to fight with their own kind to stay on earth and save the humans from the worldly flood, protect, guide and provided knowledge to the humans on earth! Was this the main reason that the Caucasian race stole the religion of the Negroid race? Because this was essentially also their religion too, if it is about their savior that they renamed Jesus Christ sacrificing himself, so that they were able to also have an immortal soul and the opportunity to go to heaven?

For them it would have been unimportant that it was also about the black Negroid race being freed of their curse of playing God and creating intelligent beings without a soul? This was also a bit humiliating that they seemed to have been second grade creation by God! But that they accepted the part of the Bible the new part were by the sole sacrifice of a black Negroid man, the son of God that was renamed Jesus Christ and that was willing to give his live on earth for both great causes? Give the humans a soul and immortality and released the curse of the sins of the forefathers of the descendants of the creators of the humans?

Was that the reason why the Vatican decided to only publish some scriptures of the first testament of the Bible to the general public and to remove some parts? Was that the reason that documents, books and important pieces were burned or destroyed in Ethiopia, Egypt and other places by the Arabs and the Romans, to hide these dark secrets of the creation of humans, the men of flesh that did not have a soul originally and were created to only serve one purpose which was to serve the Negroid race as slave workers?

At the end I really think it would be better not to include the assumption by me of a presumably mystic secret of first not having but later having through the intervention of Jesus Christ a soul, of which I did not have any evidence, but just a gut feeling or an unexplained knowledge, to the to be prepared presentation by me. I better not go too deep in the religious or mystic aspect in the presentation of the mystery of the different races it is already complicated enough and decided to now concentrate on the pile of work on my desk!

After a half an hour or so my husband walked into my office, looking radiant and full of energy! But this was not always like that, eighteen years ago he was diagnosed of developing Diabetes 2, which according to me started two years earlier with him getting a lot of stomach ache and headaches because he constantly claims that he lost his appetite and did not eat regularly and or properly. But he just started his own business and I guess that running your own business comes with a lot of stress. Nine years ago he had a stroke and two years ago he began again struggling with his health because he was diagnosed with colon cancer, I remember that I was urging him to go to a doctor because his tummy was getting bigger and harder and his fart smelled like something died in his stomach! He was convinced that I was exaggerating, but I knew something was wrong! So I forced him to go to the doctor with me and when informing the family doctor of his symptoms, she immediately wanted him to do a colonoscopy. The doctor attending us where he took the colonoscopy test, informed us after the test that they have diagnosed that he had colon cancer and that he needed to start immediately with chemo therapy for a few weeks and then followed by an operation.

We were devastated, since he was the one after having the stroke and me warning him that I definitely do not want to be a widow yet, who was the most concern of keeping a healthy life style, to be there for us. By walking and swimming nearly every day and also using various diets and herbs to keep him healthy. What went wrong is this something hereditary I asked myself. Or is it again stress as doctor has warned him since 18 years ago when he was diagnosed with Diabetes 2. Which stress symptoms has started for sure since 20 years ago.

"I am very sorry to inform you that you have colon cancer" Doctor Han informed us sitting in his office after he had taken the test, showing us pictures of my husband's colon.

"How bad is it?" I asked the doctor, because I could not understand what the pictures are supposed to tell us, looking up at my husband, who just was very silent with the bad news of the doctor. I grabbed his hand and fingers and pressed them hard, reassuring him that we are in this together.

"Pretty bad I'm afraid! I am going to schedule a treatment immediately of chemo to first contain the problem area and then afterwards you should seek for a surgeon that will perform the operation as soon as possible. Because we have to contain the damage now, before it is too late" Doctor Han answered.

"Could you recommend someone?" I asked doctor Han.

"I can give you a list of all the surgeons that preforms such operations" Doctor Han suggested.

"That will be of great help. Is there any way possible that we can skip the chemo therapy?" I asked.

"Skip the chemo therapy? No mam that is not possible, we have to shrink down the cancer and then remove it! Why do you not want him to do chemo therapy?" Doctor Han asked.

"I just do not believe in chemo therapy" I answered.

"Well these are our only options. Do you have kids? Because they could be at risk also" Doctor Han asked us.

"Yes five, they are all grown up" Den my husband finally spoke out firmly. And I looked at him, yes we need you to be strong, that is the only way we were going to fight this, my eyes were telling him.

"I would advise that they all take a colon test. I would also suggest that you speak to a dietician Den to adjust your diet as soon as possible" Doctor Han suggested.

"I am pretty sure that I am eating very healthy doctor" Den answered.

"What do you call healthy?" Doctor Han patiently asked Den.

"Well I do not eat fast food, but good home cooked local dishes, I also eat a lots of fruits and vegetables. I doubt that there is something wrong with my diet!" Den said with conviction in his voice.

"Local dishes has a lot of fat which is completely unhealthy for you. Also in all these dishes there is the pork tail which is proven to be the cause to various stomach and intestines sicknesses. And in this situation that you are in you may want to hold on raw vegetables, and bread that has glucose in it" Doctor Han responded.

"What is he then allowed to eat doctor?" I asked confused.

We called a meeting at home to inform all the kids of the situation and also informed them that the doctor suggested that they all should perform a colon test. The kids were very devastated with the news and my daughter Rona suggested that we pray to the heavenly Father that their father and my husband regain back his complete health. So we formed a circle and hold hands and prayed to our Father in Heaven. My husband assured all of us that he felt the presence and the hands of the healing father on him, when we were praying which made him feel very good and confident that he was going to be alright.

It was also Rona that suggested to pray to our Father in Heaven for the survival and regaining of the full health of my youngest son Andrew when he had an accident, some twenty years ago when she was only 12 years old and he was just 4 years old. It amazed everyone that he was very athletic, could run very fast, was doing pushups with ease and had very strong arms, of which he could throw a ball very hard and very far. We all were convinced that he would be a great baseball player or pitcher when he grew up. For more than three months I have been dreaming of a little child laying down on our street covered with a lot of blood, but I could never see it's face or if it is a girl or a boy. So I decided to visit all the families that have a little child, playing in the street, just warning them that several cars are sometimes riding as crazy in our street. And that they should take the necessary precaution of not letting their little children play in the streets alone. My youngest sons were not allowed to play in the street without us or their bigger sisters being present, so it never occurred to me that it would be one of my own youngest kids who were going to suffer a terrible accident.

We were just preparing to go on vacation to Holland with the kids. I had a day off and went out with the two older girls to buy some additional clothing to make the trip. Arriving home little Andrew was sitting on the front veranda together with their nanny and Emil a nephew who came to visit us on that day. As soon as Andrew saw our car pool up in our street he flipped over the veranda rail, landed on his feet and ran as a lighting bowl to the garage door to open this for us. He slide the door so fast and with such an ease, which was amazing even I could not do that because the nine foot long and over six foot high, iron door was very heavy. He wanted to be able to say something to me and stepped out of our yard into the street. I was just about to scream to him stay were you are and then without us realizing it the door some way or other got out of its rails and came tumbling down on Andrew, he tried to run and hold the door with his hands, but it was too late!

The door fell on the upper part of his body! There was so much blood on his face and me and my oldest daughter Ella could not get the garage door of him and I started screaming at the sky: 'No no no not my child, don't you dare do that to me God, please please don't, if I lose my child I will lose myself and will not be able to fulfill any mission you still have for me! Don't do this to me I beg you God don't'! I was pleading to God! And then if by a miracle my eldest daughter Ella lifted the heavy door on her own and pushed it against the wall. I saw Andrew lying there his face covered with blood and it was the same sight as in my dreams, of a child covered in blood on the pavement of the street. I kneeled down and picked Andrew up as in a trance, my eldest daughter screamed 'No mom, don't touch him leave him there, we need to call an ambulance!" Emil my nephew just came running down as he heard me screaming and I said to him, 'Drive me to the hospital, we do not have any moment to lose'. The nanny was just about to call 911 for an ambulance, when I told her tell them we are on our way! When we got in the car, the first thing I did was start talking to Andrew, telling him to open his eyes. He opened his eyes and wanted to lift his head and say something but he could not and I told him to lay still but not to sleep!

When we arrived and the doctors took him over from me to take a scan of the damage of the accident, they were amazed that he was still conscious, seeing the apparent head trauma that he had suffered. I told the doctors that I did not want him to doze off and kept talking to him all the time, what according to them helped that he did not fell in a comatose state. But the doctors gave up on him when they saw the results of the scans and advised that he would probably slipped into a coma and if he lived, he would have severe brain damage, next to that he had also broke his right arm.

At home Rona immediately asked everyone to start praying for Andrew, they made a circle and started to pray! The next morning when I called home to see how everyone was doing Rona told me that after they have prayed and she went to bed, a man as a spirit that was indulge in light came to visit her in her room late in the night and told her that her little brother will be just fine. After staying at the hospital for a couple of weeks, Andrew survived the ordeal and did had some issues of remembering things, but with time he recovered nearly completely, he just did not liked to run fast or throw hard balls anymore, because he claims that he gets a headache or dizzy and his right arm just remained stiff!

Rona was since she was little a very mysterious child that seemed to see and talk to not visible persons. When we asked her to describe the persons that she speaks to or showed her pictures, it seemed that some of them were known as deceased family members. But when she gradually got older she stopped communicating with these spirits. Which made us very happy because it was sometimes very creepy, when she just start speaking with someone who is not physically present, but only we knew that, she did not seem to be aware of that, so I had explained to her that my mother also communicated with the dead or spirits and that I sometimes can receive a message from deceased family members or someone I know but only while I am at sleep. But that you have to ask the spirit to only contact you in urgent cases in which you can really make a difference or help someone else. Because these spirit would have to respect the fact that you are living in a material and this present world and have to concentrate on the day to day aspects of this world. She asked me how can she recognize if the person is real or a spirit and I answered her that my mother used to tell us that spirits does not seem to touch the floor, they just seems to float upright!

I never had the psychic ability to talk in real time with the death, surely not with someone that I do not know, I also believe that I would have not maintained my sanity if that would have happened to me! It was always in a dream that only people I knew and had died or going to die had conveyed a message to me that I just did my best to understand and remember and past it to the one they have asked me to! It was not scary at all, just a conversation if though they were still alive and paying me a visit. But as it seems I do sometimes get visions of things to happen, or insight of something that already happened, maybe from people that died or going to die? I do not have any clue how it works! There was a dear friend and old colleague of my husband a Dutch European white lady that has informed me that she can feel that I possess paranormal powers and that she can help me developed these powers and I looked at my husband and told her 'no thank you'! I think it is best that as Den has advised me not to mess with the mystic world, if it comes to me, that's fine, but I am not going to seek for more! Because I really feel that I am now being protected most probably by passed away family members and I also feel that if I cross a line that is not supposed to be cross I will have no one to protect me!

But still I was really astonished that she could perceive that I had some psychic abilities, because I normally do not discuss these feelings with complete strangers, afraid of being ridiculed and not understood! She then explained to me that she was in a group called white witches that were experimenting with the occult, white because they were doing good and improving lives! It seemed hilarious that black witches were supposed then to be doing wrong! And that she can teach me to protect myself! I told her that I do not have any control of what I receive as information in dreams and sometimes it is just a feeling of doom that I have and that I really wish that I did not have, in particular if I cannot do anything to change the fate of the person in question! And that I am definitely not in the pursued of being a psychic that various people can contact to assist them, because I would not want to take on that responsibility!

When I was just 12 my eldest sister Siena was killed by her own husband Jose, it was his intention to kill his entire family and to commit suicide afterwards! Due to a very unfortunate misunderstanding Jose got fired at work and he could not process the injustice that was according to him done to him! Jose could not find another job and was getting really depressed and upset that his life and that of his family will be ruined. Jose could also not get a grip on things and was very devastated with his misfortune, my sister Siena was also pregnant of their fifth child. As a way to have an income Jose decided to put their house for rent. A few weeks before the day it happened, they came to live with us, our house was very small, so my brothers and Jose emptied, cleaned, repaired and painted up the small shag that we had in the bag of our small yard, were my mother and my father put all kinds of old stuff and were my mother used to wash our clothes in the washing machine! They put two twin beds in the shag, one for my sister Siena and her husband Jose and one for all the four small children, from one to four years old!

Jose has asked my mother to help him because evil was pursuing him and that he had liked to get married in the Church to receive the blessing for his family from God! It was a really special and beautiful day when they got married in the church and Jose told my mother that he finally felt at peace with his fate and was ready for a complete new beginning.

But when the day was coming to an end I felt really afraid and anxious, afraid that something bad was going to happen and that I somehow needed to save the children of Siena! So I begged my sister Siena to let the children sleep with me and my sister Mitta, so that she and Jose can continue celebrating their marriage! She laughed and said 'Isa we are married for more than five years, now we got a Church blessing, we do not need a honeymoon'. Then I went to the children and said to them, 'come sleep with us, let mama and daddy be alone tonight, I will tell you lot of stories!' Jose was against my proposal, he said that it was very important that the family be together for this evening! But two of the kids, just loved my idea and my sister Siena agree that they can stay with me, the oldest and the middle one! The youngest, still a baby naturally wanted to sleep with his mother and the other one loves to be with his father.

I went to bed with the kids but after telling them some stories I could not really sleep I felt that something really bad was going to happen, but I could not put it into words! Normally I will be awaken by my mother but that morning I was awake before my mother it was a Monday and most of the people in the house were asleep just before five in the morning! I felt a definite urge to go and see if my sister Siena's children were alright in the shag in the back of our house! When I wanted to open the backdoor my mother who just got up said to me, 'Don't do that Isa it is too early to open the door, it is really dark outside you know' and I asked her 'Can I go and get the kids of Siena mom, maybe they need some warm milk or something?' she looked at me and was very puzzled, since when did I became so eager to help and more stranger than that, I normally hate to wake up very early in the morning! 'No Isa they are probably still a sleep, you out to go get some more sleep also its too early' and I climbed up back in my bed, but was not able to sleep. Then a half hour later one of the kids got up and I got out of bed with him and ask him 'Do you want to go see how mom and dad are doing?' But he said instead 'I am hungry, can I have some bread and tea aunty?' Nearly another half an hour has passed and my mother finally allowed us to go outside a few minutes before 6 am! I immediately start making music and ask the other kids that were now also awake to sing and dance, my mother came outside and said "Isa keep it quite you are waking everyone up!' And I responded, 'Everyone should be up mom, it's a school and working day, can I wake the two other kids of Siena, they are missing all the fun!' I screamed! My mother shook her head and said 'You must start preparing in a half hour to go to school Isa' and then went back inside, so I decided to go closer to

194

the shag and encourage the other children to sing harder and to call out the name of the two other kids of Siena! And then after just a few minutes Jose came out and just ignored us and went straight through the back door inside our house. I immediately went to the door and opened the door of the shag and saw my sister Siena laying down as if she were asleep on her bed as an angel, I knew in my heart that she was gone, I got the youngest kid that was still asleep in my arms and yelled at the other one that was awake and was just starring at his mother, my sister Siena, to follow me outside!

Soon afterwards it was like hell had broken lose, everyone was screaming inside. I did not even noticed that the other kid was still in the shag, because I was concentrating on the baby to see if he was breathing and ok! Two of my sisters and my mother got into the shag, they were screaming that my sister was dead, but could not find any wounds! Apparently Jose had cut both of his arms at the crack were you normally give blood and blood was all over him and dripping of him, meanwhile he was confessing that he had killed my sister and seeing the blood they thought that he had stabbed her or something.

In those days there was a police station in every neighborhood. Jose just walked himself to the police station and confessed that he killed his wife and that it was his intention to kill himself and his whole family, but that he was confused because his daughter and another son was not with them in the room, but in the morning hours he decided that the two boys that were with him also needed to be saved and deserved to die to have a new beginning. But at the last moment he could not killed the two boys as planned in the early morning hours, because he could not concentrate with all the noise outside! The police did find some kind of poison that he had prepared, that he most probably gave his wife and was maybe planning to give to the boys. He never explained precisely how he killed my sister and how he have planned to kill the kids, only that it was his duty of saving his family after receiving the blessings for his whole family from God in the Church!

I really did not exactly knew what was going to happen, I just knew that something bad was going to happen to my sister Siena that night and that maybe I would be able to save not her but only her children! I also knew that it would be Jose that was going to harm my sister, but how could you explain to someone and at my age that the one that loves you is most probably going to harm you! But I also had the feeling that I had accomplish what was intended for me to accomplish, which was to save the children, sometimes I wonder that it maybe was my own sister Siena who did that, telling me on a not conscious level in my dreams what I needed to do to save her children! My mother used to tell me that a person's spirit knows at least two to six weeks that he or she is going to die and that that person is already transcending to the afterlife! But why did she not contacted my mother, my mother had better psychic abilities, maybe my mother could have saved her, but I think that she knew that my mother loved Jose as her own son and that I was always a little afraid of him, like I knew as soon as I met him that he would bring darkness in our lives. But also maybe she did not contact my mother because of the fact that it was her time to leave earth and no one could have actually saved her? And she did not want my mother to carry that burden?

"I have a brand new project of a client that I need you to revise the feasibility report and come up, if you believe that this project is feasible, with a business plan to execute this in Curaçao" My husband Den requested. I was very happy that he was now completely healthy. And hoped sincerely that I would have him for much more years on my side as my hubby.

"Sure babe" I replied. I love working on business plans, were I can indulge myself in the thought process of the initiator and help him or her to fill in the loopholes, get a better idea what are the area of opportunities and also assess all the involved financial risks. Sometimes a client needs us to start from scratch doing all the research ourselves, which is a lot of work, but also very satisfying.

After comparing and researching various aspects of the topic of the "The Mystery of the Different Races" of which I decided that I definitely needed to write a book and now was working on a presentation because apparently the local black people does not really like to read! I was very enthusiastic about the presentation that I have planned to present in approximately two months to a first group of 12 to max 14 persons that are interested to attend my presentation! I had also planned a second and third presentation, with a week interval, to have sufficient time to adjust the presentation if needed! This was very exciting for me, it has been a while since I have addressed and stand before an audience. The subject was very intense so I would have to repeat some facts to get the message through. I also needed that everyone present would be open minded to really hear me out and judge in the end if the facts that I am presenting, where the culprits of executing and keeping this a secret are based on a developed conspiracy theory on my part are also sufficiently backed by me with the needed facts, although it will redefine all what we have learned in life from school and our churches!

But now I needed to prepare all that is needed for me and Den to take our grandchildren to the Beach House for our big family reunion vacation. When my children were kids they also wanted to go to these big family reunion vacations, were mainly the grownups gets a bed to sleep in and all the kids were delighted to sleep on the floor! Now that they are all grownups they would come at the Beach House but would only stay one night, the Barbeque and Party night! At the second night at the Beach House a nephew decided to bring a projector and organize a film night in the large back veranda for the kids, which had relieved me of the task of entertainment of the kids for this evening. We the older generation were just sitting and making jokes on the front veranda in various groups. One of my nieces was stating that she cannot understand why our local men are so obsessed with the white and with long straight hair Latin American woman.

"Can someone explain to me why our local men are so obsessed with the white with long hair Latin woman?" Zury asked.

"Do not generalize, not all local men are obsessed with the Latin woman! It is not common in our family! But sometimes you, our local girls are a little annoying and to demanding! But we still love you and choose you!" Tyrel a nephew answered, with a big smile on his face. While the group began laughing!

"But still a lot of local men are actually doing just that, choosing and regarding the Latin woman as their ideal partner, giving our local girls or woman the feeling that they are not beautiful enough! And that does make me mad that our men are doing just that!" Ray stated.

"This was since the beginning of time on earth, were the black man apparently was mesmerized by the pale color and the long straight hair of the white woman!" I commented.

"What are you talking about aunt Isa, what beginning of time?" Tyrel asked.

"Be sure to attend my presentation!" I answered!

"You are mean aunt Isa!" Tyrel responded.

"That is a good teaser aunt Isa!" Zury commented! Then my brother decided to start discussing the subject of the possibility of us as a nation to really submerge in the Dutch nation, by becoming a real province of Holland. The reason being that this would alleviate the 25% of people on Curacao living for quite some years now, under the poverty line! Which had also influenced a spike in the criminal activities of much more younger men or actual boys, as from 13 to 16 year of age who are fed up living while seeing their mother or their sisters turning to the oldest job on earth which is prostitution, to put food on the table and pay all the bills of the household!

"Ray do you really belief that if we gave everything to the Dutch that they will relieve poverty on Curacao?" Roy a family friend asked.

"Look at what they did to Bonaire and Statia dad, these people are not helped at all and are only humiliated by the Dutch Government!" Tyrel whom is actually the son of Ray commented.

"What else can we do, unemployment is through the roof and there is no economic growth, to the contrary we are going backwards on job opportunities! And also the huge amount of crimes that our people mainly the youth is committing to just survive!" Ray answered.

"We can fight for our independence!" Tyrel answered.

"You want us to be a second Haiti?" Ray asked.

"There are various other countries that had reached positive developments, why do everyone has to put Haiti as an example of being independent?" Tyrel asked in annoyance.

"You know I saw a documentary on the TV where I believe some American Evangelicals that were convinced that if the Haitians turn to God they will be saved. They were interviewing some elderly Haitians why Haiti cannot have prosperity and that they had stated that the Haitians had offered their soul as a nation to the Devil, because God would not help them released themselves from their oppressors. They were the first nation that fought in union to abolish slavery for their people and also the first Negroid nation that gain their independence as a black nation in the western world. The Haitians are also very well known to perform black magic, the whole zombie stories of people waking up after several days or weeks that they had been buried, comes from Haiti!" I commented.

"Do you really believe that they sold their soul to the devil?" Ray asked laughing.

"You believe in God don't you, well if you believe in God you automatically must believe in the Devil!" I replied.

"Yes the Yin and the Yang philosophy!" Commented Roy.

"But seriously guys I do not believe that we have it in us to become independent, more over that we have too much problems and also cannot seem to be able to unite in obtaining our goals!" Ray answered.

"You know sometimes I do believe that maybe we just got to throw our hands in the air and give them everything! Because it does not seem that they are going to stop pushing us to the brink, until we do that! So maybe Ray is right!" I commented.

"I would have never belief that you aunt Isa would have suggested that" Tyrel my nephew commented disappointed.

"You know before I knew what I know now I was fighting with all my heart to maintain what I believe is my home and my only country! But now I feel that we as descendant of the Negroid black people that were enslaved are actually real world trotters and can live wherever there is sufficient sun for us to recharge or maybe on another planet!" I answered laughing.

"Aunt Isa does this also have something to do with the secret in your to be presented presentation? Tyrel asked.

"Yes it does! I also wrote this on our family app and apparently there are not many of you that read what I wrote!" I answered with a smile.

"If I open my app and I see a lot of conversation I usually ignored it, sorry aunt Isa! But I do not want to wait some months to find out, come on tell us something!" Tyrel requested.

"Yes, tell us now, I also do not want to wait!" Ray also requested.

"Why do you actually need months to give the presentation, if you already have the prove?" Tyrel asked.

"It's a lot of work to put it on paper or document this for a presentation, I am also piling up more evidence!" I said smiling.

"What are you guys talking about?" Roy asked.

"And please go with the short and simple version! As is your natural style, give it to us straight! We will survive!" Ray added with a smile.

"O.k. the short and I hope simple version! It occurred to Ray that there were too many differences in the races and that everyone has straight hair beside the Negroid race! The theory of evolving from hominoids or big apes or monkeys does suggest that all humans should have straight hair as the apes or monkeys also does! The Negroid race which is also the first race on earth, does however not have straight hair and also does not have the DNA of the hominoids or apelike man gene in their system! The other races have two DNA in their system, the Negroid DNA and also hominoid or apelike man DNA in their system! So all the other races have DNA of two species and are therefore hybrids! So the Negroid race that does not have hominoid or apelike man DNA does not belong in the evolution theory, which actually means that scientists, now that they can analyze DNA, do not really know where the Negroid race came from! This not having of the monkey gene DNA is also reflected in the rhesus negative factor blood type, because being of the negative blood type actually means not having an origin from earth! But it seems through tablets found named Sumerian Tablets that the Negroid race or our ancestors, yes I know that we are more a mixed race, with bits and pieces of various races but as a mixed race we still fall under the Negroid race category, ok hold on tight! According to these tablets that seems to tell the same story as the Bible, the Negroid race were a technological more advanced race that came from another planet of another solar system. Our ancestors, whom called themselves the Anunnaki came to earth to find and mind gold to repair their atmosphere that was deteriorating! The ones who were supposed to mind the gold decided after thousands of years of mining to quit the job and run away as fugitive or deserters! So the one in charge of the mission decided to instruct a scientist on the mission to create or to genetically engineer slave workers, using their own DNA and also the DNA of the hominoids or ape like man already living on earth! So the evidence of the Negroid race being the Anunnaki is in the DNA of the other races! After the mining was done the Anunnaki in charge decided that the created slave workers and the deserters or fugitives should be annihilated by an earthly flood! But not all the remaining Anunnaki agreed that this was the correct thing to do! It is recorded on these tablets that this group were weeping very hard because of their love for these created humans. And a war begun between the two groups, which resulted in a group of the Anunnaki returning back to their planet with the gold and another group staying behind with the created humans or other races all with the straight hair, to save and protect them! On the earth remained also the first group of Anunnaki or Negroid deserters or fugitives! Not everyone survived the flood, but for sure the three major races with the Anunnaki that protected them and some of the first group of the Anunnaki called the fugitives or deserters! The left behind Anunnaki that decided to protect and saved the created humans, were being adored and called 'the Gods' by the saved humans! This relationship of guiding and protecting the created slave workers or other races of the world stayed like this till the 1500! Yes you heard me correctly, till the 1500 A.D. same time period of the Trans-Atlantic African Slave Trade! The created slave workers or the other races or humans with the recognition point of straight hair, but mainly the white European races decided to take revenge and killed and or enslaved the descendants of the Anunnaki or the Negroid race in the so called Trans-Atlantic African Slave Trade! And with this act they changed the world order, the world history and white washed our religion and our legacy! They reversed the roles in an act of revenge, the Negroid race became the slave workers without a prior history! The only history that was allowed to us the descendants is of being their slave workers! The same history that they had as being created and to start off as slave workers of our ancestors! They also decided to murder or annihilate various Negroid people out of revenge of various of them being slaughtered in an earthly flood! They as the white race became the ones in power, the superior ones with the help of the stolen knowledge of the Negroid race that were kept by the Vatican Church and also certain evidence that are being kept secret by the Smithsonian museums and research centers that is controlled by the white Jews of the United States of America! The Negroid race held till the 1500 and the 1600 very important positions in Europe and all over the world, the Caribbean, the Americas, Africa yes all over the world! So they did not bring us from Africa were according to their versions we were just running wild, to the Americas or the Caribbean, we were already here! They did brought however many Negroid people from the European countries, were they were the first European Kings and Queens, doctors, lawyers, astronomers, philosophers, musicians and murdered them or make them or their children slaves in the Americas and or the Caribbean, together with the ones that were already on these to them new found territories! This Trans-Atlantic African Slave Trade was a sort scam to distort what was really going on and to take revenge or payback of the Negroid race for creating them with the only purpose to be slave workers and to be afterwards as was the plan discarded as garbage in an earthly flood! So their hatred of us is very deep, it seems that the time that has passed did not as yet heal their wounds! In particular the Dutch and the American high society and the Government, maybe they are afraid that if we regain the unification of our people they would lose their power! We seemed without knowing it, to be a force to be reckoned with! So I believe that if we came from another planet, after exploring the universe for gold, I do not feel the need to hold on to a little island, if they want to have it for whatever reason let them have it! I want my people to expand their wings and go and conquer with their knowledge and other abilities a little piece of the world for themselves! By the way they also have the Negroid DNA in their system so if they really hate us, they actually must also really hate themselves!" I finished the short version of my findings!

"Is this for real Aunt Isa?" Satie another nephew that just joined us in the beginning of my explanation asked.

"Well this is what I found out, the long version take you through it step by step, with pictures and others as evidence!" I answered.

"So you believe Aunt Isa that the whole enslavement thing was a revenge of creating them as slave workers? And that was also the reason that they took everything from us? Now these are then more reasons that I strongly believe that we are supposed to fight to maintain what we have now, although it is a very small island it is now according to their own international legal rules and law our Island, aunt Isa! What would be the added value if now we know who we are and that we probably were here before they came, if we cannot use that to really get our total freedom if now there is evidence that we can lead our country ourselves?" Tyrel asked.

"I guess you are right, maybe I should also fight for what is ours! I just believe that my task would be completed when I wright a book about this and it would be up to the upcoming generation, your generation to decide what you are going to do with this information and if you are going to keep accepting all this bullshit from the Dutch government! I answered Tyrel.

"But what if that they are not at all interested in the island and its possible benefits, but that their major goal is to keep us as Negroid people controlled and occupied with different by them made up challenges to obstruct us to take care of ourselves and our family, so that we will not be able to conquer a little piece of the world or maybe also other planets?" Tyrel asked again.

"Then we should definitely go for full independence! They have announced various times that they were going to send by courier our exit from their Kingdom if we expresses that we will not abide by their rules anymore and will have to inform our people to choose for independence!" I answered.

"But what if they really do not want us to become independent?" Tyrel asked again.

"We should then definitely prepare for a fight and maybe call in reinforcement" I said laughing.

"Reinforcement?" Tyrel asked, frowning his eyebrows.

"Well the other Anunnaki's or Negroid race that or living on another planet and also the ones who has deserted their task and were considered fugitives at some time on planet earth! Although they seemed to have chosen not to meddle in this affair of the creators and their own creation, they are now aware that they also are being oppressed in their own countries in Africa" I answered.

"Yes, why did the Anunnaki that left not returned back to save us when we were being killed and enslaved?" Satie asked.

"Well our ancestors were warned that the humans are the other races were 'wicked and evil' as stated in the Bible and also on the Sumerian Tablets! Still our ancestors choose to protect, save and shared knowledge with these created humans or other races. Maybe they thought we got what we deserved as the descendants of the Anunnaki that fought against their own kind and stayed behind to save and protect the created humans or other races! I honestly do not know! It was also known that the Anunnaki or these Negroid races could see the future and knew that their descendants were going to be killed, dehumanized and enslaved! Our ancestors sure had a lot of confidence in their created human's ability to ultimately forgive us for their sins or they also saw in the future that we will not be oppressed anymore!" I answered.

"So we the Negroid race came from another planet? I knew that there was something not quite right, with all these different races! And we are sure the ones that definitely does not seem to fit in the group! And all of the mysterious pyramids and other impressive building were then really build by our ancestors! And many of these information are stated in the Bible?" Ray finally commented.

"Oh yes, it is also stated in the Bible that they are coming back! And that they will take a nation of 144.000 people to live on their planet! You know I always thought that the December 2012 date prediction actually means a new beginning and not an end of the world! And I also felt that maybe the counting is incorrect or maybe it was not correctly counted, due to the constant changing of the counting system of the days and years in the past. But that means that the time for them to come back is still probably very near, maybe 2021 or maybe even 2121 who knows!" I commented.

"Was that before or after nothing happened in December 2012?" Roy asked smiling.

"Oh way before December 2012, I also never thought that the world was going to end I always knew that something big was going to be revealed to the world. The word Revelation does mean the reveal of a secret, a really big secret! Maybe that secret would be the reveal of whom the Negroid race really are or the reveal of how the other races were created and this not only for a few but for all to know! And that probably they themselves would come and make that announcement to all living on earth! At least that it is what is stated in the Bible " I replied.

"But aunt Isa that is in two to three years!" Tyrel commented.

"So you believe that in 2020 or 2021 the Anunnaki or the alien Negroid race that went back to their planet, will come back to reveal or certified all the secrets of planet earth and the creation of the human slave workers and who the Negroid race is?" Roy asked.

"Definitely! I personally believe that the end of the days as we know them on earth are very near! Their coming are supposed to be preceded by various natural disasters as is predicted as it seems in the Bible or other known predictions! All these natural disasters are occurring because we are creating an imbalance on earth! But my presentation does not go that far, it only covers the reveal of the secret that the Negroid race are indeed not from this earth, that they are the Anunnaki and that they created the other races!" I answered.

"What is then the need of knowing this now?" Tyrel asked.

"Tyrel I believe that regardless if you can use an information immediately or in the future, every information is food for your soul! Particularly if you have felt that you were held back to realize all your dreams and the pursuit of your happiness! And in any event you should be prepared and not panicked, commit suicide or start a war against your own kind, when it is coming down. Because all the movies that has been made are actually stating that the aliens wants to eradicate us! That is also stated in the Bible, that God was not pleased with his creation of humans and wanted to eradicate them. I believe that the Bible is a handbook for us as descendant of the Anunnaki or Negroid race, our history, present and future! Maybe here and there it has been distorted but you have to see through that! And you have to take everything literally" I explained.

"Could we be that nation of 144.000 people aunt Isa?" Satie asked.

"I do not have the slightest idea! But I assume everything is possible! Definitely if it were in the 1950 when we were considered by the UN as the most humble and visitor's friendly nation in the world! Because they the Anunnaki would certainly come as visiting aliens to our planet earth!" I answered smiling.

"Do you really believe that we are the Anunnaki Isa? I have heard about the Anunnaki that they were giants and we humans are very much shorter than they are! Plus they live for thousands of years and we can only live for a maximum of 125 or less! The Negroid race actually has a shorter lifespan than all the other races! And the Anunnaki are also geniuses, I do not believe that they are many Negroid geniuses on earth Isa!" Roy commented.

"You are right that the depiction of the first created full grown up humans seemed smaller or maybe half the size of their creators or the Anunnaki! But it is stated by scientist that the first of the three new races, the Caucasian, the Mongoloid and the Australoid race that actually the first of the new races was the Australoid race or the Australoid Aboriginals and they were in ancient times definitely not taller than 1.25 meters long and very skinny! The Asians or the Mongolian race were also very short and skinny!" I explained.

"But there are other depictions that the Anunnaki seemed three to four times the size of the humans!" Roy commented!

"The Egyptians Pharaohs also sometimes depicted themselves as very much larger than the rest of the Egyptians but this was a way to put emphasis on their importance and power!" I replied.

"Ok, maybe that is the explanation for that then, but how about the fact that they were genius?" Roy asked.

"Well I do believe that we are all also 'geniuses' and that this has to do with the pineal gland. And what is actual a genius? A genius has the ready ability to receive information of the Universe that others will need books or an internet connection to gather these information and learn them by heard, for ready reference! So the brain of a genius works like a real fast internet with connection to all information ever existed in the universe! And how do you connect? You connect through the pineal gland or what the Egyptians called the third eye that can provide you with all knowledge of the universe! Imagine that our pineal gland situated in our brains with the black matter called melanin in it has the possibility to have a so called 'internet connection' with all the knowledge available in the universe! We knew how to connect, now we have lost the knowledge how to connect and also how to read the communication or information received, but sometimes we do connect and receive by chance information's! The education that is now being provided to us, is to slow for our brains and when we try to slow down our brains we get lost or lose the connection, which is then considered being dumb. Our mind is just not wired the same as the mind of the other races that has a lesser amount of melanin! You know we could have a 24/7 direct connection with all the universal available knowledge, without paying any monthly fees! But unfortunately we lost the knowhow how to connect properly and decipher what is presented to us! This is also not evidence but the way I perceived it as the truth, based on the knowledge of the Egyptians of the third eye!"

"That is an interesting way of explaining that, but how come that there are only white geniuses then?" Tyrel asked.

"Well as just explained, I believe that their internet connection is slower, enabling them to receive and decipher part of the knowledge received! The darker you are the faster your internet connection is and if you did not learn to accept and decipher what you are receiving you can get lost. Reason why we experience that we know more without actual learning and or studying all the required know how by heart! We just know it and many times cannot explain how we got the info or the calculations needed to explain the solution! I remember once I was getting only a perfect

10 for algebra, then the teacher told me I need to write done in details how I got to the correct answer, because others were thinking that I am cheating. As of that day, the highest score that I got was 8 and that in at least twice more time to finish the tests. The vast majority of recognized geniuses like Albert Einstein also do seem to state that they are just receivers of information readily available according to their testimony also stored in the Universe! So there is actually nothing special being a genius, it is just that your receiving station is in perfect condition!" I explained.

"But knowledge is power!" Tyrel commented.

"I believe that this is true, sometimes I know the answer without really ever studied that particular issue and when others asked me how did I know that, I always said it just seemed logical to me!" Ray commented.

"But I really do not know how come the Anunnaki lived for over thousands of years and that the Negroid race and also the humans or other races also could have lived longer in ancient days, but that this was eventually changed as also stated in the Bible and maybe also on the tablets! Also the Egyptian Pharaohs lived very long for thousands and thousands of years, as is documented by them. Maybe it has something to do with the atmosphere of the earth that shortens the live of the Negroid race, from generation to generation or maybe they made a special potion that they could take to live longer or maybe it was a special diet or maybe they travel out to space and each time they came back, for them it seems like a few months, but on earth centuries has passed? I really do not have a clue and that is still a secret that I did not as yet encounter any plausible explanation" I answered.

"The secret of living long and youthful is a secret that people will kill for! Maybe they will also kill if the secret of the Negroid race came out" Tyrel replied.

"They paid someone to kill Martin Luther King, nearly killed Nelson Mandela by keeping him imprisoned, maybe the government I mean the Dutch Government also paid someone to kill our leader Helmin Wiels! Did these black leaders know the secrets that these countries were trying to keep to themselves and therefore got killed?" Satie asked with a horrifying face!

"They also killed Tula!" I replied.

"Maybe you would be in danger too Aunt Isa!" Tyrel commented.

"We all got to die some day and I am sure happy to die if needed for the publication of this truth, at this point and time of my life. It would have been different if I still had young children, because I would never want to put my life in jeopardy and leave them behind as small children!" I answered.

"You are a hero if you are willing to die for this truth Aunt Isa" Tyrel stated.

"Oh no I do not think I am a hero, because I definitely will take the necessary precautions to safeguard my life, your grandpa and uncle Den are the real hero's" I answered.

"How come?" Tyrel asked.

"Your grandpa saved me from the hands of incompetent doctors, that just wanted me to last for a few months, risking to go to jail for my life. And uncle Den saved a girl at his school when he was a teenager, by catching her and avoiding that she felt of a cliff, while endangering himself of also falling down with her!" I replied.

"I have heard about you and grandpa, but I never heard what uncle Den did, that is new to me!" Tyrel stated.

"Oh Den does not like to talk about these things so much, it was another girl that told me at school that Den had saved a girl from falling down a cliff. But he did however confirm it when I asked him!" I commented.

"Where is Den?" Ray asked.

"I believe he is already asleep, you know that Den does not mess with his sleep, if he is tired he just climbs in bed!" I answered.

"Yeah, he always does that doesn't he, we're partying at your home, everyone is having a good time till two in the morning and where is Den, fast asleep since midnight or 1.00 am or not? Ray asked laughing.

"We are both like that, we love to party but 1.am the latest 1.30am is our check out time. But as host I am the one still doing my best for all our guest! And still if we are working on a project or studying for a test, we could stay awake till the morning if necessary" I said shaking my head.

"Oh yes, because you both are essentially nerds!" Ray said smiling.

"We are not nerds! Ok maybe we are" I said laughing. And the whole group started to tease me being a nerd, wannabe something else.

"Satie, what did you meant, that maybe Helmin Wiels the killed senator who was first completely against the Dutch Government and then suddenly changed and became a defender of the Dutch Government, was really killed by the Dutch Government whom he was now defending? That does not make any sense!" Roy stated.

"Maybe Helmin was just playing along to let them think that he was on their side, so he can gather more insight information. And we all know that governments in the past paid assassins to get rid of people who knew too much or were going to betray them! And the Dutch Government certainly does has a suspicious behavior in regards of their agenda for us as a nation and this without knowing the secret of the Negroid race!" Satie answered.

"You know that when they announced on TV that Helmin Wiels got killed and also showed the headquarters of his political party and all the members of the party, I just said to my kids 'the killer is among them of his own party' and I also knew at same time that they were going to frame others for his death! Afterwards the partner of Helmin Wiels also stated the same that the killer or the ones in charge of killing Helmin are in his own party!" I commented.

"We know that you have psychic abilities Aunt Isa so tell us who killed Helmin Wiels?" Tyrel asked.

"Well as I said before, when they were announcing his death I received some kind of a mystic message and that was it! But as you all know I love resolving crimes by coming up with my own theory, it is a hobby of mine!" I answered.

"Do tell us your theory then aunt Isa!" Tyrell asked.

"First I do not even believe that it was the ones that they said shot him, I think that they definitely were framed! But the framed killer had a lot of murders on his conscious, he was a professional killer but he did not kill Helmin. Then the person that was also calling him to meet him at the site where he was killed was also framed according to my theory, I believe that he knew something was going to happened maybe that they will beat or scared Helmin but definitely I do not belief that he thought that they were going to kill him, otherwise he would not have constantly called him! Because both of them were involved in an issue of receiving money in the USA and it appears that Helmin changed his mind to accept this money! And maybe he thought that it was stupid and dangerous not to accept this money, because maybe they really needed the money for campaigning for the upcoming elections and a scare would convince Helmin to accept this money?"

"Yes I remember that there were FBI agents that were investigating the opening and receipt of a lot of money by Helmin and another party member in the USA!" Tyrel added.

"According to my theory this plot to murder Helmin was in combination with the Dutch and maybe the USA Government, some elites on the island and insiders of his own party!" I commented.

"But who of his own party?" Tyrel asked.

"My hunch is that one or maybe two close party members knew that he was going to be killed and participated full in the killing!" I replied.

"But why would they do that, have their own party leader killed?" Satie asked.

"Power and money!" Ray replied.

"Exactly!" I confirmed.

"Do you think that Helmin Wiels knew of the secret of the Negroid race or that he was very close of knowing the truth of who we really are?" Tyrel asked.

"I do not know exactly what he knew or was on the brink of finding out, but remember that Helmin Wiels was rewinding our brains of thinking that the white or Dutch people are superior to us! For this reason he was purposely denigrating the Dutch race as a strategy to get them down at the level that the Dutch has put us and that afterwards he would have built us up to believe in ourselves! And that is what sure all the other leaders were doing, informing their Negroid race that we are all equal and were getting their people to follow their lead! It is a doctrine of these white countries to impose on our people that they are an inferior race, more likely still a hominoid or apelike being in development and everyone who tries to proof the contrary and is in a critical political position as a leader could get killed or imprisoned!" I commented.

"So this is your theory! But how does that psychic thing actually works aunt Isa?" Satie asked.

"Well most of the time I dream about things to happen, or a deceased person or a person that is going to die informs me of something or give me a message for someone else, but sometimes it is that I just experience like someone is in my head and tell me things, that I just many times blurred out! But I do not have any control of it, I do not seek the information, I just receive it!" I answered.

"You know Isa I still cannot see how the Negroid race can be the Anunnaki, they lived for thousands and thousands of years!" Roy commented the same observation again.

"My conclusions are based on the fact that the Negroid race were on earth for over 200.000 years as established by scientist. And that according to the scientific 'Out of Africa' theory all the other races emerged through interbreeding or the merging of the DNA of the Negroid race and that from the hominoids! The Anunnaki came to earth from another planet as described on these Sumerian Tablets some 400.000 years ago! Scientist are not able to establish the origin or any evolutional existence of the Negroid race on earth, it seems that they do not have an earthly origin or that they were dropped off in some way or other on earth! Same scientist cannot really explain the reason of both DNA of the hominoid or apelike being and the Negroid DNA found in all the new races that existed not more than 30.000 years ago! Because this could not have been possible through interbreeding, two species as the same case when a donkey and a horse bore a mule, the mule will be born 99,99% sterile! So my conclusion is that the only possible explanation is that much more technical advanced beings genetically engineered the new races with their own DNA and the DNA of the hominoids and made a hybrid specie that they call humans! Which is exactly what is stated on the Sumerian Tablets that the Anunnaki used their own DNA, to create the humans or the three other new major races, just the same that scientist has acknowledged that there must have been some merging of DNA of two species! Scientist were or are still working under the presumption that 30.000 years ago, there only existed a primitive life, which according to their data would have made it impossible to perform a mix of two specie by genetically engineering this. So their only other left explanation would be interbreeding to create a new specie or the hybrid or the humans. You know Anunnaki actually means 'those whom from the heaven's came!'

All of this ties in with the scriptures in the Bible! The three new major races also seems to match the Bible version of the sons of Noah, which are Japheth which I believe is the predecessor of the Caucasian race, Shem the predecessor of the Mongolian race and Ham the predecessor of the Australoid race! It seems that it was also stated in a much older versions of the Bible or it's dictionary that the Negroid race is not a created human race, belonging to Ham, which many other religions belief or pretend that the Negroid race belong to. And also other important facts and documentation, but that would definitely be the much larger version!" I explained!

"Very, very interesting! When are you giving these presentations Isa?" Roy asked looking very intrigued.

Chapter 5.

The presentation!

Being aware of the fact that the subject that I was going to present will be a very delicate one and that this would shake up the base of what is believe to be the truth of all invited to attend, I was very careful and wanted to assume the responsibility that I had to guide them and to reassure them that this knowledge had only strengthen my own believe in one Almighty God and his begotten son our savior Jesus Christ!

I was also still a Roman Catholic, because I had acknowledged that the Roman Catholic Church had just copied the religion of the Ethiopians, the Egyptians or in essence the Negroid race, they definitely put their own flare on it, I did not mind that, because the core of both religious believes should be the same. And I do belief that it does not matter where you pray to God our Father or with whom you pray to him, as long as you pray to him with an honest heart and express your gratitude to him for your blessings! As he our Lord had declared: 'For where two or more are gathered in my name, there am I amongst them!'

All invitees were informed as from the invite that the whole presentation will take about three hours. Since the education that we got were in my view incorrect and correcting and unwinding these information will take a lot of time and explaining all of this will also take a lot of time. And then after a short introduction I began with the presentation.

"Did you ever wonder why there are actually various races on earth, with really unique differences if we all are supposed to come from the same source? According to the Bible we all came from Adam and Eve, according to various myths, other religious believes and ancient documentation it was 'The Gods' of each nation that created his own nation or races differently and according to scientist it was either through evolution, what they call the 'Evolution Theory' which theory does have a missing link or chain evidence. The other theory of scientist is based on DNA and it is called the 'Out of Africa Theory' or what scientist regards as 'the first original people on earth' the first Homo Sapiens or the black Negroid African people! Did you also know that the word Homo Sapiens means 'the wise man' in Latin?!

At one of our family gatherings this same subject came at the table and my brother brought up that it seemed impossible that all the different races came from the same Adam and Eve. The differences in the races were according to his view too much to have come from the same ancestors with or without the influence of the sun! Different noses, lips, hair texture and body structure! I was immediately intrigued on the subject, why was there indeed so many differences in the appearance of the races, in particularly between the white Caucasian race and the black Negroid race? So I decided to do a research how the races had developed, by consulting various different sources of creation or emergence of the races as presented in the Bible, existing myths, scientific findings and other ancient documentation and discovered that in particular the Negroid race also had an added mystery to their origin! Because scientist seemed incapable to establish the origin of the Negroid race as evolving from the hominoids or the apelike beings on earth! Which actually means that the Negroid race does not have an earthly origin and if the Negroid race does not have an earthly origin, then from where did they came from?

Before I continue I would like to state very clear that I am not a scientist and that I also do not want to pretend to be one! My official education is Finance and Administration and as a Financial Controller and Financial Manager I usually prepare Financial Statements and Reports and also prepare Business Plans in which I do various research to establish the feasibility of a project. So on this particular project I use the knowledge and ability that I have to gather information, to gather all scientific available information wherever these where and filled in the blanks with other not scientific available information or documentation.

I am also not a very religious person, but I firmly believe in one Almighty God and his son that we call Jesus Christ! The process that I used was first to collect all and any information I could find of various scientist, anthropologist, various religious documentation, myths and any other relevant documentation on this topic of the races and their creation. Some of the information gathered were at first hand very much out of this world, but I kept an open mind and kept digging up more unbelievable information! Then I tried to find a correlation of all the relevant findings, from all the different sources. And then I connected all the dots and the truth just hit me right in the face!

Was this the reason that my ancestors were nearly eradicated from earth and were also nearly sentenced to a perpetual enslavement as a race on planet earth? Did these other races decided that the Negroid black race should be systematically maintained as being on the bottom of the Pyramid of Achievements, because what the Negroid black race has done in the beginning of their own existence?

But if this was the truth, who came up with the plan, how did they pulled it off and how did they achieved keeping it a secret for so long? At this point and time I would like to request you to also keep an open mind and to join me in, my journey through time and space in search of the undeniable truth of the origin of mankind.

Scientist has established that there are four major races on earth of which all the other sub races are derived from! These races are the Negroid race, the Caucasian race, the Mongoloid race and the Australoid race! Scientist has also proven through the Mitochondrial DNA or Eve DNA, that the first anatomically what we now call the human race or Homo Sapiens was the African race or the Negroid black race. The Negroid black race came into existence according to scientist at least 200,000 are more years ago, where skeletons were found and dated in Ethiopia Africa, Ethiopia actually means in Greeks burnt face people, but this nation called themselves Nubians of the Kush nation! Scientist called the fact that there was first only one race on earth in Africa and that from that race other races emerged 'The Out of Africa Theory'! But why does scientist only have an explanation of how the other races emerged and not from what or where from the Negroid black African race or the Ethiopians emerged on earth?

Ethiopia was also long considered by ancient societies through their writings as 'the cradle of humanity', 'the Garden of Eden', 'the Mother of Mankind' way long before scientist established their 'Out of Africa Theory'! But how could ancient people had the knowhow to establish this fact, that it was in Ethiopia Africa that humanity begun? Who gave them this knowledge? In the Bible there is also on various occasion the mention of Ethiopia Africa! It was also well known in ancient times that it was the Ethiopians that started the religious believe in only one almighty God of the whole universe! Yes the Universe, these ancient Ethiopian Africans had vast knowledge of the universe, there is documentation that they took time to study as of ancient times the stars and the planets in the universe! But why would ancient seemingly primitive Negroid Africans study the universe? And for what purpose?

Did you also know that all the days in a week are based on a planet in our solar system? And that the naming of these days as such is more then thousands and thousands of years old! Older then the civilization of the Greeks and the Romans! The first day Sunday is the Sun, the second day Monday is the Moon, Tuesday is Mars or as stated in Spanish 'Martes', Wednesday is Mercuries or as stated in Spanish 'Miercules", Thursday is Jupiter or in Spanish 'Jueves', Friday is Venus or in Spanish 'Viernes', Saturday is Saturn or in Spanish Sabado! Spanish is actually the language that is more in common with ancient Latin! Do you also know what Latin actually means? Latin is derived out of the word Ladino, in ancient times Ladino meant the people that were black Negroid or commonly called in Europe as the Moors!

Did you also know that the Moors had vast knowledge of counting of seconds, minutes, hours and also the knowhow that, that will constitute a day which is the cycle of the stars and the sun! And that the earth revolved around the sun, way before it is stated to be known by the Greeks in our history books! The Moors could also speak various languages! Had knowhow of astronomy that this current world is only now discovering! And did you also know that these Moors were also known as the initiators of various religious believes, according to ancient documentation in Europe? Did you also know that it is the same Moors that started civilized living in Europe, by building castle, roads and other infrastructure?

But let me continue first with the Ethiopians, the first nation on earth, this ancient nation had also the knowledge that a day had 24 hours to complete a cycle on its own axes and that the Earth travels approximately 365 days around the sun to complete a cycle called a year! But how could it have been possible that such an ancient civilization had such vast knowledge! It is documented that they had all these knowledges before the white Roman nations claimed these knowledges as their own discovered ones! These Ethiopians also knew that the earth was round and not flat as the white Romans believed it to be! It was also known that the Romans claimed that the Ethiopian black Negroid race could perform 'black magic', because of their mysterious abilities, that could not be explained by the Romans!

So the Negroid black or Ethiopian African race was in existence according to scientist at least since 200.000 years ago! According to same scientist the emergence of the other races occurred some 30.000 to 10.000 years ago, when according to their findings, the first race the Negroid race decided to migrate for no apparent reason out of Africa to the North and encounter hominoids or apelike beings that were living a very primitive live on earth in Europe and Asia, the Neanderthals and the Dinosivans and decided again for no apparent reason, to mate with these hominoids or apelike beings and that this mating produced the other three races, the Caucasian race which is a mixing of two species the Neanderthal and the Negroid black race, the Mongoloid and the Australoid race, which are a mixing of two species the Dinosivans and the Negroid black race!

Which resulted as is concluded by scientist in these new races being hybrids because they apparently have two DNA in their system, the black Negroid DNA and also the hominoid or apelike being DNA! The common theme of these new emerged races with the hominoid or apelike being is the straight hair! The Negroid race has wooly or curled hair, but the apelike beings or hominoids had straight hair, a more lean or sluggish body and a flat behind! So now we have a scientific explanation with the help of DNA why only the Negroid race has wooly hair and the other races all have straight hair, a less muscular body and also a more flat behind!" I was explaining, when a hand went through the air!

"Do you mean to tell me that we have been called apes but that it is them that are the real apes?" Humberto a friend asked a little furious while he was staring at me demanding a suitable explanation!

"These are scientific facts! Which indicates that the Negroid race does not have the hominoid or apelike being DNA in their system but that all the other races does has the apelike or monkey DNA in their system!" I answered, what else could I say. He deserves to express his boiled up frustration of being ridiculed as being an ape by others that actually did carry the ape or monkey DNA. Humberto lived for many years as a child in the Netherlands and he is a big man with a pretty dark color and he had confided to me long ago, that he was bullied a lot as a child at school of being a monkey or a gorilla!

"But in the days that the knowledge of DNA was not yet discovered there was also as mentioned before another theory the 'Evolution Theory' of Charles Darwin, which all scientist recognized that it has a missing piece or link of chain evidence in regards to humans, that all the races also the Negroid race should have solely evolved from only the hominoids or apelike beings to humans! But as DNA evidence shows the original Negroid race does not have the hominoid DNA in their system, only the other races has the hominoid DNA next to the Negroid DNA in their system! Due to the discovery of DNA this evolution theory is definitely not applicable for the Negroid race! Which in fact means that the hominoids or apelike beings did not have the ability to ever evolve on their own to Homo sapiens or modern humans with all their current capacities and abilities! It is due to the mixing of the Negroid black race DNA that the hominoids essentially became humans or homo sapiens with all their current capabilities!

'"Ok!, hold on, do I need to understand that without the DNA of the Negroid black race, there would have been no other races or other humans? But only us and the ape-like man?" Humberto again asked with an astonished face.

"Yes, that is the scientific conclusion Humberto!" I answered.

"So, this gave rise to another theory 'The out of Africa Theory', on which scientist based their theory on the two DNA found in the other races! Scientist believe that there was an intervention or interbreeding of the two species, the Negroid race and the Hominoids or apelike beings that created in fact hybrids or the other races! Knowing these facts could it even be possible that the black Negroid race or the first nation the Ethiopian nation or the first Homo sapiens which in Latin means the 'wise men' on planet earth, starting off over 200.000 years ago as proven by scientist with all their actual intellectual capabilities, did not achieve greater accomplishments? As is documented the other races, coming in existence only some 30.000 to 10.000 years ago, some 190.000 to 170.000 years later then the Negroid race, with also the hominoid DNA or monkey gene added in their system, as asserted by scientist and not by me, of whom the hominoids were definitely living a very yes very primitive live as a specie for millions of years, apparently according to our history books, achieved much more then the Negroid black race without the hominoid or monkey DNA or gene in their system? As is also established by scientist no more new developments or perfection of the first Homo sapiens was achieved since the existence of the first Homo sapiens at least 200.000 years ago till present day. Was not the Homo sapiens recognized as the 'wise men' in ancient times? Was not the first 'wise men' not the Negroid race or the Ethiopians? What is the information that we are then missing here that there are no recorded accomplishments of the Negroid race for the world in our history books as they were supposed to be the first 'wise men'?

Because standing straight and talking were as it seems not accomplishments of the first race or the Negroid race, they were apparently doing this as of the beginning of their existence on planet earth, as is proven by scientist!

Must we then assume that the hominoids or apelike men were, although they were living a very primitive live for millions of years and could not speak, somehow had more hidden intellectual capacity, due to the size of the brain of this particular hominoid or apelike man, as pointed out by scientist as the possible explanation of its intellectual superior capabilities and achievements in comparison to the first Homo Sapiens, the so called first 'wise men' or the Negroid race? Is the intellectual capability really established according to the size of the space were the brain mass should be seated? Are for example elephants more intelligent than us or a mouse because the size of their brain?

Another interesting fact to debunk the theory of the presumed lower intellectual capabilities of the Negroid black race, is that it has been established by modern scientist that making music and the connecting rhythmical movement through dance, both requires a high intellectual capability of the person accomplishing this, which we all know comes very natural for the black Negroid race. It has also been proven by scientist that great athletic accomplishments and or coordination in sports like basketball, baseball, football and other sport games requires very highly intelligent calculations that are being performed in seconds or as the speed of light, in the brains of the persons playing these games, to coordinate the actions of his or her body. As we all know the Negroid black race does excel in music, dance and sports.

But why are then still the vast majority of famous scientist with very high recorded IQ white Caucasians and all known important inventions or other spectacular achievements all credited to the white or Caucasian race or the other races that have hominoid or monkey gene in their system? Didn't the presumed mating or mixing of the DNA of the Negroid, the first 'wise men' and hominoids had any deteriorating effect on the other three races, the Caucasian, the Mongolian and the Australoid race? Apparently not, on the contrary, this hominoid or apelike being gene had vast improved their intellectual capabilities in comparison with the Negroid race, definitely if you are inclined to believe and accept the presented world history.

Does it make scientific sense, that the Negroid race is behind in their development and achievements as a race, being the only race that originally did not have the hominoid or apelike being DNA in their system? It seems to be a huge mystery how this could have developed the way that it did, since scientist are telling us that the Negroid race were primitives living in the wild for at least 200.000 years! It was only in 1500 AD that the Caucasian white race according to the history presented to us, had taken the wild running Negroid African people out of the jungle and enslaved them and brought them to the civilized world of the Caucasian race to save their souls from eternal condemnation!

So it definitely seems that the black Negroid race existing according to scientist for over 200.000 years did not have any real contribution to the advancement of mankind or humanity according to written Western European and American documented history books or films. Moses, Adam, Eve, Mary, Jesus

Christ, Columbus, Einstein, Mozart and the vast majority of other historical important or religious people and other ground breaking discovery or invention for the advancement of mankind all apparently as is depicted in the presented history books and films in Western European and American education system, came from the Caucasian race only. How could it be even possible that the black Negroid race as established by scientist to be the first race or the first Homo sapiens or the first 'wise man' on earth since 200.000 years ago, did not have any contribution at all in the development or advancement of mankind on planet earth?

Where the black Negroid race contently wondering for hundred thousand of years in the woods and using only very simple tools to catch their meals as the hominoids or apelike beings who could also not speak, but only grunt did? Do we need to conclude that if this was the case, there is essentially no differences in these two species, even though one of the species got to walk completely upright and could articulate and speak, made tools, living facilities and wrote or made drawings and the other specie the hominoid that could not really walk upright and only grunt, did not really use any tools and made no drawings and did not make a living facility but lived in nature developed caves?

Can we then also conclude that the first black Negroid race or Homo sapiens were in essence intelligently actually more incompetent than the for millions of years very primitive living hominoids or apelike beings on earth? And that it was thanks to the mix of the DNA of these hominoids or ape like beings that the Negroid race were actually upgraded to more intelligent superior hybrids or the new emerged races?

232

Or were the first Homo sapiens or the black Negroid race just only one step ahead of primates or the other known extinct Hominoids or apelike beings as is seemingly depicted by the evolution theory? Is what in the evolution theory is also subtle suggested correct namely that the black Negroid race had actually stopped to evolve? And that apparently in the "Out of Africa" theory a magic happened when two species the Homo sapiens, the 'wise man' or the Negroid race interbreed with the hominoids or apelike beings, of which the hominoids according to scientific documented findings were a specie that was not intelligent or capable enough as the homo sapiens and that out of that mix was supposed to emerge a hybrid race with more intelligent capacity than the original homo sapiens or the specie that was regarded as the original 'wise man'? Do scientist also really want us to believe that the Caucasian race as last depiction in the 'Evolution Theory', actually must be interpreted that the Caucasian race is the only fully developed and completed human intelligent being? What is the reason that the 'Evolution Theory' the theory from apes to humans was regarded as missing a link or chain of evidence? Was it because of the fact that it seemed that the Negroid race with its woolly or curly hair did definitely not fit into this theory?

But how come the Negroid race whom is supposed to be a 100% 'wise man', since 200.000 years ago did not accomplish any wise achievements for the world? What was the first race, the Negroid race or the first Homo sapiens or wise man doing in the time frame of at least 170.000 years? But still it remains as if the Caucasoid race with the hominoid DNA or gene existing for more or less 30.000 to 10.000 years is far more intellectually developed then

233

the Negroid race? What had happened that it seems like the Negroid race was stuck or actually thrown back in time? Or was the history of the world and the achievement of the Negroid black race completely wiped out or stolen, but why or by whom?

According to the own history of the white Caucasian race, they were still living in the stone ages some 8.000 to 6.000 years ago. While there are now evidence that a group of early civilizations were already living in golden ages at least some 10.000 to 50.000 years ago or more? Who was that civilization? Was that the civilization of the first Negroid black race, existing on planet earth for more than 200.000 years? That would have been the best assumption since the Negroid black race was the first and only race on earth, living as an intelligent being as is confirmed by scientific facts since at least 200.000 years ago!

The Bible also suggest that humans were created maybe some 6.000 to not more than 10.000 years ago. The new races as recorded by scientist existed for approximately 10.000 to 30.000 years ago. But the Negroid race existed according to scientist at least 200.000 years ago. Does the Bible imply that the Negroid race is not a created human by God?

Adam and Eve apparently would have been according to the depiction of the Roman Catholic Church, white with straight hair and pointed nose or definitely a Caucasian! But in the event that the Bible or the interpretation of the Bible is correct, if Adam and Eve were indeed white, this would automatically eliminate the existence of the Negroid race as created humans or as the sons or daughters of Adam and Eve! Because this is a scientifically impossible achievement, two white Caucasian people can never bore a Negroid black child! So in the event that the Roman Catholic Church is right, were did the Negroid race came from, since this race could never have come from the creation of the first humans the white Caucasian Adam and Eve?

But it is a scientific fact though that in contrary to white people, two black people can bore a white child or what we now call an Albino, a person with a genetic disorder or a deficiency of the pigmentation called melanin, which causes that the child has blond hair, pale skin and blue, green or grey eyes. But that same Albino child of black Negroid parents will never be born with straight hair, a seemingly flat butt, thin lips and a narrow high nose! So the white Caucasian Adam and Eve or the Black Negroid Adam and Eve or another of the other races just seems to exclude the existence from the same source of one or more of the other major base races! Or was Adam a Negroid or a Caucasian and Eve was the opposite a Caucasian or Negroid, the mixing or interbreeding of the two races as explained by scientist? But that is not what is stated in the Bible, because God made Eve with the rib or in scientific terms the DNA and genes of Adam! So Eve it's actually in scientific terms, a cloned female version of Adam!

According to the Bible, on earth there were only the angels or the watchers of God and the fugitives or the ones that abandoned the mission of God and also the created humans by God! So could the Negroid race be considered somehow to be the angels or the watchers of God or the fugitives that abandoned God that as recorded by the Bible decided to mate with these created humans,

235

because these created humans were fair and beautiful? Does fair means being of white or pale color?

And from that union or mixing of the white Caucasian children of the Caucasian white Adam and Eve and the Negroid black angels or watchers of God or the fugitives came the two other base races? Or more precisely the emergence of the two new additional races the Mongoloid and the Australoid races? But even if that would have been possible, how come that they maintained their unique features as a group or a race? Was there no more mixing of all the races together, which would have dissipate the existing of various unique races and make it at the end, only one race 'a mixed mambo jambo race' existing on planet earth?

Another interesting scientific question is, where did the black Negroid race came from, as scientist has already established in 'The Out of Africa' theory that the first Negroid black race did not have any trace of other hominoid or apelike genes in their system, which upon the evolution theory on earth is based upon. So the conclusion is that the evolution theory does not seem to be applicable at all to the first base race, the first Homo sapiens or "wise men' or the Negroid black race? And if the Negroid black race its origin or evolution if any is not from earth, from where is it then? And how did they landed on earth? Maybe from the heavens? Could they really be the angels or watchers of God or the fugitives that did not want to follow the orders of God? As it is depicted angels just look like us and could transport themselves for ancient concept in mysterious ways, reason why they portrait them with wings as birds that just could fly off?

Or could they be the aliens that other more futuristic scientist are claiming that the angels were. Angels or the God's that protected, guided and brought knowledge to the humans? Angels or the God's that build impressive structures and had their Golden Age and afterwards for some or other reason abandoned planet earth? But what if they never abandoned earth, what if they are the ones whose presence on earth cannot be explained by common scientist, what if the Negroid black race are actually aliens from another planet that came from the sky or from the heavens? What if it was them that were more technically advanced beings or homo sapiens or 'the wise man' and decided to genetically engineered humans by mixing their own DNA with the DNA of the hominoids or apelike men already on earth?

So to recap according to scientist DNA evidence has proven that the first anatomically human race or Homo sapiens or the black Negroid race, they started off without, yes without any evolutionary progress from apes or hominoids! But all the other base races that has evidence of existing not more then 30.000 to 10.000 years, their DNA proves that they do have hominoid or monkey gene in their system, next to also the Negroid or Homo Sapiens DNA in their system! So actually these new emerged races has as stated earlier DNA of two different species in their system, so they are what we call hybrids! The question is how did these new or the other later emerged races got both DNA or gene in their system?

The way that scientist explains this, is that the hominoid gene got in the system of the other races, when the first race, the Negroid race migrated to the North and decided for whatever reason to interbreed or have intercourse and procreate with hominoids or apelike male or female! These hominoid were covered with a lot of long straight hair, with a flat but, that could not speak, but only grunt or make other noises. That specie was missing the needed bone in their neck what would have given them the ability to articulate and be able to speak. They did also not involve themselves in the making of tools, arts, games, dance, music, painting and or writings. They only concentrated on the basic, like getting food for survival and were living a very primitive live in only nature developed caves. It seems that their arms were also nearly as long as their legs! In contrary to the first race on earth the Negroid race, which were categorized as having the "sacred geometry" or the "golden ratio" of the human body, which is the perfect body to excel in sport activities! These hominoids could also not really stand up straight as the upright walking and standing homo sapiens or Negroid race did!

It seems that the long straight hair that covered the entire body of the hominoids, were protecting them from the cold in the North. Same straight hair, that contrary to the Negroid race that had very curly or wooly hair, all the other three mayor races have! So scientist do confirm through DNA findings that there was a mixing of the DNA of the first Negroid black race with wooly hair or the original homo sapiens and the DNA of hominoids or apelike beings with straight hair and with that mixing of DNA not one but three, yes three additional major races emerged, the Caucasoid, the Mongoloid and the Australoid race and all with straight hair!

The only problem is that this could not have been through interbreeding or mating between the Negroid race and the hominoids! Because when two complete different species interbreed, the offspring will be born for 99,9% sterile, just as when a horse and a donkey born a mule! So this scientific explanation for the creation of three new races based on the "Out of Africa" theory with DNA of two species, the Homo sapiens or Negroid race and the hominoid or the apelike being, through interbreeding or mating is scientifically not possible! So the only other explanation would be that this was done through scientific genetic engineering! But could this have been possible some 30.000 years ago? And if so, whom would be capable of doing that? Some futuristic scientist also claims that it was the aliens that visited planet earth and were called 'The Gods' by ancient humans, because of their unexplained capabilities, that genetically engineered these hybrids or younger races, by using the DNA of the Negroid race and the DNA of the hominoid. But why would they the aliens bother to do that, put two species or DNA together? The Negroid or the Homo sapiens or the 'wise man' DNA combined with the Hominoid or apelike being DNA, to create the younger races, for what purpose would they have done this?

It is evident that both scientist also the futuristic ones and religion acknowledges that there was some mixing of species or DNA! Because the Bible also have the angels or watchers of God and or the fugitives, mating with the created humans by God, or the children of Adam and Eve! Scientist has the Negroid race mating with the hominoids! And futuristic scientist has 'The Gods' genetic engineering these new races, with DNA of the Negroid race and the Hominoid DNA, both according to them already on earth! But they do not explain the reason why nor do they explain were the

Negroid race came from, since their DNA or blood heritage is not from earth!

So as already stated scientist has established that these three new major races only existed some 30.000 to 10.000 years ago and the Bible also speaks of the creation of humans for no more than 10.000 years ago! Could it also be that there is a correlation of the Bible and scientist in regards of the three sons of Noah whom replenished the earth after the flood? Could Japheth be the progenitor of the Caucasian race? Shem the progenitor of the Mongolian race? And Ham the progenitor of the Australoid race? If this is the truth, is this also evidence that the Negroid race is regarded in the Bible as a race not belonging to the created humans by God on planet earth? Who are the Negroid race then in the concept of the Bible? Are they really the angels, the watchers of God or the so called fugitives and who are the fugitives as described in the Bible? Well these fugitives are described as the angels or watchers that disobeyed God!

It is believed by anthropologist that the ancient Egyptian nation came from the first nation on earth the Ethiopian Negroid nation! There are unfortunately not many ancient documented information from Ethiopia, due to the fact that the Arabs a Caucasian race, destroyed most of it! But it is documented that the ancient Egyptians, which nation emerged from the ancient Ethiopians, had their own Bible "The Kolbrin Bible", their own ten commandments and also their own Virgin Mother with her son, named Isis and Horus, existing before the stories of Mary and Jesus Christ for sure over more than 5.000 years! It is also established by scientist or anthropologist that the ancient Egyptians were a black

Negroid nation! You can also noticed this on the depiction of themselves as carved and painted on their walls, the braided hair, the use of earrings and chains which is an African custom, the not high and narrow nose in both bridge and root and the color of black or brown of their skin! The Egyptians documented on their walls the creation of humans on earth. According to their version it was their ancestors that created the humans and they also stated that their ancestors came from another planet in the Orion Belt Constellation. Right next to the wall of the depiction of creation of humans the Egyptians had also depictions of some rhesus monkey, as part of their creation myth of humans on earth.

The Egyptians had also documented on their walls how they build the Giza Pyramids which actually mimics the Orion Belt constellation, of where they claimed as stated before that their ancestors came from! So the Egyptians are stating that they are descendants of aliens from another planet! Many of the documentation of the Egyptians were also destroyed or secluded only for their eyes by first again the Arabs as stated a Caucasian race nation that invaded Egypt and later by the Romans also a Caucasian race nation that destroyed a very important library the Library of Alexandria in Egypt and took various documentation, which are presumed to be carefully guarded in the secret library of the Vatican in Rome!

You know why also the Negroid race were called a Nigger? The Egyptians Kings used to were crowns that depicted a snake that they regarded highly as a symbol of the Nagar or Negus which stands for the ones who have and can give power, wisdom and protection! When you pronounce the word Nagar in ancient times, you do not pronounced both the a in the word or to be precise you pronounced Ngr, which stands for the word Nigger, which was later changed to Negroid, since the word Nigger was readily used to humiliate first the slaves and afterwards the free Negroid people! This word due to this misuse unfortunately lost its significance of being a word of most regarded value and appreciation in the past! The Negroid people in particular the Negroid man however still call themselves Nigger as being a proud personification of power, wisdom and the ones who protects! And also pound their heart with their hand in a closed fist, in a gesture of recognition and appreciation of the fact of being a nigger or being whole, which gesture is now also a common ritual practice in the Roman Catholic Church ceremonies.

Although as stated before nearly all documentation of the first black Negroid nation or the ancient Ethiopians or the Nubians, and the Egyptians were destroyed by the Arabs, whom were ransacking the northern part of Africa to steal the wealth of these Negroid nations since 600 AD, it is recorded by other nations or countries that Ethiopia was regarded as the "Cradle of Humanity" of which also the "Garden of Eden" myth was anciently known to be a myth that originated from Ethiopia or from the Ethiopian Negroid black people, way yes way before the existence of the now known Bible. The ancient Ethiopians or the first Negroid black nation on earth, were known to be a very religious nation, who believed in monotheism. This is the belief that there is only one God or Supreme Being! One God that created the whole Universe and established universal laws, that all must abide to.

The Ethiopians had a governing system were a High Priest was the ruler of the nation. The ancient Egyptians also began the Egyptian nation with same governing system, but later changed this to a Kingdom were Kings and Queens or to be precisely Pharaohs ruled and were the High Priest were demoted as advisor to the Pharaohs. The Ethiopians also build the first Pyramids, Obelisk, Castles and various more interesting structures. Maybe not so grand and impressive as those of the Egyptians but still the first ones on planet earth! The Ethiopians also build buildings as from the rock or mountain itself, from the top till the bottom and till this date scientist cannot comprehend how they could have done this. On various places in the world same kind of buildings or structures are found. The Ethiopians were also known as a nation that have the ability to foresee the future, resurrect the dead and perform miracles, which many of the other nations regarded as Black Magic, or the Black ones doing their magic! The Ethiopians or Nubians have a believe system that is based on the knowledge that there is a constant battle of Good and Evil and that it is each and every one of us it's task to ensure that Good always will prevail! But that it is ultimate your choice to choose for the Good or the Evil and to then bear the consequences of your choice!

As is documented by anthropologist the Ethiopians had also the same religious believe of the coming of a black savior, that was the son of a virgin, for many yes many thousands and thousands of years at least five thousand years before the presume birth of the now known Jesus Christ and that same savior died on a cross for the sins of man! This religious legend was apparently copied by the Romans, since it is documented by the Romans that their ruler needed something to unite and control his people. There was a group of black Negroid nomadic people who called themselves Hebrews, that had carried through the turmoil of different civilizations of various God's being adored, the same religious believes, which is the believe in only one God and his begotten son that we now call Jesus Christ for over more than five thousand years as their religion. It seems that maybe this religion of a savior or a Christ was something that the ancient Ethiopians, the ancient Egyptians or various other different Negroid race groups or nations that all had as their religious ancestors beliefs!" I was ramming up showing also different slides of the findings of renowned anthropologist and suddenly, various fingers went in the air!

"Do you mean to tell me that Jesus Christ and the Virgin Mary did not exist?" Latisha a friend of my niece Angie asked.

"Well no, to the contrary they did exist, because a savior or the son of God does or did exist on earth, the name that he is called or the period that is claimed that he came to earth, that is what is not historically correct!" I answered.

"But the counting of time or dates had been stopped to adjust everything to B.C. Before Christ and A.D. for Anno Domini, the year Christ was born, it could be one year or two off but not more!" Commented Rupert the husband of a colleague of my daughter Rona.

"Yes that is correct and that was done first in Rome after they stopped the persecution of the first now called Christians but in fact were the black Hebrews in approximately 400 AD! If I am not mistaken, it was a monk that came up with the idea in 500 AD or so and they went back and re-dated everything of importance to reflect the new counting system as proposed by this monk!" I explained.

"So according to you Isa, the Romans or the Roman Catholic Church just invented a new Jesus Christ and his mother the Virgin Mary, to fit that particular period, so that they could claim it as their own religion?" Marcela a dear friend of mine asked, a little annoyed.

"Well anthropologist found evidence of references to much, very much older same stories dating to at least 5.000 to 8.000 years ago, of a savior named differently in different cultures and his virgin mother who was born on or about the 25th of December in a stable or a cave, was beaten or hanged to death or crucified, descended into hell and rose from the death and afterwards goes to heaven, for the sins of man! Fact is that such a savior did exist, what his or his virgin mother's name really was or in what year precisely it all happened is not quite clear! It definitely did not happened 2.000 years ago as stated by the Roman Catholic Church or the Vatican!" I answered, feeling a little guilty, this was what I was most afraid of! The possible disruption of the faith of some good people as my husband Den had warned me!

"So Aunt Isa, a Jesus Christ or another name or savior was on earth and this all did happened just not on the date or the year that is mentioned that it happened?" Angie my niece asked.

"Yes, precisely!" I answered relieved that at least they are following the essence of what is important.

"But what about the first Christians or the Jews or Hebrews they all acknowledge the birth and the dead of Jesus Christ" Latisha insisted.

"Well actually the Jews or the white Jews did not acknowledge Jesus Christ as the savior!" Rupert answered, before I could have!

"I am aware that this is a very difficult subject, but can I reassure everyone again that Jesus or whatever name you wish to give him and his virgin mother did exist and whatever we call him, he sacrificed his live for our sins that is written in stone!" I said, trying to calm everyone and convincing them that I am not here to disrupt their faith or belief in God or Jesus or the Virgin Mary! That is a scared belief that I myself do not have any doubt of.

"So to resume, as established by scientist the other races emerged on earth only some 10.000 to 30.000 years ago! Most scientist or anthropologists recognize 3 to 4 basic races in existence today and that these races can be divided in at least 30 subgroups. Mainly all scientist agree that the first race on earth in existence at least 200.000 years ago is the Negroid race or that the Negroid race is the zero based race or the original Homo Sapiens! And then 30.000 years ago other races developed next to the Negroid race. But who are the races next to the Negroid race and who are all these races as ethnic groups? Let us first begin with the Negroid races, being the Africans, the African American and the African Caribbean. The Caucasian races, being the Europeans from East and West, the Russians, the Indian Sub-Continent, the American Indians, the European American, the Arabic and most of Middle East people. The Mongolian race being the Asians, the northern Mongolians, the Chinese and Indo-Chinese, the Japanese and Korean, Tibetan, Malayan, Polynesian, Maori, Micronesian, and the Eskimos. The Australoid races being the Australian Aborigine, the Melanesians/Papua and the people of South Asia.

Each and every race have different features, as stated before the new three races all have straight hair, a more lean body structure and a flat butt! Only the Negroid race has curled or wooly hair, thick lips, a natural more muscular body or the ladies very curved hips and both a nice but! The Negroid race also have a forward jawline, as also the Australoid! The Caucasian race has as only race a very high and narrow nose and their jawline is more inwards! The Chinese has a more flat face and nose and a more like closed eyes! All of this without considering the color of the skin, because the color of the skin according to scientist does actually not determine your race, what determine your race is mainly your skull and the other facial features and your body!" I explained, showing the pictures of the different features of the races and nearly all the persons present started raising their hands to ask questions again.

"I have never noticed before that there were so many differences in the skull structure of the different races, it is pretty amazing and very strange that we never got these specifics in the biology lessons at school! But now I am also asking myself, how did these differences came to be, out of the first race which was the Negroid race?" Carlo one of the invitees pointed out.

"As already explained, these new races all have two DNA one from the Negroid race and one from the hominoid or apelike man and therefore are considered hybrids. Being the Neanderthal DNA for the Caucasoid race! And for the Mongoloid race and the Australoid their study shows this is the hominoid or apelike being the Denisovan DNA in their system! Which explains according to scientist the differentiation of the other races with the original race the Negroid race, as having primarily straight hair as a heritage of part of their ancestors hominoids or apelike being genes, the Neanderthal and the Denosivan! The question is now how is it possible that the DNA of both species be in one new specie or a hybrid" I was explaining!

"You mentioned that before aunt Isa but what is a hybrid?" Angie my niece asked.

"A new specie out of two other existing species, as I had explained earlier as like a mule from a horse and a donkey" I answered.

"But a mule is born sterile, so the other three races could have impossible developed, because they would have been sterile too!" Eduardo a friend of my husband commented.

"Yes the scientist explanation is that the races emerged out of the mating or interbreeding of the Negroid race with the Neanderthal hominoid and the Denosivan Hominoid. But that, as is my conclusion and as also stated by Eduardo would not have been possible. And they must have known that, but assumed that there was no other way possible some 30.000 years ago. The only possible way to generate new races, was if the other races were created or in scientific terms genetically engineered! But by whom by God as is explained in the Bible or by 'The Gods' or aliens as explained by futuristic scientist?

Connected with this mystery of the other races having also hominoid or apelike man gene in their system is another scientific mystery of the differences in the human races, is why there are also many differences in the human blood types? And why a natural abortion occurs when a Negative Rhesus blood type mother is carrying a Positive Rhesus fetus. The science behind this, is that the biological system of the RH- mother reacts as if there is an 'invasion of an unknown enemy', which is actually her baby in her body, but why, the biological system reacts this way is still unknown, to nowadays scientist! This only occurs to rhesus negative mothers, because a positive rhesus mother can carry a negative rhesus child and of course a positive rhesus child!

There are in essence four types of blood the A, the B, the AB and the O blood type and also all these blood types could be of a Positive or a Negative Rhesus factor blood. Most humans on earth have the O blood type 60%, A is 20%, B is 16% and AB blood type only 4%. Of which most human beings 85% has a Rhesus Positive factor blood type and only 15% a Rhesus Negative factor blood type. The Positive Rhesus factor is actually comprised of some protein which is also found in the Rhesus Monkey or as commonly called the hominoid or apelike being gene! Can we then conclude that all the other new races should have then a positive Rhesus Monkey gene, due to the hominoid gene injected in one way or another into their blood and DNA system?

This all ties in the evolution of apes theory, that hominoids evolved from apes or maybe more precisely of the rhesus monkey and then eventually in humans or Homo sapiens! But the original Homo sapiens or Negroid race does definitely not have a rhesus positive factor blood but a rhesus negative blood type, due to the absence of the hominoid or apelike man gene in their system! So where did the Negroid race came from as they definitely do not seem to fit in any way or form to evolved on earth? And are the scientist really suggesting in the 'Out of Africa theory' that the Negroid race is not from planet earth? Could it be the truth that the Negroid race are in fact the aliens or 'The Gods' that came from another planet to planet earth as stated by the Egyptians and that they created or genetically engineered the other races? Is the Bible also suggesting that the Negroid race are the angels, the watchers and or the fugitives or fallen angels that came from heaven or from the sky or from out of space? Other African ancient civilization also acknowledges that their ancestors came from another planet from a complete other solar system! So could this really be the truth? What other data or documentation are out there to confirm that the Negroid race could have come from another planet and were the ones called 'The Gods'? And also how did the other races emerged since this could not have been possible through interbreeding of the Negroid race and the hominoids as already confirmed, because of the 99,9% sterile offspring.

Ancient very old writing dating from at least 20.000 years ago in cuneiform, called the Sumerian Tablets that were found in 1841 and that were translated recently tells an interesting story that brings it all together. According to these ancient tablets that are older than the documentation used for the conception of the Bible, more technological advanced beings that called themselves the Anunnaki, or 'the ones whom from the heavens came', came to our planet earth! It seems that the Anunnaki came from another solar system and planet some 400.000 years ago to earth to mind gold. This gold was needed on their own planet to restore their atmosphere that was deteriorating! The same stories that are described in the Bible of the beginnings and the creation of the humans and the deluge is also written on these discovered very ancient Sumerian tablets.

It is written that the Anunnaki decided to create slave workers, due to the fact that their own kind decided to flee as 'fugitives' because the work of mining gold was too demanding. The word fugitives or fallen angels that were not complying to the duties as given by God is also mentioned in the Bible! It is also stated that due to the need of manpower to continue the work of mining, they genetically created slave workers, by improving the DNA of the existing hominoids or apelike beings on earth with their own DNA to create not one but various Adam's or hybrid males.

It is also stated that various errors were made in the creation of these slave workers called humans by them, which actually means man of flesh, the hu or hue actually stands for flesh! It is also stated that they later made a female version or an Eve for each of them to have as a partner or we may say a wife, because they saw that the males were depressive and therefore not progressing with the work of mining! It is also stated that they replicated or cloned their first creations of these males and females creating in essence groups with the same features or qualities, creating in this way in fact what we now call races or to be precise the three different younger major races to do the work of mining for them!

251

So in essence these ancient old tablets also states, as in the Bible and as acknowledge by scientist, that there was some mixing of DNA, the DNA in this case of the Anunnaki and the DNA of the hominoids or apelike beings already existing on earth to create a fleet of workers for them to save their own planet are in fact the known by us new emerged races some 10.000 to 30.000 years ago! As stated before all the other races has a mixing as established by scientist of DNA of the Negroid race and the DNA of the hominoids or apelike beings existing for millions of years on earth!

Can we then conclude that the Anunnaki or the aliens or the ones called 'The Gods' whom is as recorded on ancient tablets of not originating from this planet earth but of another planet and solar system or as stated by the Bible came from the sky or heaven and used their own DNA to essentially upgrade the capabilities of the hominoids or apelike beings on earth to create new beings or races as essentially slave workers, are in fact the Negroid black race? Which evidence is now apparent in the two DNA system of the emerged hybrid races some 10.000 to 30.000 years ago!

So is this really what the so called "Trans-Atlantic African Slave Trade" where the Negroid race were nearly wiped out of the surface of planet earth, dehumanized and or enslaved with the intention of a perpetual enslavement, ripped from their history, legacy and their religion was all about, the ultimate revenge or payback for creating the other races as upgraded hominoids to work as slave workers and to later be disposed of when their service was completed in an earthly flood as is stated in the Bible and also on these Sumerian Tablets?

It is also mentioned that it was a job of trial and error and various mistakes were made when they created the human slave workers or the new emerged races! It is written on the Sumerian tablets, that they created by mistake 'idiots', that they created some 'without skin', that they created some with not good functioning limps, that they created some without genitals and so on. But due to time constraints they decided to use all the created slave workers with the errors made in their gene system and duplicated or cloned them to have various groups doing various needed work, next to the mining! So in fact they were cloning or creating various groups or as we now described the various new different races!

Could being without skin actually means having a pale or white color, which many races on earth have be interpreted as having a permanent genetic disorder now called Albinism, the inability to produce sufficient melanin to darken the skin! Another genetic disorder that also seems to identified according to a scientist John Langdon Down, another entire race due to the characters of the disorder, is the Mongolian Idiocy, a mental disorder or commonly now renamed as the "Down Syndrome". This disorder gave limited intelligent capabilities to the ones suffering of this genetic disorder and also changed their facial appearance! In 1866 this English Doctor, John Langdon Down discovered that children born with this genetic disorder had the exact same facial expression, like seemingly closed eyes and flat face as the Mongolian race?" I kept on explaining. And Eduardo raise his hand.

"Is that not offensive to state that the Mongolian races were created as idiots?" Said Eduardo.

"I am very sorry, it is not my intention to offend, but I do need to point out the facts and similarities, to prove my point of the possibility of the Sumerian Tablets being accurate!" I answered and then continued with the presentation.

"As stated before, when the Anunnaki observed that the slave workers needed a life companion to lift up their spirit, so that the job can be done more effectively they decided to clone a female version or an Eve for each slave worker, just as also is stated in the Bible! With the exception that in the Bible it is stated that only one Adam and one Eve were created!

The Anunnaki called themselves as a group the Anunnaki or 'the ones who from the heavens came', but where called 'The God's' by the created human slave workers or other races. But in those ancient days, being called 'God' was the same as being called the Master, the Lord or the one that you must obey and gives you commands! It was also the intention of the Anunnaki after the mining of the gold was done, to completely wipe out their as denominated by themselves 'imperfect' creation in an earthly flood, just as is also mentioned in the Bible, that God has repented the creation of humankind.

But a group of the Anunnaki did not agree that the humans should be annihilated, this group was weeping and struck by greave as described on these tablets for days and they decided to defend the humans and fought against the other group that had decided to annihilate the humans and also stayed behind on earth to save the by them created humans from the earthly flood! Also just the same that is explained in the Bible of Noah and his family being

254

saved from an earthly flood send by God to get rid of only the wicked or evil humans!

The depiction of these Anunnaki on same tablets have them having braided hair and beard with beads in them, the males also wear earrings just as the Egyptians and other African nations. It also seems that they were on earth according to the translation since 400.000 years ago. So could the Negroid race that scientist establish to be as it seems dropped on earth at least 200.000 years ago, whom are regarded as the first homo sapiens, be the Anunnaki or the so called 'wise men' that created or genetically engineered humans or more precisely the other new races as slave workers some 30.000 to 10.000 years ago, by using their own DNA and the DNA of the hominoids or apelike being found on planet earth, effectively creating hybrids or a complete new species with two DNA on planet earth?

Just as modern scientist has established through their findings of the DNA of hominoids and the DNA of the first Homo sapiens or the Negroid race, both present in the new three major races! And also just as the Bible has acknowledge the creation of humans in the image of their creators? Is using their own DNA stands for in creating the humans in their own image?

Can we then conclude that the Anunnaki as stated by these Sumerian Tablets, that were here first and stayed behind to save the created humans, from a worldly flood were the first established nation on earth the Ethiopian nation, the first homo sapiens or 'wise man' or Negroid race? Same Negroid race who's origin is also not from planet earth as, as subtle as possible is suggested by modern day scientist? So at the end must we understand that the humans or the other races were essentially created to only serve one purpose, which was to be slave workers of the Anunnaki or in essence of the Negroid black race?

Was the African Trans-Atlantic Slave Trade therefore their ultimate revenge, by making the enslaver their slave? And wiping out their history or origin and taking over the place of their creators by white washing all the facts of their existence? Making sure also that the descendants of the Negroid enslaved ones believe that they had no past, but only as being primitives or their slaves? As also they had no past but being primitive hominoid and the slave of the Negroid race? Starting of first by annihilating most of the powerful Negroid males in Spain and continuing all over Europe. Taking all the children and the woman Negroid as slaves and bringing them over to the Americas to serve now them as the Masters. Using all their energy and passion to take care that the descendant of the Negroid race does not find out who they really are? Using also all their myth and power to secure that the Negroid race be kept on the bottom of the pyramid of achievements? As they were also created to be kept on the bottom of the pyramid of the Anunnaki or the Negroid black race?

Could the Anunnaki really be the Negroid race? The race that the created humans adored and called their 'Gods' that saved them, protected them and gave them knowledge? The word God in ancient time as stated also meant my Master or my Lord or the one that had power to give me knowledge and protect me! The same denomination that is used in the word Nagar or Negus or the word Nigger, as used by the Egyptians! It does seem like the Bible is a more delicately put together but still the same basic story as is described on these much, much older tablets of the Sumerians!

One should ask oneself are there evidence of very much more advanced technological beings that were on earth that would make these tablets credible? And this beside the already established evidence of the DNA of the Negroid race in the newly emerged races or hybrids! This was essentially done to upgrade or upscale the hominoid or apelike beings own DNA and also to give them the ability to communicate or speak!

Pyramids and other impressive buildings were found all over the world, in Ethiopia, Egypt, China, the Americas and also in the Ocean near the Bahamas! There are also suggestions that outlines of Pyramids were seen on Antarctica! It is believed that the Pyramids were lightened by light bowls and that the Pyramids themselves seems to have been, Power Plants to generate energy as theorized by Nicolas Tesla a famous white Caucasian scientist! If the much more advanced Anunnaki or the Negroid race could have travelled in space to a complete other solar system, making big pyramids and other impressive structures would have certainly been nothing too difficult for them! Creating humans or playing God, the Almighty and creator of the Universe, through genetic engineering would also not have been a problem for them!

Other ancient interesting structures with very sophisticated systems like energy generating plants, sewage systems and irrigation systems were discovered on earth, dating as of more than thousands of years ago. Maps of the world and the complete constellation of the universe were found dating at least 5.000

years ago, when there were according to our knowledge no plains or satellites, to observe these! All these Pyramids have the exact same concept base work, dating back thousands and thousands of years and everyone is wondering, who had the technical know how to build them and where did they go afterwards, why is there no evidence of their existence? Did they left earth, but what if they stayed behind, who are they? Could they really be the Negroid race, the seemingly most unintelligent and primitive race on planet earth?

The majority of these Negroid black race, with presumably know how of technological brilliancy, seems to be living now as the most deprived and primitive race on earth! Why are the not captive or enslaved free Africans living a primitive live, are they the fugitives? The ones that abandoned their duties to mined the gold to save their own planet and now are still living a life as fugitives or a live as incognitos or a low profile life? As though willingly not to be noticed or taking the precaution not to draw any attention to them? But why? Are they the descendants also ashamed of what their ancestors have done or had their ancestors not shared with them the information of the abandonment of their duty to save their own planet in another solar system?

And how is it possible that we as modern humans still cannot comprehend how they build these mega structures and that we still cannot figure out the purpose of these structures, although there are various theories? How is it also possible that they were able to travel across the Atlantic Ocean many ten thousands and ten thousands of years ago? Many futuristic scientists are asking the same unanswered question, did aliens build these? Were there really aliens that visited our planet in space ships thousands of years ago and made these beautiful structures and afterwards left our planet? But what if they are still here? Are the evidence of their existence staring us in the face, but we do not dare to admit it is there? Is the evidence that was supposed to be revealed with the acquired knowledge of DNA readings not sufficient? Or is there really a conspiracy that began with a payback by the other races, leaded by the Caucasian race against their creators the Negroid race, that created them essentially to be their slave workers and was ready to dispose of them in an earthly flood?

As all the other new races have two DNA in their system, the DNA of the hominoid or apelike beings and the DNA of the Negroid race, can we then definitely conclude that the Negroid race is the Annunaki or 'the God's', the Angels, the watchers or the fugitives, as mentioned in the Bible? The more technical advanced beings that came from the sky or another planet from another solar system called the Orion Belt Constellation? And that a group left after leaving two groups of Negroid people behind on earth, two groups that hated each other guts, the fugitives and 'the Gods', the watchers, the angels or the defenders and also co-conspirators of the creation of the humans as their own slave workers, to ultimately assist in the saving of their own planet in the Orion Belt!

So there actually were two groups, the creators that decided to stay behind defend, protect, lead and save the humans from an earthly flood and also to give them knowledge! And the group of the fugitives, the group that did not wanted to do the work anymore to save their own planet, but decided to establish themselves on planet earth and kept their distance from the co-

conspirators of the creators and their creation! Do leaders of African nations the descendants of the fugitives know of this truth and decided for self-conservation to distance themselves of the group of the Anunnaki that created the human slave workers and stayed behind to save these same slave workers? Is this the reason that these African nations never claimed the safe return of the descendant of the enslaved ones from the new discovered lands? Some African nations also do mention that the enslaved Negroid race in the Trans-Atlantic African Trade Slave, are the cursed ones! Is it maybe because they played God by creating intelligent beings? Do groups of other races also know this but decided to keep the common public and in any case the descendant of the Negroid enslaved ones in the dark? If this is the case what is their agenda for keeping us the descendant of the enslaved Negroid race in the dark of who we are as the Negroid black race?

If I with limited scientific knowledge could have figured this out, in such a short period of time, scientist using the DNA reference and other discoveries most definitely should have figured this out already! But why have they all decided to keep us the Negroid race or the descendant of the so called African Trans-Atlantic Slave trade in the dark? And was this slave trade scam constructed in such a way so that we the descendant would never know who our ancestors were and were they really came from? And that our ancestors were essentially in some point in time loved by the ancient humans and regarded as 'The Gods'!

Depictions of it seems of these 'Gods' in enormous stones were found near the Pyramids of the ancient Mayas, the famous Olmec Heads, also on the Asian continents in Europe and various other places on earth. These 'Gods' were depicted with Negroid features that according to myths told, assisted the humans of various areas or countries around the world, protecting them and giving them knowledge and spiritual guidance. As is also stated by these same nations! Why is it then stated by modern scientist that it was the Indian Mayas or other civilizations who build these? Meanwhile the descendants of the Indian Mayas are stating themselves that they did not build these. That according to their ancestors, these were built by 'The Gods'!

Are these facts being systematically hidden or covered up to hide the fact that the Negroid race is a race that came with technological advanced knowledge from another solar system and planet in search for gold to safe their own planet? Is this also the reason that gold was considered for no apparent earthly reason to be of such a value since ancient times?

Permit me to ask again, could the Negroid race really be aliens of another planet, the so called Annunaki or 'The Gods' that came from the sky on earth with the purpose to mind gold to fix their own planet and that they made a terrible judgement by playing God the Almighty of the Universe and created human slave workers or what we now call the younger developed or the new races to assist them, due to the fact that their own kind have abandoned their duties?

That apparently two groups decided to stay on planet earth, one as fugitives or living as incognitos on earth and the other group that really owned their responsibility to first try saving their own planet and to also save or protect, the by them created humans or the other new races from an earthly devastated flood! And to afterwards lead and guide these humans spiritually and giving them also universal knowledge. Could the Negroid race or a group of them be the ones the ancient civilizations called 'the Gods'?

But let us take a look again into the Ancient Negroid nation the Ethiopian or Nubian nation their customs, culture, traditions and religion! The Ethiopians or Nubians as a nation had a governing system, of a High Priest and his attendants or some sort of Bishops in place, the High Priest ruled over Ethiopia, a very spiritual nation. This same system was later copied by the Vatican of Rome! As stated before they also believe in one God, the God of the Universe!! They most probably came with this wisdom of one God from their own planet in another solar system!

The Ethiopians or the Nubian nation was also the first nation that adopted 'Christianity' as their official state religion in 341 AD. Why? Was it because they recognized the similarities with their own religious believe of a savior, who was born on or near December the 25th in a cave or a stable, son of a virgin, who died as a martyr? The Ethiopians were also the first nation that used a cross in their religious rituals!

The Romans decided to establish the Christian believes as their official state religion in about 380 to 390 AD, after they first persecuted and killed from 70 AD till 313 AD, various of the first as they are now called 'Christians' which were actually the real Hebrews or the followers of the savior, the son of God. The Vatican of Rome established in Italy, try to apply same system of a High Priest or Pope in Italy Europe and afterwards the world. The

Romans came to the conclusion that they could unite and dominate by fear mongering their people and nations through a strong and strict religious believe, reason why they choose to adapt a religion that had existed for thousands of years, the religion of the Ethiopians or the real Hebrews as their own!

A very important library, the Library of Alexandria in Egypt, was burned down in same period by the Romans. It is believed that various books with tremendous universal knowledge were burned or confiscated by the Vatican. After 313 AD the Romans decided to tolerate the Christian belief and stopped with persecution and annihilation of the Christians, the Emperor Constantine of Rome gave the order to stop all persecution. Many followers of the one that we now call 'Jesus Christ' were according to the Bible, murdered by the Romans, during the persecution and eradication of the 'first Christians' or the real black Hebrews.

The first 'Christians' in Rome buried their death at burial places instead of cremating them as was customary in the Roman culture. Upon the construction of new streets in Rome in 1578, underground burial places called the Catacombs of Rome, dating since at least 400 AD were discovered with depiction of 'Jesus Christ' and his apostles, all of them with black Negroid features.

In conclusion it seemed that there was a very much more advanced civilization living in ancient times then the current now living civilization on earth and that also an old already existing religion was adapted by the Romans to be popularized as their own religion to their people. The reason as contemplated and documented was to unite and dominate the people of Rome and to eradicate the various other religions that were in Rome Italy that were adoring multiple Gods and to join all these religion together in one religion called Christianity!

Did you also know that the Popes of the Vatican of Rome actually prays' to the Black Madonna virgin and her son? Is this because they acknowledge that these are the real depiction of the Virgin Mother and her Son? In various churches in Europe also a Black Madonna and her child are regarded as the real depiction of the Virgin 'Mary and Jesus'!

The Ethiopians or the Negroid race migrated as now is apparent all over the world as is established by scientist, to Europe, Asia and America and did also established and guided separate human races or specific groups and raised various civilizations of the other younger races in each of those areas. This is also stated in the Bible as the territories assigned to the three major races, or to Japheth the Caucasian races, Shem the Mongolian races and Ham the Australoid race! In those areas as is confirmed by anthropologist they used the same basic of their religious and spiritual beliefs and their advanced knowledge of construction to build great impressive Pyramids or Castles with structures of irrigation systems, for the emerged new races or prior created slave workers as nations in Europe, Asia and the Americas.

As is believed the Negroid race were the ones leading or guiding all these new nations! But if this Ethiopian or Negroid race of nation were also in Europe, the America's, the Caribbean and in Asia, are there any evidence of their presence and why is it not mentioned in the history books taught to us in schools? The only known mentions in the History books are the acknowledgment of the Egyptians, of which the white Caucasoid Arabs now living in Egypt claims that they are the real descendants of the original Egyptians. But in fact they are the descendants of the Arabs whom were as stated before ransacking the continent of Africa to take over all the wealth and possessions of the African Negroid nations.

I know that you are asking yourself that, if the Negroid race are indeed the advanced beings called the Anunnaki, that came from another solar system, which is believe to be from the Orion Belt constellation, why is there no acknowledgement in the Western European and American history of their technical advanced achievements, the sharing of their knowledge and their protection and guidance of the other younger races on earth? And also why are a great part of the Negroid black race not sharing their advanced knowledge anymore or are living in modern days as primitives or like bushmen or in submissive positions and behaviors in the land that they were supposed to be taken by the slave masters in the so called African Trans-Atlantic Slave Trade?

Well according to the African Negroid Dogon tribe, that claims that they are the real descendants of the Egyptians, whom as stated by themselves, to save their lives from savage nations, that were only interested in taking over of their wealth in one way or the other, were forced to take to the woods and adapted to a more natural lifestyle, where they could finally exist in peace! The Dogon's had too much in depth information of the Egyptians and the Constellation of the Orion Belt, that scientist could not have denied that their claim must have been legitimate!

As it seems the descendants of the so called African Trans-Atlantic Slave Trade, were systematically cut off of their own heritage, legacy and history and also from their own religion!" I was explaining when I finally saw a hand raised.

"Did the Egyptians or the African Negroid tribe called the Dogon's really say that they came from the stars or more specifically from the Orion Belt? Why did nobody bother to investigate that, if they seemed to have legitimate information?" Latisha one of the invitees asked.

"Well the modern scientists and anthropologists just thought that these were illiterate bush men that believed in stupid stories that their ancestors told them. But they did document these stories as these were told to them, being although a little impressed by these illiterate bush men knowledge of astronomy! Africa is actually the first continent were a University was built to discuss findings of the studies of the universe or all the stars and planet and their movements. But why would ancient people be interested in studying of the Universe or the movements of the stars and planets, if they did not have knowledge of that same universe?" I replied, while continuing with more information.

"So again why is the history of the accomplishments of the technological advanced beings the Anunnaki or the first Homo sapiens or the ancient Ethiopians or the first Negroid race not duly recorded? Are they really the technical advanced race that built pyramids and other impressive buildings and statues all over the world? If not them who else could have built these? Why can't the now existing modern society, which is dominated by the Caucasian

266

race, not explain how these impressive buildings and statues were build more then thousands and thousands of years ago all over the world, in a time that they did not as yet crossed the oceans, because they the white Europeans believed that the earth was flat and that you would fall off when you reach the edge. But why does the Negroid race also not have these information's?

Is it because of the African or Negroid Transatlantic Slave Trade, were the builders and architects and the ones with the advance technical knowledge and the ones whom were Kings and Queens were killed or brought into slavery and their children systematically cut off of their knowledge, legacy, heritage, religion and also of their origin, history and role on planet earth? Is it because all the documentation was burned or taken away to the secret or private library of the Vatican? Is it also that the descendants of the fugitives or the Anunnaki that decided to abandoned their task of mining the gold that was needed to correct their atmosphere, did not wanted to be reminded or to explain to their descendants that they were the ones that failed their mission to save their own planet and adapted to a lifestyle in oblivion as seemingly illiterate bushmen?

The possibility of the Negroid race being the Anunnaki would also explain the Negroid race natural spiritual connection with the Universe and the Supreme Almighty Being or God! Does this have something to do with the Third Eye as named by the Egyptians or the Pineal gland which produces melanin? Melanin a substance that now modern scientist are regarding as a sort of black matter that is supposed to hold the Universe together? Modern scientist has also recently discovered that one's skin color is not determined by the sun but by the creation within our own body of melanin that is as already stated produced in the pineal gland. The pineal gland is located in the middle of the brain, like a sort of control center. The exact purpose of the pineal gland itself is not yet determined by nowadays scientist, since studies has shown that contrary to black or brown colored people the pineal gland of white or pale people seems to be galvanized. This same pineal gland is however depicted as the third eye of universal knowledge and wisdom in the Egyptian mythology.

It has also been established by scientist that a fetus starts off as a pineal gland and everything else grows from that pineal gland which can be regarded as the command center of each human being. If the pineal gland that produces melanin is more active in black people and is known in the Egyptian mythology as universal knowledge, why is it than that the black Negroid race intellectual accomplishments as a race could have been recorded historically so low? Landing back to the same questions, were the historical accomplishments of the Negroid black race duly recorded or has there been some alteration in these accomplishments or denying of facts or findings? And has this been done because the Negroid race is the Anunnaki, the ones whom were called 'the Gods"?

Going through all the gathered information of different anthropologist and other scientific sources, it is apparent that they all agree that the origin of all religious beliefs came from Ethiopia or the Ethiopians or the first Negroid black race! Although one is now inclined to believe that much of these religious information were somewhat altered and or adapted to fit the purposes of some power seeking or fear mongering groups! But still the Bible does have various clues that confirms the fact that the Negroid black race were the ones playing important roles in the scriptures of the Bible! Was not Moses ordered by God to take his hand out of his coat and saw with devastation that his hand turned white as snow as a kind of leprosy disease and then was amazed that God performed a miracle by curing his hand again to his original state. Does this not imply that the original state of his hand was black or of a dark color? Was not Jesus, the son of God black? Was it not stated in the Bible that Jesus had feet that looked like burned brass, thus being very dark and with hair with the texture of pure wool? Has not Joseph one of the disciples of Jesus painted Mary and baby Jesus black and does not this same picture hang in the private quarters of the Pope in the Vatican of Rome? Where not all the first acknowledged Saints Negroid people, like the famous Saint Nicolas, the guardian of the fisherman and the giver of gifts to primarily children because he wanted to see them happy, on which well-known children tales like Santa Claus and the Dutch version or festive events are based upon? Was not Buddha, The Quetzalcoatl, Krishna, Shiva and Jesus, all considered God or deities in their respective nations, black Negroid people from Ethiopic decent as is already established by scientist or modern anthropologist?" I kept on explaining and showing them pictures of the findings and names of all the anthropologist's involved.

"I have a question, how did the scientist know that these Gods or deities like Buddha or Shiva were black Negroid people. I always understood that Buddha was Chinese and Shiva a Hindu that was according to stories that I read, blue" Eduardo asked.

"Well first they all had the same Negroid face features that I have described in the beginning and also same type of wooly hair, that sometime had African hairstyle, like parted in little squares and then tightly curled or locked and pinned on their head, like as we locally called the 'sibojo' or onions hairdo, as shown in the depiction of Buddha. Or their hair were locked and let down, like Bob Marley. And it is indeed mentioned in documentation that Shiva was blue black, which actually means a very very dark black color! In recent times to misled the viewers they took away the black and only kept the blue, they also adapted his face features to more resemble the Hindu people. But the original depiction of Shiva was a person with Negroid features! I also understood that blue blood or royal blood was derived out of the concept of being a person of blue black or very black color!" I answered and also showing the attendees the real pictures of these known black Negroid deities and other King and Queens

"Can we see the pictures of the features of all the races again? And also the description of which group of race falls under which category?" Angie a niece of mine requested.

"Sure, let's go back! As you can see the only race with a long, high and narrow nose in both root and bridge, is the Caucasian race! The group of people falling under this category are the Europeans East and West, Russians, Indian Sub-Continent the Hindu's, American Indians, Arabic and most of Middle East people. They all fall under the Caucasian race, why Caucasian race because of the same skull features that were found in the Caucasus mountains, a mountain that is situated in Russia, Armenia and Georgia. The

Caucasian could be white and also black and all variations in between, they also have sleek or straight hair!" I explained.

"What I do not understand is, if the Caucasian race came from ape like beings, were did they got their nose from? Because I do not know any monkey with a high nose!" Angie asked.

"Well according to scientist, the skulls of the Neanderthal hominoids found had a very high bridge were their nose should start, which indicates a very high nose! It was established by scientist that these hominoids evolved from apes to hominoid and as DNA has shown this Caucasian race has two DNA in their system, the Negroid DNA and the hominoid or apelike being DNA or the monkey gene! It were the Caucasian white scientists that in our era had acknowledged that humans or to be more accurate hominoids came from monkeys or more specifically from the Rhesus monkey!" I answered.

"Can we also look at the pictures of the rhesus monkey again?" Angie asked again!

"Sure let me see, yes here is it! This same rhesus monkey is depicted by the Egyptians on their walls of their creation myth. Here we can acknowledge, that the ancient Egyptians possessed more knowledge than the in our time modern scientist!" I commented!

"I see some resemblance now, with the white race! But I do feel somehow embarrassed that humans are compared with animals! If I thought it was wrong when my race was compared with gorillas or other monkeys I do think it is wrong now to do the same with the white race!" Angie commented.

"There is absolutely no reason to feel guilty or a shame if you are trying to understand the scientific process on which scientist base their theories through comparisons with other animals! Because we are now dealing with scientific facts in which comparison has to be made to find the predecessor specie that could have become hominoids or apelike beings and afterwards evolved to humans according to scientist! So we are just going through the same process that they had used to base their theory upon. But what is an undeniable fact is that now we can research the DNA of all species and their similarities and also their differences!" I kept on explaining.

"If the Negroid race were indeed the Anunnaki or 'the Gods' that came from another planet, created humans or to be precisely the other races using their own DNA to be their slave workers and decided that they should be annihilated as an imperfect creation, could indeed the so called African Trans-Atlantic Slave Trade, were it was the intention to annihilate or put the Negroid race in perpetual enslavement be categorized as a revenge or payback for the injustice done to them the other new races, which was orchestrated by the Caucasian race or more specifically, by first the Arabs, then joined by the Europeans or more precisely the Vatican of Rome and later on also the European Ashkenazy Jews, the three now largest religions on earth, the Muslim, the Roman Catholic and the Jewish faith!

So was there in essence an 'Inter Galactic War on Planet Earth' for the obtaining of power over humans through religious doctrine, were the Negroid race first the leaders and the elite on earth, were now prisoners of war that were captured, killed on the spot or sold as slave in the same region or another region! The Arabs as evidence have done their part as from 600 AD, to conquer Africa and the 'Middle East' as that part of Africa was later renamed by the English! And the Vatican with the help of the Ashkenazy Jews took care of Europe and the Caribbean and the Americas as from the 1500 AD! It has been also contested in recent years by other white Caucasians that the Ashkenazy Jews are not blood related Jews or the Israelites 'the children or the chosen ones by God', but converted Jews, that did not originated from the Middle East but from the Khazar Empire in East Europe, as their DNA has also established! It is now believed that the real Jews or Hebrews are in essence from the Negroid black race, as also the Catacombs of Rome showed us!

Over 20 million Negroid people were killed or enslaved in this so called 'Trans-Atlantic African Trade Slave', which should have been named an 'Inter Galactic War on Planet Earth'! This war had more casualties then any known war in the history of the modern world! Most of the captured and or killed Negroid people were as also is evident already living in the Americas, the Caribbean and Europe! Sure there were some slaves brought over from the African continent, from for example Timbuktu, the Songhay people and other groups living as advanced African and Black Civilization, but the majority as already has been proven were already living in Europe the Caribbean and the Americas! And not one of them were illiterate or seemingly not educated Africans! Why was that? Because the seemingly illiterate Africans Negroid races that were living as primitives, were the ones as described in the Bible 'the fugitives'! The ones that had no participation in the creation of humans, for the sole purpose to use them as slave workers and to dispose of them in an earthly flood when their job was completed!

It was definitely the intention of the enslaver that the children of the enslaved Anunnaki or Negroid people or the creators of the humans as slave workers, be not educated or be kept illiterate as part of their punishment of creating them as 'imperfect' slave workers! This could also have been a strategic move to safeguard that the next generations of the Negroid enslaved ones be kept on an as low as possible intellectual level. The tactic of willful torturing and or fear mongering to break down the will and the spirit of the enslaved Negroid children would have also contributed that the confidence that the Negroid child needed to excel on an intellectual basis was diminished.

I also believe that there were some Negroid people brought over that were from the tribes living a presumable primitive lives as bushmen and that were the first group of the Anunnaki that had abandoned their work, the as already mentioned so called 'fugitives' or falling angels, as is also stated in the Bible and on the Sumerian Tablets. These group of Negroid 'fugitives' knew that the last group that stayed behind consider them as traitors, on the other hand they had to be angry with the last group for creating the humans, whom they regarded as man of flesh, which is what hu-man stands for, as they regarded themselves as man of soul! Were these 'fugitives' the group of Negroid people that were used as 'foremen' on the field to keep an eye and also punish the other enslaved group of Negroid people that stayed behind, the creators of the humans as essentially slave workers.

These Anunnaki or Africans or Negroid 'fugitives' also consider the last group of the Anunnaki or Negroid that created the humans and stayed behind to save the humans as being 'the cursed ones'! But why would the last group that saved the humans be considered as the cursed ones? Both groups must have known the fate that was awaiting the descendants of the Anunnaki that created and stayed behind to save and protect the created humans or other younger races!

Because it was alleged that the Ethiopians or the Negroid race could see the future, so they already knew what was awaiting their descendants but still made the choice to save the created humans? Did they accept their own fate as this was written down in the Bible in Deuteronomy? Is this why it is mentioned that the Europeans stated that the Negroid race were cowards that did not fight back? And that they also bought the Negroid African slaves, from other African Negroid people, it would be comprehensible that maybe these sellers were actually the 'fugitives' or the first group that deserted their duties of mining the gold and were considered as traitors of their own kind? So were these sellers also belonging to the group of the 'fugitives' that were also used to watch and punished the other enslaved Negroid people?

Is this also the reason that African countries in Africa did not claim the return of their people back to their land after the abolition of slavery? Because this group of the enslaved ones, had already abandoned Africa together with the created humans to various other parts of the world? Is that also the reason that the Africans on the mainland of Africa, Africa Americans or African Caribbean's cannot also really unite because of the denomination of the group that abandoned their duties as 'traitors' or 'fugitives'? And also on the other hand the denomination of the creators of the human slave workers as being 'the cursed ones' by the first group or the 'fugitives'? Was or is this a rift in both groups of Negroid African people that was also destined to be?

In the Bible it is stated that the three sons of Noah, Japheth, Shem and Ham were dispersed to various territories on earth and as we now can ascertain the stayed behind creators or the Anunnaki or the Negroid black race also accompanied these group as their leaders, to protect them, guide them spiritually and to give them knowledge. The sons of Noah or as we now know, the new races or the by scientist acknowledge three major groups of races, the Caucasian or the descendants of Japheth, the Mongoloid or the descendants of Shem and the Australoid or the descendants of Ham! Another point to consider is that the African Negroid races living in Africa, which presumably are the 'fugitives' do not seem to have any recollection or records of massive slaves being taken from their territories or from Africa! But these same African nations do state that the Negroid people in the Americas and the Caribbean are the 'cursed ones'! Asking them why they were and still are called the 'cursed ones' by them, they will answer that this group has committed a 'universal abominable act'!

But why the cursed ones and what is the abominable act that they have committed? Did the Anunnaki or the Negroid race that created the humans made a terrible mistake by doing just that, was there a line crossed that disturbed the nature of the universe, when the Anunnaki or the Negroid race created the slave workers or the other races? Was it not the privilege of only the almighty Universal God to create intelligent beings? Were the Anunnaki or the group of the Negroid race that created the other races, saved them, stayed behind with them to guide them and give them knowledge therefore cursed, because they were not supposed to create intelligent beings, on earth now called the other races and all that are a mix of those races? Was that also the reason that our ancestors accepted their fate of being enslaved by the ones that were first enslaved by them?

Continuing with another piece of the puzzle, in order to make their story stick of the 'African Trans-Atlantic Slave Trade', because they wanted to create the perception that they were rescuing bushmen running wild, without a sense of civilization and tied these with their records of the boats and the times these boats took the trips to and from Africa, they had to invent that the boats were redesign to carry the Negroid African slaves like sardines! Which indicates that if this was the truth, 90% of the cargo of the Negroid slaves would have suffocated and died on board, since this was a trip that took many weeks! But still using the fabricated design to carry more slaves and the majority of the slaves still arriving save and sound at the required destination the figures still did not add up, to the registered quantities of enslaved Negroid people in the Americas and in the Caribbean, that were supposed to come from the continent of Africa as a cargo from these boats!

It is believed that most of the Negroid influential male grownups though were killed on the spot in Spain or other countries in Europe, America and the Caribbean, mainly the not influential male and children and the woman were shipped as slaves to other parts of the Caribbean or America just to mix them up and to confuse the children! As they the 'created imperfect slave workers' were also confused when all languages were changed and every group was taken to another destination as explained in the Bible? The way that they finally confused the young slaves of who they were was by first changing their names, separating children from their parents and by constantly changing the care givers of the enslaved children, who came from other Caribbean Islands or parts of America or Europe that had developed different languages to communicate in! To make the situation more chaotic adult Africans or the Negroid black race that were categorized as 'the fugitives' in the Bible or on the Sumerian Tablets or the ones who were categorized as the deserters or traitors of their own kind were also thrown in the mix as the one who were enslaved.

The ones in charge of informing the African Negroid enslaved children whom they are or were as a race, were the missionaries of the Roman Catholic Church and their agenda was to make sure to inform these children or young slaves that they should be grateful that the white man took them out of the wild jungle of Africa, to ensure that they would become civilized and God abiding people that should obey their white masters for their redemption!

Obey their white master for their redemption, but redemption of what? Well according to the interpretation of the western white Caucasian people, there is somewhere in the Bible or in specific

278

interpretation of some religions, that black people or more specifically the Negros are cursed and evil and therefore condemned to slavery, till the day that they receive redemption or repent! Same question again redemption or repent, but for what? What has the black Negroid race done to be dehumanize or eradicated, as was done during the so called 'African Transatlantic Slave Trade'? Many white Caucasian people in the times of the so called African Transatlantic Slave Trade in the Americas and the Caribbean claim with passion and without any remorse, that it was their God given right as the descendant of Japheth, which according to their interpretation of the Bible is the progenitor of the White Caucasian race only, to enslave the black Negroid race, that according to them were the descendants of Ham, the cursed ones? The cursed ones, that were cursed not by God but by Noah of a disrespectful act by Canaan the son of Ham?

How would the Negroid race if they were actually the descendant of Ham ow the White Caucasian or the descendant of Japheth redemption for a disrespectful act done to the Noah and should therefore submit themselves to be enslaved by them? But was this actually the real reason for the dehumanization of the black Negroid race in the so called 'African Trans-Atlantic Slave Trade' or was it as stated before indeed payback time for the original sin, the creation of humans not by the Almighty God, but by the Anunnaki or the black Negroid race.

Because they all knew that the Negroid race are the descendants of the Anunnaki, the ones that came from another planet and created them as 'imperfect human slave workers' to mine gold which they needed to save their own planet and that the Anunnaki were essentially ready to annihilate or wiped them out, after the completion of their service to them, with an earthly flood! That my friends, would be indeed an act to which the Negroid race or that particular group of the Negroid race and their descendants, should repent and received redemption for! Because as stated in the Bible, 'The sins of the father shall be visited upon the son!'

Acknowledging these myths, citations in the Bible and other ancient documentation as real facts collaborated by the findings established by scientist, I can fully see the complete picture and can also now comprehend the actions of the white Caucasian race, that out of a sort of vengeance had set out to destroy the Negroid black race, when they found out and or truly understood the truth about their own origin, which is the Negroid black race original sin on planet earth. So they created a plot to let the descendants of the ones that created them as slave workers to experience the same that they had experienced! Although they were fully aware that they were taking revenge of the same group of the Anunnaki or Negroid black race, that fought with their own kind in order to stay behind and save the by them created humans from an impendent complete annihilation in an earthly flood! This same group of the Anunnaki that gave up to return to their own planet, stayed behind and dedicated their lives to save, protect, guide spiritually and bestow knowledge to the created humans or the other new races.

We must not forget the fact that they did this aware of the fact that they or their descendants will eventually pay a heavy price for their actions of creating and saving of these new created races or created 'imperfect' humans on planet earth! But as it seems they the Anunnaki or the black Negroid race, were not perfect also because they had committed a heinous crime, by creating intelligent beings and were also ready as a race to wipe out the evidence through an earthly flood.

Could the stayed behind Anunnaki or Negroid race that created the humans managed to undo the 'imperfectness' of their creation or of the humans? Is that the real reason that the races or groups were separated as stated in the Bible and that there were various languages designed for each group of races, not to confuse them as stated in the Bible, but to maybe give each group also a fair chance to develop at their own pace? Was this also a strategy to seclude the various races to work on and correct their 'imperfectness', giving them also a culture and a tradition to give each group an identity and a sense of belonging as a society?

Because the modern Mongolian race are certainly not 'idiots' as was described when the race was created! So has the Annunaki or Negroid race managed to correct all these mistakes when they created these humans in a haste to be only slave workers, to be able to reach their deadline to save their own planet? Or was it indeed also to confuse them or to divide them so that they would not form alliances to take revenge and annihilate the group of the Negroid black race that created them? As they the Anunnaki had the power to see the future and knew that they had to avoid that these created humans or new races that were initially created to serve as slave workers, will eventually take their revenge on their own descendants? Were they trying to postpone these actions by the new created races? And is this not also mentioned in the Bible in Deuteronomy? So is the Bible in particularly the First Testament maybe a guide for the Negroid race, were in essence their history, present and their future is documented as the descendant of the Anunnaki or the Negroid race that had created and stayed behind to save, guide and give knowledge to the created humans or as the now known as the other younger emerged races?

Accepting what I have presented as the truth, would definitely explain the whole reason behind the dehumanizing efforts in the African Negroid slavery, the taking away of the black Negroid enslaved ones of their history, identity, their culture and traditions, because they created them the humans or other younger races without a history, identity, culture and traditions. And why it was designed to never end the enslavement of the Negroid Black race, because they never wanted the truth to come out! It would also explain the reason why no apology was given by the authorities of all the countries who had participated in the African Trade Slave to the descendants of the enslaved Negroid race! And also the reason why the African countries, were the majority of the 'fugitives' or fallen angels lived, never demanded the save returned of their people! And also the reason, why there are still to this date efforts being undertaken to keep the Negroid black race isolated, humiliated and their struggle for progress constantly obstructed and systematically controlled!

The reason behind all of these actions of in particularly the Caucasian white race, whom decided to take the lead and declared themselves the 'superior race', because they have thought out the masterplan to take down 'the Gods, their creators and masters' and make them now their slave. This would be the ultimate payback or revenge as stated earlier, to the ones that had created them, used them and afterwards wanted to discard them as garbage in an earthly flood as 'imperfect creations'! Does not every piece of the puzzle falls in place acknowledging all these facts as the truth, the truth of the dark beginnings of mankind!

And why it was their passionate and unwavering mission as the created and denominated as the 'imperfect' hybrid race by the Negroid black race, to seclude the children of the Negroid black race and to cut them off from the knowledge of who they are and their innate capabilities and to also induce onto them to despise themselves as an evil, immoral and inferior or imperfect race or creation? 'Yes let us change the roles of what was done to us, to make the descendants of the Negroid black race despise their own skin color, hair texture and facial features, as the now 'imperfect' and full of evil ones on planet earth, the ones who deserves to be wipe out from planet earth, because they are not from planet earth! The ones who came to planet earth with apparently the only purpose to take and to use! The ones that had no right to rule on planet earth! The ones that we now must denominate as the lazy and the corrupt ones, because they had used us to do their duty and their work to save and advance their own planet in another solar system! Let's use them now to advance our planet, planet earth, because we are in essence the legitimate heirs of planet earth as the upgraded hominoid or apelike being that lived on earth for millions of years!'

Their vengeance would certainly be complete if the descendant of the Anunnaki or the Negroid race would admire and adored them, the same way they admired and adored the Negroid race as their 'Gods', the ones that had all the knowledge and power and therefore were the superior ones! They whom were regarded as the 'imperfect' created human slave workers, but specifically the Caucasian race had now taken the role of the superior, by claiming the religion, the history and the knowledge of the Anunnaki or the Negroid race as their own. They would now be the perfect holy ones on planet earth! A role that they desperately feel the need to maintain and would sacrifice anyone whom would dare to cross their paths to end their role as the holy and superior ones on planet earth!

The Caucasian white race insiders seemed also to be embarrassed of this secret of their creation! That they were not a creation of the one and only Almighty God, but that they were genetically engineered as 'imperfect' hybrid slave workers by some more technological advanced beings and just wanted to wiped all evidence of these facts out! Their hatred toward the Negroid race and their descendants of creating them as slave workers kept them motivated and passionate to invent ways to keep this a secret from their own race and people but still they invented ways to motivate their own people to despise and hate the Negroid race, by using the false lie of the 'Evolution Theory' that the Negroid race are still in essence hominoids or apelike beings, that will bring the human race down if interbreeding occurred! Using films and racial profiling to portrait the Negroid race as a corrupt and criminal race! To do whatever in their power to make this a reality by obstructing their advancement for survival and progress as a race!

And it all began with the creation of a master plan to completely wiped out the history of their creation, white wash or steel the accomplishments, legacy and religion of the Negroid black race! At the same time also creating the perception of a historical low contribution to mankind of the black Negroid race! Let's confuse their descendants and reverse the roles, let them believe that they are essentially still hominoids in development, not as yet as developed as we are! And that only we, the self-proclaimed intellectual superior Caucasian white race has the power in the world to lead them if they accept there by us given role of still being not completely human to be more humanlike or civilized and be accepted by the other human races on earth as a wholly and accepted race on planet earth! Could they have demanded this of the other African Negroid races living in Africa as 'fugitives' also, to keep a very low profile and to essentially keep living as seemingly illiterate bushmen?

This had as planned combined with the induced self-hatred by the Negroid race itself, led to a very high appreciation and or abnormal adoration of the white Caucasian race, by quite a lot of black Negroid people. Could this adoration have been a by chance opportunity or was this also a carefully thought out plan? It would be interesting to know who were the leaders in charge of this master plan to reverse the roles and how did they pulled it off? And when exactly did the execution of this plan begun?

Well next to the Arabs whom were as already stated ransacking Africa since 600 AD, according to the information available it seems that in Europe and in the America's and the Caribbean, it all began with the fall of Granada Spain in 1491 AD, were after their triumph the Vatican, whom were actually the legal owners of Spain, through Pope Innocent VIII, removed all the Negroid people or Moors as they called the black Negroid people in Europe, from power and Royalty in Spain and ceased all their fortunes. On August 11, 1492 a new Pope was elected, Pope Alexander VI, after the dead of Pope Innocent VIII in July 1492! This new pope belonged to the Borgia family, some kind of a rich and big mafia family in those days! Many believe that the family of this new Pope financed the assassination of the earlier Pope, whom was given blood to drink by a white Ashkenazy Jewish doctor as a failed very strange blood transfusion effort! It is also believe that they had bought the Papacy, so that their son can become the new Pope and the cruelness of the Vatican to obtain by any means worldly power through the use of religion and dominium had begun!

In essence the Vatican and the White Jews together with the Queen of Spain began the Negroid eradication and enslavement and the war to obtain world power from the Negroid race, because the majority of the Negroid race were already established as evidence proves all over the world in the Caribbean, the Americas, Europe and Asia! Was this also when the new as claimed 'World Order' was established by the so called 'Illuminati' or the Enlighted Ones, the Ones who have the knowledge and had all documentation of how it all went down? A new 'World Order' where the power of the world was taken over from the Negroid Black race? The Arabs were as already stated busy since 600 AD with the eradication and enslavement of the Negroid race in the Middle East and Africa and now the Vatican, the Royal House of Spain and the white Ashkenazi Jews had joined them in 1500 AD!

Could there be any more hidden evidence or clues intertwined in the European history that can provide us with more insight of the Negroid race being the ones in power in these European countries? Exploring monuments and other displayed pieces of the European history we can notice that there were various depiction of black saints, black Madonna and child, black famous philosophers, black famous musicians, black royalty, black Kings and Queens with their codes of arms of the establishment of various Kingdoms like the ones of Germany, England, Scotland, Wales, Spain, Portugal, Italy, Denmark, Croatia and more. And also a century's long European empire named Schwarzkopf, which actually means black head, with a logo that is used till this date of a man with an afro, which is a Negroid hairstyle!

We can also notice that the clothing of the white nobility women in the 16 century, had small cushions attached at the side and a big cushion at the back, both on the inside of the dress, combined with corsets, creating the illusion of a tiny waste and volume hips and behind! Why were these white woman pretending to have the curves of a black woman? If the black woman were only slaves after living a primitive life in the wild? And also there was no slavery practices of the Negroid race in Europe, this was only done in the Americas and the Caribbean islands! So where would they have copied that? Also the hairdo of the white nobility woman and those of the man seems like an effort to copy images of the Negroid race hair style, high volume stacked up hair with locks at the bottom or with only locks, these were sometimes wigs, because their own hair could not carry these style of a volume hairdo! Wigs that also sometimes had a very powerful white color, the color of whitening hair when a Negroid male become of age and presumably more wise and respectable? Could this curled or locked hairdo be a combination of a wooly afro and dreadlocks both Negroid hairdo that were mimicked from the previous only elite black man and woman, that were taken under false pretenses in captivity in Europe and brought to the Americas or the Caribbean as slaves, after their elite clothes were ripped from their body on the boats? There are written stories that the Queen of Spain had given these Negroid elites an ultimatum to abandon Spain on ships and establish themselves in other countries but they were taking instead as slaves and or killed on these ships or just thrown overboard in full open sea!

There also seems to be some interesting naming of ages and events that maybe will throw some more light on this mystery of the hidden facts of Negroid elites and Kings and Queens in Europe. What was the real meaning of the so called "Dark Ages" which was the period between 500 and 1000 AD in Europe, was this maybe a period when only black people were living or in charge in Europe? Did you also know that most of the white Europeans were actually living in Russia in ancient times and then started to migrate to Europe, because of the prosperity of Europe! Why was there a plague called "The Black Plague" in 1400 AD as recorded by the European civilization that killed more than 50% of the population? Was this a plague that killed the majority of black Negroid people living in Europe at that particular time? Is it for that reason that it was actually called the black plague, a plague that primarily killed black Negroid people? Why is there no mention of the Black Nobility in Europe and or the Moors who constructed the various castles and other structures in Europe? Who were, the so called Moors that were in charge of Europe till at least 1500 or 1600 AD? Who were the Moors that were cast out of Spain in the Spanish

Inquisition in 1500 AD? Were these Moors also Hebrews? Or were these Moors Muslims? Or were these Moors Christians? Or were these Moors in charge of all these religions? And were these Moors the Kings and Queens in Europe? The one with power and also mystic abilities and knowledge? What is actually the meaning of the word "Moor"? Does the word Moor or 'Moreno' as translated from Spanish just means black or brown Negroid people? And was it the same as the word Ladino, the black Negroid civilization that spoke Latin and was of black Negroid descent?

So should we ask again was there really an "African Trans-Atlantic Slave Trade" in 1600 AD? Or did a war to enslaved and or eliminate the Negroid race started earlier as of at least 600 AD by the Arabs? Which eradication war was later joined by the white Europeans lead by the Vatican in 1492 AD? And why is there mention of a period also in the European history called the "Renaissance" or the rebirth of the European nation, also in the 1500 AD?! Why a rebirth, what happened for there to be a need for a rebirth? And the rebirth of whom specifically? Could the white Caucasian race have meant that they were going to rebirth themselves? But this time not as the 'created imperfect humans' or slave workers of the Anunnaki or the Negroid black race? But reinvent themselves as the now superior race existing on earth, by white washing and stealing the history, heritage, legacy and the religion of the Negroid black race and making them the Negroid black race now their own 'imperfect slave workers'?

Going further in history, who were the historical first followers of Jesus, the Hebrews or Jews, that the Roman Empire decided to persecute and kill as recorded in 70 AD till 313 AD? Were these followers white Caucasian people? Then why are the pictures of these followers depicted as people of a black Negroid race on the walls of the Catacombs of Rome?

And if the followers of Jesus were black, who are the white Jews, or better known as the Ashkenazi Jews, that claimed Israel as their blood heritage from The Almighty God? Why did Adolf Hitler stated that the Negroid black race are the real 'Israelites' or 'The Children of God'? And also why did Adolf Hitler thought that if he starts a new religious movement, he the "Holy Hitler" could conquer the World? Why would Adolf Hitler believe that by having his own religion he would be able to conquer the World? Was it not for that same reason that Constantine the Emperor of Italy in the years 400 AD wanted to have a good religion to unite and dominate his own people? Is this also the same reason that the Arabs also wanted to have their own religion to unite and dominate their own people around 600 AD? And also the Ashkenazy Jews that decided to adapt and claimed the Jewish religion as their own religion to also unite and dominate their own people. All with the purpose to obtain power on planet earth!

The Ashkenazy Jews also falsely claimed to belong to the bloodline of the 12 tribes of Israel, the Children of God and claimed Israel as their promised land! While all the other, for thousands of years established nations in the now called Middle East region, claims that the real Jews or Hebrews left Israel as a black Negroid nation and therefore cannot accept that the Jews or Hebrews now came back as a white Caucasian nation or as the Ashkenazy Jews? Should not the from origin Arabic nations in the Middle East be perfectly aware, that the Hebrews were a Negroid nation, because they spent centuries on getting rid of these real Hebrews, the 'Children of Israel' out of the Middle East?

Based on all these facts can we then assume as I did, that the first homo sapiens or the black Negroid race or the Ethiopians of which we now know that they were a very religious or a better word spiritual nation, that believed in only one God or supreme being and his begotten Son, indeed came from a planet in another solar system, which is the Orion Belt Constellation, to mine gold to correct the atmosphere of their own planet, at least as established by scientist at least some 200.000 years ago or as the Sumerian tablets states about 400.000 years ago?

That apparently they were a technically much more advanced civilization, otherwise they would have not managed to arrive on planet earth. And that out of necessity some 30.000 to 10.000 years ago, they decided to create human slave workers to essentially mine the gold for them, as their own kind has abandoned their obligation of mining the gold. On earth they encounter these apelike beings or hominoids, that they as is confirmed by scientist decided to enhanced their capabilities, by adding their own DNA or to make these humans or man of flesh more in their likeness or in their own image. A sort of hybrids of both specie, with DNA of the hominoids and DNA of the Anunnaki or the Negroid black race! This fact is already established by scientist, but the implication of this fact is explained away by modern scientist!

It also seems that it was common knowledge at least till a certain period and later on maybe only to certain elite social groups on earth, that the humans or other new races were created by the Anunnaki or the Negroid race that were mistakenly called 'The Gods'! Reason why there were various Negroid deities or God's being adored by humans in various nations. But about the year 600 AD the Arabs a white Caucasian race, decided that they want to take the wealth, the history and the religion of the Negroid black race. By simply destroying or white washing all their records and killing or taking the Negroid black race and their children as slaves and indulging them in their culture and making them belong or be a part of their own nation and abide to their established rules.

Some centuries later in 1500 AD another Caucasian race the white Europeans decided that they also wanted to take the wealth, the history and the religion from the Negroid black race. By also destroying or white washing all their records and killing or taking the Negroid black race and their children as slaves in the 1500. The only difference was that these Europeans did not really want to indulge the Negroid race in their culture and they certainly did not want the Negroid Black race to be part of their newly concurred nation, with the same rights as they would have, so after the abolition of slavery they decided to maintain these divisions by creating 'Apartheid' or the 'Segregation Laws' as was common practice by the Dutch in their colonies and also in the American societies. Because as crazy as it sounds, there were actually no enslavement of the Negroid race or segregation practices recorded in Europe, Russia or Asia, but only in the colonized newly territories by the countries situated in Europe! Was this because the people of these European nations were actually accustomed with the Negroid black race being people of power and royalty?

I want to finish the official part of my presentation with this documented interesting quote of Count Constantine de Volney, a white French noble man, philosopher, historian and politician, he wrote in 1787, when he visited the Sphinx in Egypt: 'Just think, that this race of black men, today our slave and the object of our scorn, is the very race to which we owe our arts, sciences and even the use of speech!' Count Constantine certainly did know that all the other races would had essentially remained hominoids that could actually only grunt and not speak, if it was not for the intervention of the Negroid black race!

Is this a secret that till today is only known to a few elites, of the Vatican, the Arabs, the Ashkenazy Jews and the leaders of some countries and most probably also some of the white and rich societies on earth that formed some white supremacist groups to enforce their efforts to keep the flame of hate of the white race for the Negroid black race? Could it be that a group that is called 'The Illuminati, or the enlighten ones, the ones who know the secret why the world has apparently since the year 1500 AD changed its order in a New World Order and why everything leads back to Egypt, yes Egypt the Negroid nation were most of the knowledge was preserved and were they apparently copied all their religious knowledge from' And that was it! Anymore questions?" I concluded my presentation.

"Can we have a copy of the presentation?" Eduardo readily asked.

"I was recommended not to do that!" I answered.

"Why?" Eduardo asked again.

"Well the notes and observations of my presentation will be used afterwards for me to write a book on the subject!" I answered.

"That is great, let me know when the book is ready to buy!" Eduardo commented.

"Sure, no more questions or any comments that I can use to improve my next presentation?" I asked.

"It is a lot to digest, maybe it would be better if you could, shorten the information of the presentation. What I also appreciated was that you repeated various information in various concepts! Otherwise I would have not been able to follow the red line to understand it all. But I believe that you really made your case with all the presented findings that then led to your unbelievable conclusion! Which I am not sure that I am willing to accept as the truth as yet, I have make my notes and will have to double check the presented facts!" Rupert commented.

"Everything was very clearly presented with pictures and demonstration of all the different theories. I would have changed the title to put more emphasis on the Negroid race, because that is what it actually was about!" Latisha commented.

"Your definitely right it began with the quest of an explanation of the differences of all the races, which ultimately resulted in the discovery of whom the Negroid black race are! I will definitely change it for my next presentation, thanks" I answered smiling.

"What I got out of this is that we are descendants of an alien race, the Annunaki! The whole alien thing does not seem so frightening to me anymore!" Angie commented.

"It was indeed a little too long, more than 3 hours nearly 4, with a lot of information. I do not know if it would be even possible to make it shorter without leaving out and or repeating important facts, so that we can follow the flow of facts presented! But I sure enjoyed it and it was definitely not boring." Sandy a friend of my husband commented.

"Well I did left out some info due to time constraints" I answered.

"What, what did you leave out Isa?" Sandy asked startled.

"About the moon, but I do not want to make you scare of the moon! Here in Curacao the moon seems very far, but do you know that the moon seems very big and close by when you are for example in New York?" I asked with a mysterious smile.

"What did you leave out about the moon?" Sandy asked again with a very serious face.

"Well let me see if I can give you a short version, scientist could not as yet establish that there ever was a worldly flood as stated in the Bible! Evidence seems to suggest maybe just a regional flood but not a worldly flood! The Zulus a Negroid tribe of Africa however, believes in the placement of the moon in our solar system by technological advanced beings! These beings as it seems were not the Anunnaki but another group of beings or aliens, according to the Zulu's they hollowed a planet and or build a big mother space ship craft disguised in that planet, afterwards that ship craft was brought near the earth, as the moon of the earth! According to them the moon was created to observe the development of the created humans on earth. The artificial Moon also caused earthly devastating tidal waves that caused as stated in the Bible and on the Sumerian Tablets a worldly flood that destroyed according to them the 'First Golden African or Black Negroid Ancient Civilizations'! The earth due to the placement of the artificial moon was according to the Zulus also displaced from its axes, which changed the climate of earth and the occurrence of seasons was started" I explained.

"And they call these Africans, with all these knowledge uneducated or illiterate primitives, my God!" Sandy commented laughing.

"But no one collaborated this information, maybe it was just a myth or story to entertain because they do not have any television in the jungle in Africa!" Rupert said laughing.

"Wait a moment I am not yet finished, in 1970 two Russian scientist after studying the moon for various years, published an article entitled: 'Is The Moon the Creation of Alien Intelligence?'. These are some of their observations: 'the moon seems to be too big, ¼ of the world's size to be a satellite of the earth; the moon is too far out for the gravitational pull of the earth to maintain constantly the same distance from earth; the moon does not have its own axes, only one side is seen from the earth, which is not natural; the moon seems hollow and why there are 'moon quakes' that seems like an old machine puffing along to restart?' Various scientist agrees that there seems to be no explanation for the earth having a moon and such a big one for that matter, with also such strange behavior!" I explained.

"You know, I just saw a documentary that states that the first Americans on Apollo 11 that landed on the moon, did not seemed happy or enthusiastic at all, as the first people being able to land on the moon. In contrary they were very uncomfortable as though they were going to puke, when they were interviewed after arriving back on earth! It seemed that they have seen strange unidentified lights on the moon and they also mention that the moon sounded like a bel when they landed if though it was hollow inside as you stated. Many believe that they had an encounter with the third kind on the moon!" Carlo commented seriously.

"You mean to tell me that we are being watched from the moon by other aliens? Do you know which ones and how many are there Isa?" Sandy asked looking a little afraid.

"Well that is what it seems like and I do not have any idea by whom we are being watch and how many kind of aliens if there are more of them out there! What I do know is, if my ancestors were also aliens, it cannot be that scary." I answered with a smile.

"Ok! What else was there that you left out Isa" Sandy asked.

"Do you want to hear them all?" I asked, because I believe that everyone was exhausted.

"Yes, yes please" Nearly the whole audience replied.

"O.k. let see, the Big foot or the Sasquatch that a lot of people are seeing around the world could actually be one type of the 'extinct hominoids' or apelike beings, that were living on earth a long time ago! And also that the Anunnaki seems to call every one of their own kind sister or brother, which is the same way African Americans address each other. And that the Catholic Church does also use the word sister for their nuns and brother for the male monks, at least in Dutch, which I found very interesting! Also that the Egyptian Pharaohs has a snake on their crown called a Naggar, that represents power, wisdom and knowledge. When you spell Naggar you actually should leaf out the a or say Nggr, which the word Nigger is derived from. Nigger the ones who have power, wisdom and knowledge. Have you heard of the Knight Templars? Well the Knight Templars were essentially Roman Catholic monks that were trained to fight and kill for the Vatican of Rome! That if you notice, have the same kind of clothing as the 'black Pete's in the Dutch Saint Nicholas tale. That the Vatican ordered various white Caucasian painter in the 1600 to make various paintings as depictions of the Bible stories were every good personage in the Bible was depicted as a white Caucasian and the evil ones the demons and the Devil as black! That various rituals, clothing and head pieces currently used in the Roman Catholic Church are from Egypt or Ethiopia! Even the Amen is derived from an Egyptian myth of the 'God' Amun Ra! That in the real versions of the compilation of books named the Bible, woman played a much more important role than is portrayed, but that the Vatican wanted to reduce the importance of woman in their sacred book and made it their own 'Man only club'!

And as last topic that I left out, that there are also African Negroid groups called the Bushmen of the San tribes that according to their stories were living in massive underground man made sophisticated caves that had some sort of artificial light or sun all day long, for about 100.000 of years! According to their stories they had everything they needed underground and that they went underground to escape something! Their DNA has proven that they were definitely secluded from the rest of the Africans or Negroid race for a very very long time! They also have a lighter skin color than the other bushmen! It is also known that the Albino population in Africa, were having a hard time coping in their tribe and that lots of them were therefore isolated! Various man made sophisticated underground caves has been discovered in Africa and all over the world! These caves were build which such a sophistication that these could have been used to take cover when there would have been the great flood or deluge on earth! Or could it have been the runaway Annunaki, the fugitives that were trying to hide and therefore build and lived in those man made sophisticated caves, for thousands of years? And that is it guys, any more comments or questions" I asked before finalizing.

"I would like to recommend you to get your facts checked with a Catholic priest, see what their comments or other observations would be in particular with regards to your findings in regards with the Bible and the Anunnaki and their involvement if any!" My dear friend Marcela suggested.

"Thank you all for your comments, I will definitely take all your suggestions in consideration, with the exception of the last suggestion to discuss this with a Catholic priest! I do not want to disrespect any priest and know that I will never convinced a priest that aliens came to earth and we the Negroid race are their descendants" I said smiling.

"Mom the Vatican has a large telescope named Lucifer to study the Universe and the stars! Maybe they know more than they are letting us know!" My daughter Rona commented.

"I know that my love and I do believe that the Vatican or the Pope and the Cardinals and other higher groups at the Vatican in Rome are definitely aware about these secrets, but I do not believe or dare not to believe that a common priest, at one of our local churches is in on these very dark and ugly secrets!" I answered.

"You could be wrong remember that it was the missionaries which were actually priests or monks and nuns, which as you stated were the ones in charge to teach the young slaves who they are, that they had no history and that they should obey their white masters!" Rupert commented.

"Well although I do not have any prove to the contrary , but what I believe is that most deeply devoted religious people are very credulous and if the Vatican has instructed these priest, monks and nuns that the Negroid race is evil and has evil ways and that it is their task to get the evil out of the children of the Negroid race to save them from condemnation and to do everything in their power to let them forget their past heritage and bestow them with the knowledge that they should despise their own self and adore the white race to obtain redemption for the sins and ways of their fathers, they would without questioning do what was asked of them. Any last questions or comments?" I commented and asked.

"Maybe you could write a public letter to the Pope or the Vatican requesting them to admit or deny the existing of aliens coming to earth and creating humans and that these aliens are in fact the Negroid race and that they with other influential groups decided to enslave the Negroid race to take revenge on their creators?" Sandy requested.

"To tell you the truth I thought about that, because I really believe that the current Pope is trying to clean things up! But when discussing this further with other family and friends I understood that it would be very difficult for the Pope to admit this! Because they have created through centuries a total mess and if the current Pope does want to admit some secrets it will have to do it piece by piece and that will take a lot of time! But the ones with the full knowledge what had happened and precisely how it happened will be definitely the Vatican or the current Pope! Any other questions!" I asked.

"I think all my questions on the topic were answered, since the presentation was very thorough I only have some personal questions, what do you hope to achieve with this presentation and do you hate white people and did you ever had negative encounters of hate from white people and last do you think that white people will stop hating or hate us more, when this secret comes out?" Eduardo asked.

"Well I have prepared my closing personal remarks that may answer your questions! Anymore questions?" I asked before continuing with my closing and personal remarks.

"To answer the question if I personally experienced the hatred of any white people! I personally do only recall one negative personal incident and or encounter with a white Latin American male to tell you the truth! I did not even recognize at first instance that I was actually being discriminated! We were on vacation in Venezuela me and my then boyfriend Den, we went to a night club with two local girls that we had just met that morning when we were buying shoes where they worked. Den went to the bar to get us some drinks and a young man approached me and said to me while dancing in front of me, pretending to be sexy or something 'Oye mulata'! The two girls pushed aside the young man and said to him 'Mulata tu Madre'! Which means your mother is the mulata! I was astonished by their violent reaction, since I did not feel that I was being threatened or humiliated and was also from time to time called a mulata in Curaçao by some Latino's living there! Since I was led to believe that, that was what they called amicably all brown people! But according to the two local girls, white man comes hard on brown woman to seduce them and treat them like a whore, because neither the black nor the white man in Venezuela will ever choose them as a wife since they are considered a bastard or a mixed race! A mulata is actually a mule, which is the offspring of a horse and a donkey, the girls explained to me! And that as a mule I will not even be able to bore children for my husband and was therefore regarded as a non-wife material.

The white people regard themselves as the superior horse that mated with the inferior donkey or the black race and had a mule, the brown ones, who actually do not belong to any race in their culture. And to believe that I thought that it was a good thing that I was a mulata since I considered deep down in my soul that if they as whites considered me as a mulata I would be the legitimate bridge to join the two races together, the black and the white race.

Yes I thought that the fact that I am brown or even light brown in the eyes of the white people made a difference in regards of my experiences with them, that I am considered by them nearly one of them? I really still do not know! Or maybe it was the fact that I was just oblivious of their maybe racist observations and did just not seemed to notice their discrimination intentions as was observed by others! I was actually regarded since a small child of being an optimist and always was smiling at everyone that approached me! Although I did struggle for a long time, with the fear of trusting and accepting white people, because of the knowledge of the things that were done to my enslaved ancestors. But personally I do not recall discriminative actions, nevertheless I still do believe in the stories that others told me of being discriminated, humiliated or neglected if though they do not exist by some white people.

I do sincerely not believe that I ever hated someone in my life, certainly not an entire race, what I do know is that before I knew this secret I did never forgave them as a race, how could I after what their race did to my race or my ancestors for no apparent reason I thought, in the so called African Trans-Atlantic Slave Trade, but now that I know that their reason was motivated by vengeance and that my ancestors did actually wronged them first, by creating them to serve only one purpose to serve them as slave workers to save their own planet and then afterwards to be disposed of, I can understand their deep seated hatred and their actions, towards my ancestors and my race the Negroid black race.

But still most of my relationship with white people was that they seem to like and appreciate me, but I still kept my distance, because I also do believe that our values and the way we approach life as descendants of the Negroid enslaved race or nation is different. And this made me think that maybe the enslavement was a necessary lesson in life to get my ancestors back to their core believes and values, the same core beliefs and values that was mentioned by the United Nations that our ancestors had as reported in the 1950, very humble, warm but still proud people, that were willing to share their home and meal with complete strangers or visitors.

Maybe the enslavement on earth after thousands of years of living in a world of being the superior ones and most probably maybe without themselves being aware of it, abusing this fact had made them forget who they were or supposed to be! Everything has a meaning in live, a lesson to be learned a page to be turn. Now that I know the reason of the actions of the white Caucasian race and admit the wrong doing of mine ancestors the Negroid black race of creating these new races as slave workers, I can understand their taken action in the past and definitely move on.

I do also believe that the majority of white people are not participating in discriminatory actions and do consider all the races as equals, but with different values, beliefs, culture and customs! Which sometimes can definitely be very annoying and result in conflicts and people cursing one and other out of frustration! But this happens in the best of families that do still love and care for each other!

I do also believe that the truth is the truth, as ugly as it may be and that one should accept this! Because as long that you do not accept this you cannot move on. We cannot live a life with lies of our origin or how we came to be or to exist on earth, as hard or ugly our conception was, it is our truth and we just have to own it, because if we don't that will hinder our progress and or development! If you could just acknowledge that in spite or regardless that you have been created to serve a purpose you have managed to surpassed that stadium and have now your own purpose to fulfill. And we certainly must not forget the fact that a huge portion of humans on earth are hybrids or consist of two species the Negroid or aliens DNA and the DNA of the hominoids or apelike beings living on earth for millions of years! The Negroid race DNA is in each of us, so hating the Negroid is like hating our denying yourself!

And that there were further mixing as is evident in our DNA of the Negroid race mating with the other created races on earth as of the beginning of mankind as is also mentioned in the Bible! So if our ancestors found the created races attractive and equal enough to take them as their mate, they were definitely not considered inferior in their eyes, because out of that mating came their own children, that they apparently loved! Although I do consider myself primarily as a descendant of the black enslaved Negroid race, my own family is a mixture of also various races, from different Caucasian ethnic groups with always the Negroid race in the mix!

At the end I do strongly believe that the revealing of this truth must not induce more discourse, are fighting to be the one that gets the title of being the 'superior one' but to encourage us as the Negroid race to acknowledge that our ancestors had wronged the ancestors of the other younger races first! And a process of acceptance of our ancestors wrong doing and the Caucasians to accept their ancestors and their own wrong doing must start so that the healing can begin, in which we all at the end can come together as one, one as the earthlings of planet earth! Let us make our ancestors proud, that despite the fact that we, their descendants had to go through the horrible ordeal of being terrorized, killed, enslaved, dehumanized, and continuously humiliated and oppressed, but we still had overcome. The price for their creation of the humans to essentially serve only as slave worker has been paid in full by us their descendants! It is for us now time to set things straight and accept and own our responsibility as the original humbled, warm and loving Negroid black race to guide and protect this whole new mixed of hybrid civilization on planet earth! We must also understand that this will be a process, a process of healing of both races, the Caucasian white race and the Negroid black race!

But for now you my beautiful black people can now definitely lift your head op high and be proud if you were ever called a 'Nigger', because that word stands for the ones who have wisdom, power and the ability to protect! So be sure to thank gracefully the one that acknowledge that you are a 'Nigger' in the future! It is important that you do not let them get you down, keep your positive energy and your spirit high! You know now the real meaning of this word, so let the word that they are using as an insult, be the word that will give you power, because they are acknowledging without they knowing it that you really are as a race! Be proud of your ancestors the major architects that build impressive pyramids and other structures all over the world! Be proud also that your ancestors came from another solar system to save their planet and also saved the by them created humans, which means that your ancestors were never 'Gods' but hero's!

Praise the Lord also because you were blessed with a divine design; you are black or dark because that gives you the ability to recharge yourself with energy and rejoice in the sun without being burned; you are black or dark because you have a great quantity of melanin that is needed in your pineal gland to connect you with free available universal knowledge and wisdom, that makes that you can excel intellectually; you have wooly hair because your hair serves primarily as an antenna that can assist you to tap into that universal knowledge and spirituality; you have a broad and flat nose and a forward jawline and thick lips because that gives you the ability to articulate with ease and also sing heavenly; you have a natural muscular body that gives you the ability to excel in all kinds of sports; you have a decent behind because that makes you attractive or sexy and also serves you well if you need to sit long as now is the case and you do not have a cushion to sit on! So go out there and do not worry if anyone says that you are inferior, they are the ignorant ones, because now you also know your own truth and your real roots! Your roots that started on another planet and that your ancestors were pioneers that had embarked on a mission to save their own planet! And at the same time do not ever lose your humbleness, your grace to forgive, love and protect! Because that was what our ancestors did they forgave the humans for an act that they foresee in the future of enslaving and dehumanizing their own descendants and still decided to love and protect them! Why, because they accepted the burden that they or their descendants had to pay being the ones that had wronged the other emerged races first!

Thank you guy's I really appreciate your presence and full participation, God Bless you all!" I closed my presentation with my personal remarks and comments, while the audience were applauding and still commenting with laughter of my comments of their behind! I was really exhausted but knew that many participants will want to continue to talk about the subject. There were a few persons that did not ask not even a single question, so I decided that I would definitely target them for some feedback.

"So Marco, did you really not have any questions?" I asked.

"You know I am actually shocked Isa, I was always full of the evilness and cruelness of the white people and I truly hated the white Dutch people for oppressing us, but now I do see from where they are coming from. I am still very shocked and processing this Isa, see my hands trembling?" He asked.

"I was also mad for quite some time and very confused to what their cruel and seemingly inhuman ancestors did to mine ancestors, but now I understand why! You will find your peace with it Marco I am sure of it!" I replied.

"I really did enjoy this Isa, although there were some scary parts! You know I have battle a long time with inferiority complex due to my color, nose and hair, but I immediately began to feel good about myself, when I understood who I am, thank you for that" Eveline an older friend of one of my nieces commented.

"This was a very revealing presentation Isa! You know I watch the Discovery Channel and had some doubts of my own of the whole Adam and Eve and creation thing! Although I do also believe in

God or a supreme being! I also read a lot about the Anunnaki but never put them and the Negroid race together, although I really need to verify some facts, still I am very impressed that you came up with the idea to put one and one together that was really brilliant! Good job! History of mankind should be rewritten when this discovery is made public. I am very honored to be one of the first ones to attend this presentation Isa" Rupert commented.

"My sincere and humble congrats, you convinced me! If the new races have the DNA of the Negroid race and the DNA of the hominoids in their system, there is only one way that it could of got there, because interbreeding is definitely out of the question!" Eduardo commented.

"Aunt Isa when is the following presentation, I would want to be present again and also invite some friends to attend this! I have learned a lot, but I am not sure that I understood it all and I just do feel energized and actually would want to inform others myself of this secret!" Nerdy my young nephew requested.

"The next presentation is next week, but I would want to maintain a small group so there is only one to two more spaces! In the meantime I noticed that you made notes, so go through them and used the internet to broaden your knowledge!" I answered him. Then I went to my friend Cory and her husband Berny. They were a religious couple but not a fanatic one. They were very silent through the whole presentation and I was really wondering what their views were!

"And how was it?" I asked them.

"Incredible, incredible Isa! I was very appreciative that the religious part was covered brutally honest but delicately if that is even possible, but still maintaining its basic core intact! Because from the beginning till the end you reassured us that there is a God and his son Jesus Christ our savior or whatever name we wish to call him!" Corry was commenting.

"Do you know the other names that Jesus Christ was called Isa? I would sure want to know these names" Berny Corry's husband jumped in.

"Oh yes, various other names! But those names are not important Berny, you stick to the one you know and used to call upon him! My father was called Edgar by my mother and his acquaintances, Gary by his friends, Booboo by his brothers, Gregorio by his colleagues and his real name, the one on his birth certificate was Jose. For many years I did not even know that other person called him by those names, but he definitely knew that it was him that they were calling or referring to" I explained to Berny, giving him comfort that it should be okay to call our savior Jesus Christ as he has done for the most part of his life.

"You are right, thank you for explaining that!" Berny responded and I saw the relief on his face.

"Yes, it is just a lot to process, but we should actually be happy because all the religious wisdom and know-how did come from our own race and ancestors and now we can understand that the presence of God is felt in the complete universe! All of it has yet to sink in, because it was a lot to digest! Everyone knows that the Roman Catholic Church and the Vatican has a lot of dark secrets, but really not one of us could have thought that there could be such a big secret hidden in plain sight! We thank you to make us part of this, Isa!" Cory answered and she and Berny her husband hugged me and shook my hand in appreciation.

Chapter 6.

With the hope of a new beginning!

Again and again I have brushed off the feeling that there must be a damned powerful reason or conspiracy by the Dutch European government to systematically suppress and oppress us as a nation! The nation of the 'Yui di Korsou' or as the 'Children of Curaçao' as we call ourselves in particular the descendants of the enslaved Negroid black race! But what could that reason possibly be, it could not be an economic one, as they had tried to project to us, because our economy is too small! And if there were no reason, we were then definitely playing the victim role, was always the main reason for me to brush it off again and again, because there just did not seem to be a powerful enough reason for me to understand or to sustain this feeling of deliberately being oppressed and or controlled for a specific unknown reason by the Dutch government!

But now that I know this huge secret, that has answered the question that had defined my life, which is the real underlying reason behind the African Negroid slavery and the afterwards institutionalized created systematic discrimination or segregation by the Caucasian white race, we can now fully comprehend the attitude of these Governments towards the Negroid race! Because our ancestors had created the humans or other younger races with one purpose only which was to be their slave workers and to actually dispose of them after their service! Although a group, our direct ancestors as descendants of the enslaved ones, choose not to destroy these other younger races and fought for their safety, at the same time they also choose the faith of their own descendants on planet earth!

Our ancestors were regarded as 'The God's' by the by them the created and saved humans and gave the created humans on earth spiritual guidance and knowledge! But at a certain point the by them created humans turned against them and decided that they who were at the top of the pyramid will be now at the bottom!

They had tried to take every possible measure to ensure that our fate was sealed to one way or the other, be of service to them, as they have been of service to us, to progress what they consider their planet, as they do consider themselves as the legitimate heirs of the hominoids or apelike men, that were first living on earth. Changing or white washing the history and our name and taking away our heritage so that we cannot ever find out who we were or in essence are! The Arabs were the ones that started it in Africa and later a select group of elites leaded by the Vatican, the Queen of Spain and the white Jews joined forces to initiate the prediction that is stated in the Bible under Deuteronomy!

The Bible would definitely have various explanations of the different situations in regards with the faith of our race, the black Negroid race. One of the questions that was asked to me by various attending my presentation on this subject on the island, was that if I have found out whom the nation consisting of 144.000 souls that would 'descend to the heavens' or other planet could be and if that could possibly be the descendants of the enslaved Negroid race known as 'The Children of Curaçao'? or as translated 'The Children of the Heart of the World'? A nation that is still

313

considered themselves as a nation of 'Dushi Hende' or 'Sweet People', a nation that in its core is still unselfish, ready to share, enjoy life in its fullest as a form of expressing their gratitude to God their creator and has the ability to be very welcoming to total strangers visiting their Island or home! But unfortunately I did not find any information to ascertain who that particular nation could be! But if we as a nation go back to our core values and believe system of our ancestors, I am definitely sure that we as a nation could also aspire to be that chosen nation, when the time arrives.

It is very strange that when you know in your gut that something is not quite right, that something is definitely being hidden from you, that this specific something is considered a secret that definitely has something to do with the enslavement of your ancestors, the attitude of the Dutch Government and your race although you are in fact a mix of various races, you feel in your heart and soul that you definitely belong to the Negroid black race and for so long you were feeling confused and did not understand why all the hatred and humiliations of your race, why all these strategic and systematic efforts to keep your people oppressed, deprived of a fair chance to happiness and success in life!

Why all the conspiracies of the Dutch government to destroy your leaders to keep you going around in circles and circles without knowing what is happening and how you can possibly break this vicious cycle! And all their tenuous efforts to keep you controlled at all cost, that has in time instilled fear for your wellbeing and or life! Meanwhile you look around and every other race is getting a fair chance and treated with a much higher empathy degree than you or people of your race in the country that you are supposed to be part of! Why does for example the Netherlands calls every Dutch European citizen 'Autochthone' which actually means the 'authentic natives European Dutch people' and we belonging to the Dutch Kingdom are categorized as the 'allochthone' which actually means that we are officially considered second class citizens in our own Kingdom? Or is this not our Kingdom?

Practically the same thing happens in North America, why does only the Euro Americans get the honor to be called Americans? Even the perceived natives or Indians or denominated as 'Native' Americans and not Americans? Is that not an institutionalized discrimination of the other American citizens as second class citizens, of which many are citizens since generations? And did this official division of ethnic roots really began when the now called African Americans were no longer officially segregated and not officially called a Negro but instead a newly adapted citizens denomination, the 'African' American? And that to cover up the intentionally singling out of the 'African' American which was actually put in place for the tracking and control of the Negroid race, all other ethnic groups were called an 'American' with a preface of their ethnic identification! But what was the reason that the American Government desperately needed to keep track or in some way have control on the African Americans?

And you keep asking yourself, again and again, will we ever know what it is that keeps their systematic and institutionalized attempt to isolate, identified, control and keep track of our race and also their instigated hatred towards us as a race with so much passion from generation to generation? Is this a normal natural behavior or is this a deliberate instigated information that is being passed on to them and that is inspired by a secret not known to us the Negroid black race?

Is there something that we are not allowed to know about our own ancestors or our race the Negroid black race, that we are treated as a race in such a denigrating way? That nothing is granted to us! That the only use that we have for them is to serve them in one way or the other as entertainers for their ready amusement? That our lives as a race or nation is just constantly being controlled and made complicated by the white Caucasian race governments!

They always also seem to find a way to incorporate in a legitimate way that we cannot fully participate in the wealth of the world! They seem to find a way to single our race out through propaganda as being the ones unworthy of any trust and protection! Shoot first and then ask questions! That we are actually a nation within their nation that is in essence categorized by the governments as 'wanted dead or alive'! But why would that be, as we are perceived as the unintelligent ones, the ones who are still hominoids, what danger or threat could we possible be for these countries and their citizens, for them to treat us the way they treat us? If we are considered as unintelligent are still being hominoids, why are we then not treated as is expected as an endangered species on planet earth? A specie that they should actually have compassion with? A special not yet human species that needed to evolve and gain sleek hair to belong in their evolution theory?

And suddenly you find the missing piece and all the other pieces of the puzzle seems to fall in place and you acknowledge the wrong doing of your own ancestors and you feel relieved and in peace, because now you know and understand why! You know that it really did not only existed in your head, that you are your people were not playing the victim role as a race! That there is and was a reason for controlling and tracking each and every step of your people and its leaders! A reason that is built on fear of us the ones who had the power, because they definitely do not want to have to give up or lose their power in the world, that had led them to first enslaved us, rip us from our history and our heritage and fill our hearts with fear and doubts of who we are, single us out and control us as an entire race! Doing their utmost to keep us occupied and struggling so that we will not have the time nor the peace of mind to find out who we are as a race and why our destiny as the descendant of the ones who were enslaved in the so called 'Trans-Atlantic African Trade Slave' was sealed, the moment that our ancestors committed the mistake of playing God!

At the end, it must be recognized that our ancestors accepted their responsibility and fought to protect and stayed behind to save the humans that they created, they also shared their knowledge with the by them created humans! Being fully aware of the fate that awaits their future generations, because they had the ability to foresee the future, but still they sacrificed their own descendants! It must have been because they saw that in the future the created humans as a whole will eventually forgive them and their descendants and be grateful that they were created or upgraded, protected, saved, loved and guided spiritually by our ancestors!

The question that arise now is, had not the white Caucasian race in the name of all the created humans or the younger emerged races taken their vengeance by making the descendant of the Anunnaki

317

or the Negroid race their slaves on earth? Is the score not finally settled with this act of enslavement of the former enslaver? Taking away the history of the descendant of the Negroid black race and replacing this with a history of only being their slaves, the same that was done to them by creating them with the only history to be work slaves of the Negroid race! Creating also the illusion that the Negroid race was imperfect or still an inferior hominoid, as was done to them by the Negroid race by branding them as 'imperfect' upgraded hominoid!

And will finally also the guilt and the blame game, be completely eradicated by both parties if this truth finally came out? Enabling everyone to mourn and accept the guilt of the sins of their forefathers and be finally ready to close this chapter of the dark pages of the ugly beginnings on planet earth. I really believe that it is time that the strategic efforts, manipulation and propaganda of certain Governments or other institutions or organizations of some countries, to strategically in stow roots for a misplaced discrimination and isolation of the Negroid black race, by implying that the Negroid black race is an intelligently inferior race, a race that has corruptive and or criminal tendency, a race that is not trust worthy, a race that is lazy by nature, a race that only is interested in the pleasures of live, a race that preferably belongs in prisons to prove their point, must definitely be stopped!

Because really, enough is enough, it is definitely time for the truth to be acknowledged, the truth that the black Negroid race is definitely not an inferior race, the truth that all the other races has the Negroid DNA in their system and that it was put there by them the Negroid alien race essentially to upgrade and not downgrade

318

the hominoid or apelike beings DNA to a new specie or hybrid, the human race! Planet earth was a planet of apelike beings or hominoid and would have remained the Planet of the primitive and not being able to speak apes if it was not for the intervention of the black Negroid race! Their reason for making this upgrade was not an unselfish act, but their reason to safe, protect and guide these by them created humans and at same time sacrifice their own descendants, definitely was!

So it is without a doubt, the time for all of us as earthlings to now understand and accept our bitter beginnings and to be grateful for our existence on earth! We now know that the Universe does not only exist of us on planet earth! We are also already aware that the other specie or maybe species in the Universe are keeping a close watch on the developments of the created humans or the new specie in the Universe! Can they trust that the humans, that are not an original creation by God the Almighty, but an accepted creation by God the Almighty, through the sacrifice of his only begotten son, that we as earthlings now call Jesus Christ, co-exist in the Universe with other intelligent species?

Would they the Anunnaki or the Negroid race that created the humans, fought with their own kind for the protection and saving of the humans and that had the ability to foresee the future and were therefore confronted with the ultimate choice of the sacrifice of their own descendants, that would be enslaved and dehumanized, not foresee an ending were they could be finally very proud of their earthly creations or the humans, which would have proven to the group that left and wanted to destroy the

319

humans in an earthly flood, that they were wrong to brand the humans as an 'imperfect creation'?

The stayed behind Annunaki and or the creators, must have had tremendous faith in the created humans ability to at a point in time forgive them and at the end live in peace with their descendants on planet earth! It was a choice that our ancestors made in their believe of ultimately doing the right thing, by sacrificing their own descendants to enable the humans the time needed to redeem themselves as worthy intelligent creations in the Universe, because they believe it was the right thing to do!

It was a process that our ancestors foresee that had to take place, to enable the healing of the inflicted wounds by both parties and for us the Negroid race to let go of our arrogance as the ones in power by having all the knowledge on earth and regain back our humbleness and for the other races to obtain the respect they deserve as the new specie in the universe from us the black Negroid race, because they had saved our ancestors planet and we had secured their lives on planet earth, which would finally lead to us all ultimately coming together as one! Yes, it is definitely time for the hope of a complete new beginning, a start over and unification of all the races on planet earth coming together as one, as the Earthlings of Planet Earth in the Universe!

Epilogue

It definitely was meant to be!

A wise priest said to us once at school, that it is the man who falls in love and chooses his beloved partner and that the woman is enchanted and honored that she is the loved and chosen one, to become one with her partner! But we as young rebellious girls protested and some of the girls told the priest that that was definitely in the past, now we are the ones that will choose and seduced the man of our dreams! But the priest replied that, that will always be the case and that we as girls should respect ourselves and respect the process of the man making his choice on his own, because then he is committed to you, his choice. And that we as girls should considered ourselves blessed, because it is God that actually guides the man to choose his forever love, so that they as a couple could accomplish the life purpose that he has in store for them as a couple, together as one!

Me and Den were walking alone as the last ones of a group of friends, after attending a birthday party, because as usual we were discussing world history and politics and as always I was fascinated that he knew so much on this topic. I was just directing a question to him, when he suddenly grabbed my hand and pulled me closer to him. Disappointed I was thinking 'Oh no God, please not him!' and was just about to push him away, when he gently grabbed my chin and slowly raised my face so that I can see right in his eyes and then he softly deposit a warm kiss on my lips and whispered afterwards in my ears 'That is a kiss I stole from the girl who stole my heart!' It seemed if though I was just floating in the air and not having any control of my body and I could not let go of his hand, like our hands were just glued together and became one.

But nevertheless after experiencing this I could not surrender my love to him, because at the age of 15 I have already committed myself not to be distracted by having a boyfriend, a husband or even kids in my future, because I truly believed that my only purpose in life was to finish my education and go to Africa were it all began, to research the reason why my ancestors were enslaved and why my people in Africa are still essentially living a primitive life! But Den did not give up on the love he felt for me and I definitely did not want to lose him as my friend and protector and just after my 16th birthday, I surrender my love to him and was committed to dedicate myself to our now together as a couple established new life purposes or goals.

I honestly believed that maybe in another life or another soul will take over and try to resolve this issue of why our ancestors were enslaved. My life as a young woman in love with a man that really wanted me to be happy without any grievances and sad thoughts of the past concerning the fate of our ancestors was to say at least astounding. It was as though a heavy cargo has been lifted of my shoulders and I begin to have trust in life and in all people on earth and really started to flourish fully as a very happy and confident woman, as Den had predicted would happened.

So it definitely seems that the priest was actually right, that it is the man that needs to fall in love and choose his forever love in which he is guided by God to choose the right woman, whom will be enchanted by him. And I am blessed to have Den for me to love and to hold, as he is as it turned out, also nothing other than a direct blood lineage of the 'Anunnaki', 'the ones whom from the heavens came', so there actually was no need for me to go to Africa to where it all began, he Den as representation of Africa or the 'Anunnaki' was right here in Curaçao and came to me!

I truly believe that it was the grace of God that Den has chosen me as his forever love, to protect, guide and help me through time, with the patience of a saint, for me to lose the fear and the distrust I had in general for men, but more specifically the white Caucasian male since a child, he molded me into the best possible version of me, which had enabled me to finally obtain the spiritual insight that there is not a lot of differences in the core values of different cultures or races when it comes to love. Den also taught me through his deeds of the perseverance and patience that is needed to hold on to love and not to give up on love, from which I gained the maturity that I needed to duly fulfill my lifetime quest.

The lifetime quest that I had established since I was a young teenager, which was to find out whom our ancestors were, why they were enslaved and why it seems that there are still efforts made to keep us oppressed and to be able to analyze and comprehend the underlying reasons and to communicate this in a compassionate but true and honest way to the world, in the hope that this will restore the relationship and heal the wounds between the white Caucasian race and us the black Negroid race, which at the end turned out to be the spiritual life purpose, that God not only had chosen for me, but for both of us Den and myself as a married couple, to accomplish in this lifetime together as one!

Made in the USA
Columbia, SC
30 November 2023

26905040R00193